Praise for *The Light of Evening*

"This is a book with an emotional punch that doesn't hit you in the face but rather comes at you on reflection: the plight of mothers and daughters who love each other dearly yet never feel like kindred souls. *The Light of Evening* returns to the rural Ireland of O'Brien's earliest work but carries all the emotional complexity of her later books."
—Ellen Emry Heltzel, *Chicago Tribune*

"Philip Roth has called Edna O'Brien the most gifted woman now writing fiction in English, and it is hard not to agree . . . With *The Light of Evening* . . . O'Brien once again takes mothers and daughters as her subject, and yet she manages to make it all seem fresh."
—Brooke Allen, *The Wall Street Journal*

"One is left with the wrenching image of young and old necessarily parted, and yet always straining toward each other as well, across a vast and impossible distance."
—Alice Truax, *Vogue*

"O'Brien writes about women who are not strong; they are subject to doubts, panics, vanities and confusions—and they know all this, and it still does not make them strong. Dignity is their solace, and dignity makes them foolish, and they are always undone by desire. They are, as you may gather, completely honest, completely courageous, and heroic on the slenderest and most absolute of terms."
—Anne Enright, *The Guardian*

"Where others turn away, O'Brien rushes forward, her knives drawn for clean parsing of the real feelings that pass between two people. The bookshops are lousy with mother-daughter novels. *The Light of Evening* stands apart, refusing to give mere comfort. O'Brien doesn't just believe in the power of the bond between generations. She fears it."
—Claire Dederer, *Slate*

Also by Edna O'Brien

Murdo MacLeod

A NOTE ABOUT THE AUTHOR

EDNA O'BRIEN has written more than twenty works of fiction, most recently *Girl*. She is the recipient of numerous awards, including the Prix Femina, the PEN/Nabokov Award for Achievement in International Literature, the Irish PEN Lifetime Achievement Award, the National Arts Club Medal of Honor, and the Ulysses Medal. Born and raised in the west of Ireland, she has lived in London for many years.

EDNA O'BRIEN

The Light of
Evening

PICADOR

FARRAR, STRAUS AND GIROUX

NEW YORK

for my mother
and
my motherland

Picador
120 Broadway, New York 10271

The Library of Congress has cataloged the Houghton Mifflin hardcover edition as follows:
O'Brien, Edna.
    The light of evening / Edna O'Brien.
    p. cm.
    ISBN-13: 978-0-618-71867-2
    ISBN-10: 0-618-71867-2
    1. Mothers and daughters—Fiction. 2. Women novelists—Fiction.
3. Ireland—Fiction. 4. Psychological fiction. I. Title.

PR6065.B7L54 2006
823'.914—dc22   2006006045

Picador Paperback ISBN: 978-0-374-53878-1

Designed by Melissa Lotfy

1 3 5 7 9 10 8 6 4 2

Prologue

There is a photograph of my mother as a young woman in a white dress, standing by her mother who is seated out-of-doors on a kitchen chair, in front of a plantation of evergreen trees. Her mother is staring with a grave expression, her gnarled fingers clasped in prayer. Despite the virgin marvel of the white dress and the obligingness of her stance, my mother has heard the mating calls of the world beyond and has seen a picture of a white ship far out at sea. Her eyes are shockingly soft and beautiful.

The photograph would have been taken of a Sunday and for a special reason, perhaps on account of the daughter's looming departure. A stillness reigns. One can feel the sultriness, the sun beating down on the tops of the drowsing trees and over the nondescript fields, on and on to the bluish swath of mountain. Later as the day cools and they have gone in, the cry of the corncrake will carry across those same fields and over the lake to the blue-hazed mountain, such a lonely evening sound to it, like the lonely evening sound of the mothers, saying it is not our fault that we weep so, it is nature's fault that makes us first full, then empty.

Such is the wrath of the mothers, such is the cry of the mothers, such is the lamentation of the mothers, on and on until the last day, the last bluish tinge, the pismires, the gloaming, and the dying dust.

The past is never dead. It's not even past.

—WILLIAM FAULKNER

Part I

Dilly

"WILL YOU PIPE DOWN *outta that," Dilly says. "I said will you pipe down outta that Dilly says."*

Demon of a crow out there before daylight, cawing and croaking, rummaging in the palm tree that is not a palm tree but for some reason misnamed so. Queer bird, all by herself, neither chick nor child, with her omening and her conundrumming.

It gives Dilly the shivers, it does, and she storing her precious bits and pieces for safety's sake. Wrapping the cut glasses in case her husband, Cornelius, is mad enough to use them or lay one down before Crotty the workman, who'd fling it on a hedge or a headland as if it were a billy can. Her little treasures. Each item reminding her of someone or of something. The bone china with the flowers that Eleanora loved, and as a child she would sit in front of the china cabinet rhapsodizing over the sprigs of roses and forget-me-nots painted with such lifelikeness on the biscuit barrel and two-tiered cake plate. The glass jug a souvenir of that walk in the vast cemetery in Brooklyn in the twelfth month with the tall bearded man, searching the tombstones and the flat slabs for the names of the Irish-born and coming upon the grave of a Matilda, the widow of Wolf Tone, and pausing to pay tribute to her.

She is asking her possessions to keep watch over the house, to mind Rusheen. Asking her plates with pictures of pears and pomegranates, asking the milk-white china cups with their beautiful rims of gold, dimmed here and there from the graze of lips, a few cracked, where thoughtless visitors had flung them down. That raver for one, who ate enough for four men, raving on about Máire Ruadh, whoever Máire Ruadh was, some lore that Eleanora was versed in. Books and mythologies her daughter's whole life, putting her on the wrong track from the outset.

The suitcase is already down in the hall, secured with a leather strap because one of the brass catches is a bit slack. Lucky it is, that Con had to go miles away for the mare to be covered. She wants no tears, no sniveling. Amazing that he had got softer over the years, particularly in the last nine months and she laid low with the shingles, often walking in her sleep, anything to quell the pain, found by him out at the water tank, splashing water on herself to ease the ire. "What did I do wrong?" he kept asking, putting his cap on and off as he loitered. "Nothing, you did nothing wrong," she answered, canceling the tribulation of years.

Insisted that he take Dixie the dog with him, knowing that at the moment of leaving, Dixie would also lie down and whine with a human plaint.

Dilly thumps the armchair cushions in the breakfast room, talks to them, reckons that the swath of soot at the back of the chimney will stop it from catching fire. She knows Con's habits, piling on turf and logs, mad for the big blaze, reckless with firewood like there was no tomorrow. The big note she has written is propped up on the mantelpiece: "Be sure to put the guard over the fire before you go to bed and pull back the sofa." For some reason she winds the clock that has been already wound and lays it face-down in its usual place, ticking doggedly.

Out in the dairy she scalds basins, cans, and milk buckets, because one thing she does not want to come home to is the aftersmell of milk gone sour, a lingering smell that disgusts her and reminds her of sensations she daren't recall.

Madam Crow is still squawking and Dilly shouts back to her

as she goes out to the clothesline to hang a few things, his things, her things, and a load of tea cloths.

A cold morning, the grass springy with the remains of frost and in the hollows of the hillock a few very early primroses, shivering away. Funny how they sprouted in one place and not in another. They were the flowers she thought of when she thought flowers, them and buttercups. But mostly she thought of other things, duties, debts, her family, the packets of soup that she blended and warmed up for Con and herself for their morning elevenses, comrades at last, just like her dog, Dixie, and Dixie's pal Rover before it got run over. Poor Dixie pining and disconsolate, off her food for weeks, months, expecting her comrade back.

The March wind flapping everything, the clothes as she hangs them, the shreds of plastic bags and silage bags caught on the barbed wire making such a racket, and tears running down her cheeks and her nose, tears from the cold and the prospect of being absent for weeks. Yearling calves plastered in mud and muck where they have rolled, dung everywhere, on their tails and on the grass that they crop, the two younger calves frisky, their kiss curls covered in muck, playful, then all of a sudden mournful, the cries of them like a bleat as their mother has sauntered out of their view. No mound or blade of grass unknown to Dilly, all of it she knew, the place where her sorrows had multiplied and yet so dear to her, and how many times had they almost lost Rusheen, the bailiff one day sympathizing with her, saying it hurt him to see a lady like her brought so low, the bills, the unpaid bills, curling up at the edges, on a big skewer, their names that time in the *Gazette*. Yes, the poor mouth and fields going for a song, and her daughter, Eleanora, her head in the clouds, quoting from a book that all a person needed was a safe and splendid place. Still, her visits were heaven, a fire in the front room and chats about style, not jumping up to clear away the dishes at once, but lolling and talking, while knowing that there were things that could not be discussed, private things pertaining to Eleanora's wanderlust life. How she prayed and prayed that her daughter would not die in mortal sin, her soul eternally damned, lost, the way Rusheen was almost lost.

There was the time, the once-upon-a-time, when the gray limestone wall ran from the lower gate all the way past the cottages to the town, girding their acres. But no longer so, fields given away for nothing or half nothing to pay rates or pay bills, timber taken without so much as a by-your-leave and likewise turf from the bog, every Tom, Dick, and Harry allowed to cut turf, to save turf and to carry it home in broad daylight. How many times had they come within a hair's breadth of losing it. Still, her pride was salvaged, Rusheen was theirs, the old faithful trees keeping watch and enough head of cattle to defray expenses for at least six months or so to come. Not starving like unfortunate people in countries where rain, drought, and wars reduced them to gaping skeletons.

Madam Crow still in her roost with her *caw caw caw*s, the morning still cold, but not the bitter cold of a week earlier when Dilly had to wear mittens for her chilblains, had to drag the one storage heater from room to room to keep things from getting damp, to keep wallpaper from shedding, her ornaments stone cold like they were frostbitten. And that stab of memory when she put her cheek to the cheek of a plaster lady called Gala and suddenly back in that cemetery in Brooklyn with the bearded man, Gabriel, and the kiss that tasted of melted snow, but God the fire in it. Gabriel, the man she might have tied the knot with except that it was not meant to be. Putting memories to sleep, like putting an animal down.

In a way she was glad to be going, glad that Dr. Fogarty had got a hospital bed for her, after months of delaying and procrastination, he believing there was nothing wrong with her, only nerves and the toll of the shingles, telling her that the shingles made people depressed, that and other bull, how shingles took a long time to abate, and she telling him that they never abated, that they were always there, worse before rain, barometers of a sort. Patsy, who had done a bit of nursing, coming twice a week to her rescue, bathed the sores, remembered a few things from her nursing days, what ointment to apply, keeping watch to make sure that the scabs had not looped around her back to form a ring, because that circular loop was fatal. Patsy giving them their Latin name, *herpes zoster*, describing how the pain attacked the line of the nerves, something Dilly knew beyond the Latin words when she had wept night after night, as they oozed and bled, when nothing, no tablet, no prayer, no interceding, could do anything for her, a punishment so acute that she often felt one half of her body was in mutiny against the other half, a punishment for some terrible crime she had committed.

"How long more?" she would ask of Patsy.

"They have to run their course, missus," Patsy would reply, and so they had and so they did and most mornings she would twist round to look in the wardrobe mirror to make sure they had not spread, that the fatal ring had not formed. She'd never forget the moment that Patsy let out a big hurrah and said, "We're winning, missus, we're sucking diesel!" because the little scabs had changed color, had got more wishy-washy, which was a sign that they had decided to recede and in time their skins would fall off.

Then the next ordeal, a matter so private, so shaming it could not be discussed with Patsy and scarcely with Dr. Fogarty himself. She asked him to take her word that she was spotting blood and to please not examine her but give her something to stem it, balking at the thought of having to undress and be seen half naked and her insides probed.

"You won't feel pain . . . only discomfort," he had said.

"Don't ask me, doctor, don't ask me to do it," she had begged, and he could not understand the fears and eventually her blurting it out: "We were reared in the Dark Ages, doctor," and he tut-

tutting that, then opening a rickety folding screen for her to go behind and undress herself.

Before a week, him calling in person to speak alone with Cornelius in the sitting room, and their coming out and telling her that she would have to go to Dublin for observation. Observation for what? As if she were a night sky.

Indoors she pulls on her fawn camelhair coat and brown angora beret, then drags the butt of a worn lipstick across her mouth without even consulting a mirror and listens for the beeps from Buss the hackney driver, who has promised to be there at eleven sharp. Dipping her fingers in the holy water font, she blesses herself repeatedly and says to the house, "I'm off now, but I'll be home soon, I'll be home soon." To her amazement Buss has stolen a march on her and come into the kitchen unawares, and flustered now, because her hour has come, she says with almost girlish effusiveness, "You're the best man, Buss, and the best shepherd in the land."

Jerome

THE TALK IS OF DYING, of death, as they drive along, not just old people but young people in the prime of life taken, as Buss keeps telling her: Donal, a father of four, at his petrol pump five days previously, suddenly complaining about a pain in his chest and dead before morning, poor wife and children shell-shocked.

"Is it the climate?" Dilly asks.

"Is it what we're eating, is it that we're eating the wrong foods?" Buss replies. Neither knows the answer. All they know is that there have been far too many deaths and far too many funerals, graveyards chock-a-block, standing room only, coffins piled up in cramped, over-filled graves.

"It's the young people that I feel sorriest for," Buss says and she recoils, seeing this as some sort of castigation of her and, feeling nettled, she grows silent.

Nothing but lorries, the Monday morning toll of them. One lorry in front and another behind, restless to pass. The one in front with a load of wettish sand that is blowing back onto the windscreen, scumming it up.

"Hard to see," Buss says, taking the bit of rag that he keeps to hand on the dashboard, intending to wipe the windscreen, when the lorry behind them decides to pass and a contretemps ensues with the lorry in front. It pulls up outside a building site, lurches across the road, sand spattered in all directions and the drivers of both lorries belligerent.

"Another bungalow going up, nothing but bungalows," Buss says as they drive along, hoping to revive the conversation.

She is thinking that at seventy-seven she is of course not young, she should be ready to go but she is not, cravenly asking for a few more years. He coughs a few dry coughs and asks if she's going just for a checkup, because he is quite happy to wait, doesn't mind one bit, his voice so conciliatory that she melts and the little huff passes.

"The shingles," she answers evasively. *Devils* he calls them, his sister Lizzie laid up with them for the best part of a year, crazy from them until the good Lord guided her in the way of the healer. A healer! The beauty of the word a balm. In a mounting astonishment she hears how this man heals with his own blood, pricks his own finger, rubs the blood onto the scab, smears it all over the patient, repeats the procedure after eleven days, and then after the third visit not even a scab, the miracle completed.

"A nice sup of blood he uses up," Buss says and goes on to sing the praises of a man with a vocation, as holy as any priest, a man who would go a hundred miles to help a person and not charge a tosser for it. All his sister was implored upon was not to scrape them, not to itch them, to let the rub, to let the blood do its work. A nicer man he tells her she could not meet, a lovely house and farm, a lovely wife, applying his gift, a gift that has come down the generations, five generations so far.

"He never studied, not a paper, not a textbook . . . the books he reads are the people that come to him," he tells her, adding that he has a special affinity for the old people, knowing how down-and-out they get and with scant sympathy from the young. She is emboldened to ask and Buss says why not and that maybe Providence had sent it their way.

The side roads are narrow, sheltered, the pebbledash houses with painted white stones as ornaments on either pier, the birds walking, scudding, singing, all the signs of spring and the saplings with that flow of purple in their veins. They have decided to chance it, the healer's farm being only twenty miles off the main road and in her now, gusts of hope, the morbid gloom of earlier brushed away. Something so sacred about this man using his own blood, as did the Savior. She thinks their car will be turning back from Dublin toward home, a dinner on, that bit of bacon she had put to soak for Cornelius simmering away, the cabbage in the same pot for flavor, cooking slowly, not like the modern fad for rapid cooking. She listens with amusement at Buss's tirade about the workman on the tractor, never off that tractor for the three hundred and sixty-five days of the year.

"He wouldn't be the best of workers," Buss says sourly, resenting a man perched on his backside, the sharp blade thinning the hedges that do not need thinning, just to rook the government.

"What hedges are they?" she asks out of friendliness.

"They're white thorn and briar, and all he's doing is to strew the road with thorns and splinters, pure spite, just to give a person a puncture."

Dilly and Jerome the faith healer are in a small downstairs room off the kitchen. There is a single bed, a rocking chair, and a black metal reading lamp, its hood resting on the pillowslip as if it too is a patient. For modesty's sake Jerome draws the slatted blind, though there is nothing in the field outside, not even an animal. She lifts her sweater, then awkwardly unhooks her pink broderie anglaise brassiere that reaches way below her ribs and peels down the elasticated roll-on that she put on, for appearances, and that has been killing her since they set out. He clicks on the lamp and trains the beam along her body, front, back, and sides and with a seer's knowledge is able to tell her when the shingles started and when they started to abate. Fortified by such accuracy she asks him for the rub, for his blood that will heal her.

"It's not only the shingles, ma'am," he says and swivels the lamp away from her, quenching it.

"I know, I know that, but if you can cure one thing, you can cure another."

"Oh God, if only I could," he says, recounting the droves of people who've come with the same hopes as her, the same dream and it breaking his heart because all he lives for is to cure people and send them away happy.

"Maybe you could try."

"A fella has a gift for one thing but not another," he says helplessly and makes to leave the room in order that she can dress.

"Is there any other healer I could go to?" she asks.

"Not that I know of . . . you're better off now with the men in Dublin, the specialists," he says.

"But you see . . . you saw," she says.

"I'm only guessing . . . I'm a simple sort of fella," he says, abashed.

Their eyes meet and part, each staring into the forlorn space, a shaft of disappointment, he because he is unable to help her and she because she is thrown back into her own quagmire of uncertainty.

Flaherty

DILLY HAS BEEN ADMITTED, registered, x-rayed, tapped, and thumped, hammer blows to her chest and between her shoulder blades, a stethoscope onto her heart and upon being told to breathe deeply, made a fool of herself by coughing incessantly; different nurses leading her hither and thither, up and down the long corridors, the smells of wax polish, oranges, and Dettol. She has glimpsed into the wards, people with visitors, sitting up, others half doped back from their operations, and she has observed the various statues and holy pictures, particularly the vast painting of the Sacred Heart in the upper hall, the carmine red of his robes so rich and opulent, a lone figure in a desert landscape.

Bidding goodbye to Buss was a wrench, goodbye to the world as it were, poor Buss tipping his peaked cap over and over again as he stood by the outer glass doors, not allowed in any further but reluctant to go.

She is in her bed now, in a corner of the ward that is quite secluded from the main section. Her little niche with a view of the garden outside, the dark thin tapering branches, still leafless, scribbling their Morse onto the night sky. The sky, not pitch dark like country sky but flushed from the reflection of cars, buses, and streetlamps. She is on edge—the strangeness of things, strange sounds, coughings, moans, and the suspense of what is yet to be. The questions they flung at her on admittance, having to rake up so much of the past. What did her mother die of? What did her father die of? She couldn't answer, which only proved how callous she had been. No, she had not given them enough love and that too a blemish on her soul. Another question that freaked her: Why had she gone in the first place to her local doctor at home? She had gone out of terror, pure and simple. Their matter-of-factness, so very heartless.

Nurse Flaherty is standing over her bed, arms akimbo, looming, as if to question why she is not yet asleep.

Nurse Flaherty is a big woman, her hair the color of gunmetal, drawn severely over the crown of her head and frizzed at the back, where it is held down with a wide brass slide. From the moment they met earlier, there was an innate antagonism between them, Nurse Flaherty that bit sarcastic, wondering aloud how Mrs. Macready managed to get the best spot in the whole ward and who was it that pulled strings, then remarking on her shortness of breath, dismissed the suggestion that it was from climbing the fourteen entrance steps, both steep and unfamiliar.

"Seventeen steps," Nurse Flaherty corrected her.

"Are you sure, nurse?"

"Seventeen steps," Nurse Flaherty said, thereby establishing her sovereignty.

Nor had Dilly liked it one bit when, as a young nurse was folding her clothes to be put in safekeeping until she was discharged, Nurse Flaherty kept commenting on them, weren't they gorgeous and some people must be rolling in it. One garment in particular had taken her fancy, so much so that if its owner ever got tired of it, she knew who to pass it on to. It was a tweedex cardigan with mother-of-pearl buttons that Dilly had knitted throughout an entire winter and rarely wore, kept in tissue paper with camphor balls for that special occasion. Then the quizzing as to where she came from, which county, which the nearest town, and having discovered the exact locality, pouncing on her, with "Are you on the lake?" It transpired that the nurse knew

Dilly's son, Terence, the optician, met him at the annual Christmas spree when nurses, doctors, chemists, and the like met in that hotel out in Dunlaoghaire for a dinner dance, such a nice young man, sat with a load of girls for the starter and later asked her up to dance, a gentleman.

But now she seems even bossier having, as she says, read the report in the doctor's file, *au fait* with Dilly's medical status, the immune system weak from the shingles, the blood pressure sky-high, vessels blocked and furred up, lumps and bumps, the ticker erratic, hence that blackout in the bakery in Limerick, and with triumph concludes that she has the full picture.

"You should have had a Pap smear years ago . . . every sensible woman does . . . it's the gold standard . . ." the nurse says, shaking the thermometer vigorously, as though aggravated by it.

"Well, gold standard or no gold standard, I didn't," Dilly says flatly, then foolishly enquires if there's something she should know and know now.

"They won't know until you undergo the knife . . . they'll know then if you're riddled with or not."

"Don't, nurse, don't."

"You asked, didn't you?"

"Now I un-ask," she says and, changing the subject, remarks how nice it is to be by a window with a view of garden and shrubs and those fine trees.

A black-and-gray striped cat has positioned itself on the windowsill outside, staring in at them, meowing and with its paws assaulting the steel window frame, determined to get in.

"She's talking to you," the nurse says.

"Send her away," Dilly says.

"Sibsibsib," the nurse says in a coaxing voice.

"Send her away."

"She won't go . . . she comes every night . . . she had kittens in a shoebox in that locker of yours a few weeks back . . . curled up inside it . . . this end was empty on account of the decorating . . . so she made it her headquarters . . . one kitten died and she keeps coming back for it."

"I don't like the look of her," Dilly says.

"Oh, she could operate on you . . . she could get to your ovaries," the nurse tells her and with a strange elation sings as she goes, "Coosh the cat from under the mat, coosh the cat from under the table."

Jangled now, Dilly is thinking who might rescue her from there. It cannot be Cornelius, nor Dr. Fogarty, nor her hard-boiled son, Terence. It has to be Eleanora. She pictures her beyond in England with the shelves of books up to the ceiling and white flowers, usually lilies, in a big pewter jug, insouciant, mindless of this plea. She recalls the letters she wrote in the nights, on pink paper, on vellum, on ruled or jotting paper, pouring her troubles out in order for her daughter to know the deep things, the wounds she had to bear:

Dearest Eleanora,

I got shaky on a stepladder yesterday and nearly came a cropper. I was painting a ceiling for when you come. I know you like a nice ceiling. You mentioned one in the Vatican done by a master and many hands. You have traveled far and yet you do not forget you have a mother. Your letter and enclosures are a godsend. I needn't tell you as you know from your own experience that men think five pounds should last a year. With your first pay packet from those misers you worked for you sent me the makings of a summer dress and a bristle hairbrush. The way you thought of me. Nowadays I don't like to spend on myself but on Rusheen. When you've lived in a place for over fifty years you don't like to see it go to wrack and ruin. As per your instructions I bought another electric blanket with the money and switch it on a half an hour before bedtime and God it's like being in the Canaries, not that I ever was or ever will be. I also paid the TV license

out of your enclosure and got the cooker fitted with two instant hot plates. The oven was not right either. If only life was
plain sailing but it isn't. Cakes used to never fail on me before
but they do now. The last one I made was a flop, more like a
pudding and suitable only with a rich custard poured over
it. I will send you one anon as a cake always comes in handy
for unexpected callers. As you know I keep the odd lodger.
It's company as well as a bit of pin money. I've had a German
and his son for some time but the little boy is gone to Mu-
nich as the mother got custody for three months. She came
to Dublin to collect him. Sad to see him go. Reminded me of
the first time you left for the convent and I watched you going down the lawn and knew that it was forever. The sped ar-
row cannot be recalled.

Dearest Eleanora,

    When do you come? I saw in the paper where you were
protesting along with others about nuclear weapons. I suppose you won't be coming until the boys get their summer
holidays. How they love roaming the fields. Did you get my
last letter? I sometimes get addled and can't remember if I
posted it or if it might be behind a plate waiting for a stamp.
Your postcard from Spain arrived. Was that business or pleasure? Mrs. Du Maurier has left Ireland, gone back to England,
had her fill of here. I had a nice letter from Bude. She left Ireland last Tuesday with all her goods and chattels even the dog
and the budgie and mind you she was lonely. She stayed here
for four days and four nights and as you know she is fussy
but she seemed to enjoy it and ate and drank everything I set
before her. When she was going she handed me an envelope,
said she would not be able to send any present as there might
be duty on it from England and told me to buy myself a gift
but I did not take it from her as I would not like her to think
I had charged her. I think she was pleased not for the money's
sake but for the principle. I don't know what was in the en-

velope but even if it was one hundred pounds I would not take it. Hooligans rotted some of our lovely old trees in the back avenue dumping heaps of manure against them. Pure spite. Your good friend poor Drue is gone. He wrote about six months ago from the north of England to say he had lost three stone and that he'd lost joints off his fingers working for the railway but he was expecting good compensation as the union was fighting his case. Yet he didn't live to see it. He would have been better off in the country with an open-air life as most people are. The way you loved him as a child, doted on him, saying you'd marry at the consenting age and he and you would live in the chicken run. We used to laugh over it. I thought they may bring home the remains as is usually done but they didn't. I'm sure he left a good bit of money but when you're gone few care. Isn't life full of twists and turns. I wish you'd come for six months. I seem to have got a big burst of energy writing this whereas sometimes I haven't enough strength to hold pen or pencil. You will find that one day as you get older. I worry about you and your traveling to the different places. Nowhere is safe now. My undying love to you.

Dear Eleanora,

Had you been here last week you would have pitied your father and I, we lost a cow, a fine Friesian, due to the neglect of a pup of a vet who had come to de-horn them but was in such a hurry to get off to a horse show in the city he had not bothered to anesthetize their temples and as a result all the animals went mad around the fields charging into each other more like bulls than cattle, roaring, bellowing, a scene out of medieval times them setting upon one another, causing each other such wounds and lacerations the whole field was like a war zone. A spectacle over which your father or I had no control, all we could do was stand inside the gate and witness the carnage that was to cost us dearly, for when the young

Friesian went down others who had been venting their rage and their itch teamed up, began attacking her and did their dirtiest and straightaway dogs came from all over and fought each other for the legs and shins and limbs of the unfortunate one who perished.

Dear Eleanora,

Yes I named you after a Swedish girl I lodged with in the States hoping that it would be lucky. Her first name was Solveig but her middle name was Eleanora. There are odds and ends you must take back when you come, eleven Doulton plates, one alas broken. Don't blame me, my darling, for being upset that time five years ago when I got the wire at midnight from that queer-as-two-left-shoes husband of yours to say you had disappeared, abandoned your children, that you were very ill mentally as he put it and going to a psychologist so I thought it must be drastic. I fell for his lie and who wouldn't but I just ask that you do not drink alcohol as drink weakens the resolve. The TV that you gave us packed up again and we got it fixed but it doesn't stay right, our sewerage also gave up and must have been stopped for years. Yesterday a chimney pot fell down and the breakfast room chimney is blocked with crows' nests so we're upside down and downside up as the fella says. I saw your photograph in the paper but can I say the outfit you wore didn't do you justice, it exaggerated your figure by twice your size, the gathers and belt made you fatter. You have many ill-wishers here. Poor Dunny died alone in the gate lodge, the rats nearly got him before he was found, it's only fit to be demolished. There has been twenty so far wanting to get possession of it, grabbers, someone broke in there one night, slept there and left it in a disgusting condition. No visitors only William on Sunday evenings, endless speeches on world affairs and after two hours of it telling me the imperial sands are shifting Mrs. M. His brother Edward got a new overcoat maybe secondhand, so as they can go now to the same Mass on Sundays as previously one had to wait until the other came home from the first Mass to hand over the coat. It seems they don't talk at all only fight, the mother's will was unclear, Edward got a field up the Commons that William wanted to build on for the remarkable view and there followed dispute and foul play, a stream de-routed, a stream that animals drank from, Edward concluded it was his brother's dirty work and the sergeant had to be called. A stranger came up here the other evening, a marvelous sunny evening and asked me to excuse his cheek but said he had never seen a house that looked so beautiful so we are not in the ha'penny places after all. The creeper makes for a splash of color in contrast with the sandstone and of course the trees are a feature. You used to have a swing on the walnut tree and talk to yourself. Your brother says he will sever all ties with us unless we do as he asks and sign Rusheen over to him. I forgot to mention that there are two cakes in the post for you, one is a flop, the other a standby. You get so little time to bake and remember you can steam bits of the reject one in emergency. You are never out of my mind. I feel the cold more than I used to and this house is big, ceilings high, one fire isn't much. Moroney's pub have got two new big electric heaters but Pa will make sure the drinking boys pay for them. The doctor is marrying his sister-in-law, a thing no papal bull would allow, but it is an old and a true saying a man's wife is never dead. Little things keep coming back to me, I remember when you were young sitting on the back step one day and saying, "Mam, I'd love nice clothes." I suppose style does give an uplift when one is young and minus the spare tire. Your father has the ulcer now for years, it's getting no better always taking the magnesia or some jollup and won't go for a consultation, says there's nobody to look after the horses, says he can't leave them to die so he has to wait. How I wish he'd get rid of them as they swallow money.

Gabriel

DIM NOW THE LIGHTS in the ward, one light from the passage, miscellaneous sounds, snores, coughs and groans, sleepers trapped in their dreams, in their nightmares, caught in them and Dilly wishing she had not come, wishing she had stayed home, sick or no sick. Thoughts, unbidden, come into her mind, like those bats that come in a window in the summer and roam and rampage the night long. Her mind a jumble. Things learned by heart at school: "The harp that once through Tara's hall . . . Gearoid Og . . . The fall of the house of Kildare." Again, she recalls setting out lonesome for America, the ship plowing the main, waves high as a house, crashing in, flying crockery, prayers and screams at the birth of that unwanted child.

A young nurse doing the rounds sees that she is fidgety, muttering to herself, stops to ask if she needs something and unwisely Dilly tells her how her mind is spinning, bats, the big ship, inspectors on Ellis Island shouting at people to "keep moving, keep moving," at which the nurse runs off alarmed.

It is only a matter of minutes before Nurse Flaherty has arrived with two sleeping pills in a little plastic cup, which she rattles gaily like a child with its first fallen tooth, rattled for the fairies.

"Oh no, oh no, I don't need them things," she says, but the nurse will have none of it. Them things give such a lovely peaceful sleep and such lovely dreams, "moonlight in Mayo" time. Dilly is adamant. She never takes tablets and does not intend to.

"Well, you're taking them now because you're up to ninety," she is told.

"Even a spoon of a cough bottle dopes me . . . it's one of my rules," she says.

"Except I make the rules here," Nurse Flaherty says, decisively.

"You see they don't give a natural sleep," Dilly says half placating.

"How would you know . . . you never had a one in your life."

"I did when I was in hospital years ago and I was befuddled for a week."

"Modern medicine is different . . . streamlined . . . six or seven good hours' sleep and you wake refreshed."

"Don't ask me, nurse," Dilly says, close to tears.

"Look, don't you rise me because when I'm risen I'm a divil."

"The doctor didn't say I was to have them."

"The doctor does his job and I do mine . . . that's how things work in St. Joseph's Ward." And filling the tumbler of water from the bedside jug, she proffers the two turquoise capsules from the palm of her hand. Dilly swallows one. It tastes bitter and the aftermath bitterer still, as she retches in indignation.

Already the nurse has the second one to her lips, outlining them as with a crayon or a lipstick. One is not enough, one botches the whole procedure, it has to be two or nothing.

Dilly took the second one and scarcely had she lain back before the swoonings began. She clutched at the rungs of the bed, only to feel them soften and the bed itself beginning to sink as before her eyes there galloped a riderless horse and the consultant who had examined her is wringing the neck of a dead Rhode Island cockerel. *I am Dilly and I am not Dilly,* she says, clutching the strings of her nightgown, up-down, down-up, like milking a cow, and the last lucid bit of her mind going, going, gone as the tablets begin to wreak their worst. She pleads with herself to stay calm. She even believes that she is mastering these onslaughts, yet at that moment some ultimate door in her has been broken open and is swinging crazily on its hinges, then a burst as in childbirth and the floodgates flung open. *I am I amn't I amn't. Feel for the bell feel for it Dilly it's somewhere, find it squeeze it Nurse Nurse. She can't hear me. They're not listening. Is this how I die is this how one dies no one to give me the last sacrament all alone didn't I rock the cradle like many another mother. Oh good God I'm slipping I'm slipping. Well . . . If it isn't himself that's in it if it isn't Gabriel, eyes the softest brown the brown of the bulrushes, the lake reeds never boast a bulrush but the bog reeds do, cottony at first before they don their stout brown truncheons. Men are queer fish hard and soft both all pie when they want you so sweet and whispery sweeter than a woman then not. Distant. Wild irises beyond in that field they're kinda swaying. Hard to beat them. The upper part of your face is kinda familiar and so is your good navy suit. You scamp you. Nothing is forgotten. Up to the time he was seven St. Columcille was a very unruly boy. Things miscarry. Letters. Gifts. The waistcoat I was making for you that black Christmas I sent posted it to Wisconsin to the wilds where you sawed trees all day long from dawn till dusk you and a Finn. Lost two fingers there. The pressed jasmine and aster that you stole in the municipal park that Sunday in Brooklyn, I have had framed. A simple dark green frame on a bed of white silk, ruching. You might have written. Every bit of your daily life interests me. I wrote this day fortnight but it was returned. Tampered with. Are you by any chance dead. A post office mistress has a specialty for opening other people's letters. Not easy for me making time to write I have a man very hard on socks and workmen need three meals a day with jugs of tea and bread in between. My darling you will always have a message from me if only a postcard when I cannot make time for a letter. I would know if you were dead. Perhaps you are on your way here. Be sure to bring a candle a Christmas candle we need a bit of light to shed on things. So many misunderstandings. I was going across to you you were coming across to me but I was motioned back told to sit down and wait and that you would be with me seven years from this day. If you would get yourself photographed front face and silhouette and*

send it to me I will send postal order by return. Make sure the pho-
tographer catches the spill of your hair and your trim black beard.
I have been told that you will be with me openly seven years from
this day. Better call at night after the lights are out. Sometimes a
well-dressed lady on horseback rides by here with leaflets to dis-
tribute, things on her mind I reckon. Once there was a child with
her riding double. Walk right round the house in case of spies and
then tap on the window a good smart rap and I'll sit up. We could
go to the boathouse in Googy Park, boat half rotten but we'll be
safe enough off over there on the island no one to split us asunder.
Write to me I am weary weary of the pen weary of asking.

Dilly struggles for air, for breath, her eyes refusing to peel open,
the very same as if they've been glued together, pandemonium,
shouting, "Get Counihan, get Counihan." She is fighting someone off, a nun, a nun's face, and a nun's white habit, stiff as plaster of Paris, the voice telling her, "You're all right, you're all right
now," and she is being led back from the stairs, back to her own
bed, hoisted almost, two of them, one on either side helping her,
not able to feel the ground, not caring, their laying her back in
the bed and such a look of consternation on the poor nun's face.

"I think I was in Yankee land," Dilly says apologetically.

"Only for Nurse Aoife finding you, you'd be in Kingdom
Come . . . thank the good Lord and our Blessed Lady and His
angels and saints . . . I'll get Doctor Counihan to come and see
you."

"It was those pills, they sent me sky-high . . . I'm back to myself now . . . I don't need a doctor at all," she says and wonders
timidly if there is a chance of a cup of tea.

No longer agitated, just a little wanderish, she sees her life pass
before her in rapid succession, like clouds, different shapes and
different colors, merging, passing into one another, the story
of her life being pulled out of her, like the pages pulled from a
book.

Part II

Mushrooms

WE WERE BEYOND in the bog footing turf, three girls and
Caimin and me. The small brown stooks like igloos in rows
along the bank, gaps in them for the wind to circulate, to dry
them out. When we'd finished someone said that the tinkers had
been driven out of the Caoisearach, sent packing in their car-
avans, themselves and their children and their ponies and that
there was bound to be mushrooms because wherever there were
horses or ponies the mushrooms always sprang up.

Creena was the smartest of us at finding them. She had eyes
in the back of her head and the minute she came on a crop she
commandeered them, folded her bib to make a pouch, to bring
them home for her mother to cook in milk as a broth. There
were two kinds of mushrooms, the domes like eggcups, snug in
the grass, and the taller ones with smudgy brown mantles that
quivered. We devoured them raw, but Eileen said they were gorgeous roasted on hot coals, held at the end of the tongs and flavored with a pinch of salt.

The Shannon Lake way below and suddenly Caimin was
shouting, calling, "There she goes, the ship bound for America,"
and we looked and we couldn't see it because there was nothing whatsoever on that lake, only round towers and islets, but
we pretended, we all pretended that we saw the ship and waved
to her.

"Westwards . . . in her beautiful white cloak," he said. He

was going to cross the Atlantic Ocean in a boat all by himself like Brendan the Navigator and be a hero and go down in the annals.

Maybe I decided then or maybe not. There was always so much talk about America, every young person with the itch to go. Nothing for us in the rocky fields, only scrag and reeds and a few drills of potatoes.

Little did I dream that one day I would be lemon-oiling the banisters of the stairs of Mr. and Mrs. P. J. McCormack in their mansion in Brooklyn and dusting the treasures on Mrs. McCormack's dressing table, the tiny glass pots with their silver tops, the silver-backed brush and comb set, the silk pincushion skewered with her hatpins, Matilda, with corsages of violets and strawberries pinned to her bosom.

Creena was making us all laugh with a dance that her aunt had taught her. Her aunt Josephine had been home from Boston, cut a dash every Sunday with a change of style for Mass, telling people that America was out of this world and that no sooner did a craze for one dance catch on than another dance took over, all crazes, all fads.

My mother found the note I'd written and hidden under the mattress. It said, *I want to go to America where I can have nice clothes and a better life than I have here* and was signed *Dilly*. She beat me for it and ripped an old straw hat that I was decorating with gauze. She was furious. I would stick at my books and stay home and be useful, I was a good pupil, the way she was a good pupil before me. Again and again she would tell it how when she was in the school she prayed for rain, downpours, so that the teacher would let her spend the night in the school because it was too far to walk the four miles home barefoot. She would tell how she used what was left of daylight to keep studying. Why should America claim Ireland's sons and daughters, Ireland needing them, so many that had died on the scaffold and many more to die including, though she did not know it then, her own son. Had I no nature to want to leave, to bolt? We were always at loggerheads, my mother and me, both being very stubborn and strong-willed.

The night before I left home, there was the wake in our kitchen as was the custom for anyone going so far away. The kitchen was full of people, two men left their flash lamps lit during the dancing. Boys danced with me, said that they'd miss me, boys that had never thrown two words to me before, over a ditch. The older men sat on the settle bed with their bottles of porter and the one bottle of whiskey that they passed around and when they got up to dance they staggered and had to sit down again. The women were by the fire consoling my mother, consoling themselves, fearing that I would never come back. Some neighbors had helped with the passage money and I was sent around the kitchen to shake hands with them and swear that I would repay them. My things were packed, a black oilskin bag with twine around it, other clothes in a flour sack, and a long tin box with the name of a whiskey and the picture of a stream near where it was malted. My brother Michael sang "The Croppy Boy" and there were floods of tears over it, tears at my going and tears at the poor Croppy Boy who innocently went to do his Easter duty not knowing that the priest in the confessional was an English yeoman in disguise who would have him hanged for his insurgency.

We left in the sidecar at dawn and as many as would fit got up with us, others walking behind, the young men haggard from the night's enjoyment, slipping off at their own gates, cows waiting to be milked, a day's work to be done. I'll never forget my mother, Bridget, kneeling down on the dirt road to kiss my feet and saying, "Do not forget us, Dilly, do not ever forget your own people." My brother came with me to wait for the mail car. He took off his brown scapulars and gave them to me, it being his way of saying goodbye. "In your letters, better not mention politics," he said. He had a secret life from us, he was a Croppy Boy, so many young men were, but dared not speak of it for fear of informers.

In the mail car I kept touching my belongings, feeling for the two coins: the sovereign and a florin that my mother had stitched in the hemline of my coat, wrapped and rewrapped in cloth so as not to look like money. People waved from gateways and walls, knowing that the mail car was bringing people bound for America.

A bumpy ride over the wintry roads and where bridges had collapsed we got out and walked, then back on again and the coachman belting the two horses with all his might, because we had to catch the train to get us to Queenstown in time for the ship.

I thought of our dog Prince and he knowing for certain that I was leaving and of my mother crying into the black lace mantilla that had come from Salamanca. I thought too of the secret places where my brother hid his weapons, his revolver and shotgun wrapped in straw, like the figures in a manger.

Little Bones

FOR NEARLY TWO WEEKS a world of water, pounding and sloshing, great waves full of ice crashing against the portholes and a horizon that could have been anywhere, home or Canada, or Timbuktu, or anywhere.

Down below where we were incarcerated the fumes were terrible, fumes of cooking and cooking fat and oil from the paraffin lamps that had to be lit all day. A hole. People bickering and fighting and brokenhearted. Some had brought their own provisions and would elbow each other for a place at the one stove, the contrary cook hitting out with her tongue or a ladle or whatever instrument she had to hand. It was her stove, her domain. The staple diet for most was dry biscuits and salt fish. I nearly died of thirst. The thirst was the worst of all. I kept thinking of wells at home, imagined putting the bucket down and drawing up the clean water that had come from the mountain and drinking it, drinking a mug of it there and then. The water casks had run out after the third day and we had to use salt water for our tea and for all else. Stewards came twice a day from up above, cursing and shouting, telling us to clean our slops, to clean our messes and the contents of chamber pots, slop buckets and cooking pots were tossed over the railings, the water a sheet of gray, mile after mile of it, the waves mouthing away, like the mouths of the millions of fishes that the sea harbored.

In the evenings the sound of the orchestra drifted down as the first-class passengers danced and sat down to their five-course dinners.

Earlier we were allowed up on deck to do our own dancing and a fiddler from Galway played with a gusto. Mary Angela surpassed herself, knowing all the steps, and was tossed from one young man to the next like she was a feather. Only Sheila suspected that all was not right because of the big skirt Mary Angela wore and the loose apron that she never took off. She said her stomach was swollen because of the salt water and the gruel. At night she sat with the men, drinking grog with them in the dark, lewd laughter and sounds, the tiptoeing to different berths, men vying for her.

I had not taken my coat off in all that time nor ventured under the blanket in the berth my parents believed they had paid for. It turned out to be a quarter of a berth, the remaining three quarters occupied by a family that turned it into a pigsty and never stirred from there. The son had frog spawn in a jar and there were frogs scurrying about before we docked.

Mary Angela was the one that struck fear and foreboding into us all.

It was the night of the storm. Wind and rain battering the hatches, the ropes creaking, the timbers of the ship groaning as if they might snap apart, a crew half delirious, shouting orders to one another up above, as the ship pitched and rolled, delved down into the depths then vaulted up, water cascading in and we thrown in heaps on the floor, everything wet, our blankets wet, our clothes wet, crockery and utensils and fletches of bacon falling about, a woman pleading with us to say the rosary because the ship and the unborn child and its cargo were in death's grasp.

Mary Angela roaring her guts out and Sheila, who was not a midwife, trying to tend to her. Word had been sent up for a bed in the infirmary, but an answer came back that there was no room, as several people had been struck down with the fever and all the beds were taken. Sheila kept telling her to push, in Jesus' name to push, and the one lamp that had not blown out in the storm swung above her on its metal chain, swinging crazily, back and forth, the bowels of that ship like some inferno. Some prayed, some shouted for the roaring to stop and at the very last minute, when the screaming rent through us, a nurse appeared in a white coat carrying instruments and a bucket and Sheila hung a blanket on the handles of two brooms to serve as a sort of screen. There came then that piercing sound, with life and despair in it, the sound of an infant coming into the world and those who had been praying stopped praying and those who had been cursing stopped cursing, all now ready to rejoice, believing that the birth boded good luck for them.

"It's a boy, it's a boy," the word went round and there being no priest on board either among us or in the state rooms, a very old woman in a shawl produced a bottle of holy water and a sponge and gave it a lay baptism, wetting the lips, the forehead, and the chest, repeating some Latin prayers.

For two days mother and child did not show themselves. They lay in the curtained corner, a yellow sheepskin rug that smelled lay over them, hidden from all, the mother's hand reaching occasionally to take a biscuit or a mug of tea, the sound of the infant sucking and burping as she rocked it to sleep.

The day she reappeared she looked frail, her face chalk white but her eyes huge like lusters, the infant wrapped inside a blanket. What had she had called it? *Fintan, she said. Fintan, they said.* She was going up for air, going up to show off Fintan to the wild sea, to the roar of the waves, to the gulls and ravens that followed with their eerie cries. No one actually witnessed the happening so that afterward there was debate and bitter argument as to the truth of things. The young men who had been ogling her and who had danced with her were now boiling with hate, ready to lynch her, older men having to hold them back from throwing her in. The first news of it came as a shout, a series of shouts, a sign that something terrible had happened. It took only minutes for a crowd to gather up there, fear and molten hatred in some eyes. Others stood silent, bewildered, disbelieving. How could she. How could she. There were men scuffling her, women goading them on, the little slut, the little bitch, their faces smack up against hers telling her the black fate she was about to meet. She stood with a peculiar half smile, her blue-black eyes startled, insisting that it was dead, it had been dead for days. No one believed her. Why had she not gone to the purser and have it buried with weights in a sail cloth, the way they had buried an old man three days previous? She had done it to save her own skin. A mother with an infant but without a father was not welcomed in the new world.

"You kilt it."

"She kilt it."

"I had no milk for it," she answered back.

"Even a pelican tears its own flesh to feed its young."

"I would have taken it . . . I would have reared it," one woman said, throwing herself down in a swoon and others did likewise as they recited the litany: "Mother of Divine Grace, Mother most pure, Mother most chaste, Mother inviolate, Mother undefiled, Mother most amiable, Mother of good counsel, Mother of Our Creator, Mother of Our Savior."

Droves of birds had come, squalling and squealing, seagulls and other birds with scrawny necks, the beat of their wings furious as they strove to fend each other off, to get down there, fathoms deep, down to where our minds could not go, so hideous was it.

Two of the crew arrived with sticks and began beating the crowd back to make way for Captain DeVere. He was a big rough man who struck fear into us just by standing there. He wore a leather jerkin and leather breeches and had a mustache that curved halfway round his cheeks. Through a monocle he looked at her, her demeanor.

"Little Irish hussy," he said.

"Your honor," she said, but she was trembling.

"Where's your porker?" he asked.

"Fintan . . . the creature . . . he died . . . the milk gave out on me."

"You mean you got shot of it," he said, and then she threw herself at his mercy and begged not to be sent back down to the hole as the men would crucify her, and looking from her to them he simply said, "Yonder." We watched her go, watched her slim back, beholden, as she trotted after him.

"Its little bones, its little bones," Sheila kept saying, as if by delivering it she had some claim on it and leaning over the railings she stared and spoke down into the curdling water, into the deep, as if she could fish it out, the ship slewing and bouncing on its way, the birds maddened with hunger.

A preacher came that night to read aloud to us and possibly to quell any unrest. He read from a leather-bound book in a very somber voice.

The basin of the Atlantic Ocean is a long trough, separating the old world from the new. This ocean furrow was probably scored into the solid crust of our planet by the almighty hand—that there be waters which he calls seas might be gathered together so as to let dry land appear. Could the waters of the North Atlantic be drawn off so as to expose to view this great sea gash, which separates continents and extends from the Arctic to the Antarctic, it would present a scene most rugged, grand, and imposing, the very ribs of the solid earth with the foundations of the sea would be brought to light and we should have at one view in the empty cradle of the ocean, a thousand fearful wrecks, with that fearful army of dead men's skulls, great anchors, heaps of pearls, and inestimable stores, which in the poet's eye lay scattered at the bottom of the sea, making it hideous with the sights of ugly death.

Ellis Island

IN THE BIG HALL under a roof that leaked, we were herded into different groups, our names and our numbers tagged onto our chests, the inspectors like hawks, looking for every sickness, every flaw, every deformity, brutes at sending people back.

I had never known, never thought, that God had created so many different races—different attires, different hairstyles and headgears, men with ringlets and small skullcaps, women the size of tubs because of the clothes, the bundles they had wrapped around themselves, and their children roped to them in case they got lost. When children cried parents gave them their dolls and demanded medicines for them, which they fed them off spoons as if they were little gods. Suspicion in all eyes. Exiled from where we came and exiled now from each other, the waiting as dreadful as the journey on the ship.

To have caught sight of New York, the tops of the tall buildings pink in the dawn haze, was to wish more than ever to be set down in it. It seemed so idyllic, barges and boats moored in the harbor, the water calm and glassy, and the birds not at all like the venomous ones that had gone down after the little corpse.

On the island of tears, we were subjected to every kind of humiliation, our tongues pressed, our eyelids lifted with a buttonhook, our hearts listened to, our hair examined for lice, then our bodies hosed down by foreign ladies who had not a shred of modesty.

Then came the test for our reading and writing skills. People stammering and hesitating as they stumbled over the words of the Psalms:

This our bread we took hot for our provisions out of our
    houses on the day we came forth unto you.
Behold thy time was the time of love and I spread my skirt
    over thee and covered thy nakedness.

All around there were tears and pleadings, people sent back to wait, others dispatched into nearby rooms, and one lady in a scraggy fur coat down on her knees, holding her husband's ankles, clinging to him, "Aoran, Aoran," his tag a different color from hers, signifying that he was being sent back, forever. The whole hall was looking at her and though she spoke in a foreign tongue, it was clear that she would not be parted from him. He tried reasoning with her but to no avail, then all of a sudden she spat onto her fingers, wiped them on his eyelids, and then ran her damp fingers across her own, to contract the eye disease that she guessed he had. The guards were on her like dogs. She whirled and struck out, they grappling but unable to hold her and her husband looking at her with a coldness, such a coldness, as if he did not love her, had never loved her, as that was the only way to make her go on.

The inspector, scrutinizing my passbook where my mother had made me copy out household hints, called a second inspector over and I thought it meant refusal. They read it together and then told me to read it aloud and I realized that I was being made a laughingstock, a greenhorn with her household tips.

Rules for Management of Family Wash:

Rub line with a cloth to ensure cleanliness.
Economize on space and pegs.
Hang all garments the wrong side out.
Place all garments with their openings to the wind.

Put pegs in thickest part of garment folding.
Hang tablecloths bag shaped.
Hang flannels in shade.
Hang stockings within one inch of toe, wrong side out.

When my papers were stamped, I smarted at seeing the words *domestic servant*, but I had passed and I was trooping out into a world that seemed both strange and carnival-like, people bustling around, youngsters tugging and grabbing at my luggage, hawkers with baskets of fruits, apples and peaches, a blush on their soft skins as if they had been randomly rouged.

The Great Hall

WHAT HAD THOSE white-tiled walls and black pillars not witnessed?

People so overjoyed at being united that they wept with relief, others with despair in their eyes, fearing the worst, and Mary Angela in a blue knitted suit, like a mermaid, molded into it, walking up and down, gauging her chances. Before long she caught the attentions of a man who had hurried in, a well-dressed man with a mustache. They hadn't even exchanged a word, only gestures, and yet she knew, knew by the black armband on his sleeve, by his gaze, that he was a husband in mourning. All she did was put one hand under her breasts like she was weighing them and he came across to her, and soon after they went upstairs to an office, where it seemed he got her papers sanctioned to leave with him. She told us that she was going to be a wet nurse to his little son. We hadn't seen her since the evening of the drowning, but we'd heard that she had made herself very popular in the upper quarters and milked Captain DeVere's goats, morning and night.

My cousin had not come.

A sign above Madam Aisha's beauty parlor offered to curl women's hair and paint their faces for a reasonable sum. Many availed of it before having their photographs taken at the kissing station. Couples gazing into each other's eyes. A lady kept begging of me, "Do something for me, my most beloved sister," except that I couldn't. My cousin had not come. Boats came on the hour, people left, and the brown puddly water kept plashing on the shore, endlessly, and it was as if I were imprisoned there forever.

If my cousin did not come I would be put in one of the brick buildings with flags flying from the turrets, put there and be kept until my parents had sent the money for my passage home. Even Sheila had gone. "Call up some Sunday if you're passing," she said as she left with three friends. She lived on 22nd Street, wherever that was. A tall man kept pestering me, kept saying, "You must be Mary Mountjoy," and I pretended that I didn't understand him, in case I was kidnapped. That was the word, Sheila had dinned into us on the voyage, not to be kidnapped and not to have cheeky youngsters run off with our luggage, pretending that we were bound for Baltimore or Connecticut, or places unknown to us.

When my cousin came it was not the reunion I expected. She said why the tears, why the sulking. Did I not know she would come? She was not in the least bit like the tinted picture of herself that her mother had shown my mother; she was much stouter and her clothes were drab.

Where we docked it was bitter cold, the remains of snow on a swerve of dirty grass, a black man with long tapering fingers played a fiddle, played the different tunes to appeal to the emigrants, jog memories of their homelands. "Enjoying yourself, honey . . . going to marry the man you dreamed of," he said to me and started to dance a jig. Mary Kate was furious and lugged me away. He laughed and called after her, "It's not a funeral, baby," and dragging me she said, "You stay near me now, you stay near me now," vexed because he had made fun of her.

Everything then so hurried, getting the ticket, getting on the train, going through tunnels, then ugly sooted buildings, depots, rundown houses, and not a word exchanged between us. I could feel she was angry with me because of my gawkiness, because of my accent and my oilskin bag, bound with twine. She talked to herself, mumbled, as the train rumbled along. Then all of a sudden her mood changed and she kissed me and hugged me and said my mother and her mother were first cousins and that meant that she and I were second cousins and would be buddies. We were going to the borough, the borough being much nicer than the city, leafier and closer to nature.

The boarding house was in a street of houses that were all identical and in the dusk they looked mud-colored, but afterward in daylight I saw that they were more the color of rhubarb. We had to tiptoe. There were umbrellas and a walking stick in a china holder in the hall. She said he was a blackamoor. He had a brown face, his red eyes rimmed with silver ore. The kitchen was shared with many others, their foodstuffs on different trays with their names and a very old icebox that grunted and had odd things in it, like soft cheese in muslin and a bowl of beetroot soup. She made me stick my head inside it to feel how cold it was. Ice was precious. In the hospital where she worked packs of ice were put over the heads of the lunatics so that they could rant and rave without being heard. She had kept me some eats—bread with meat paste and a cold rice pudding. A lady came to fetch something out of the icebox but didn't throw us a word. After she left Mary Kate stuck her tongue out, said she didn't like her, she was foreign, all the other lodgers were foreign except us. We didn't stay long in the kitchen, it being communal, whereas her bedroom was private. We had to go through another bedroom with a couple and a baby and my heavy laced boots creaked awful.

It was topsy-turvy in her quarters, clothes, shoes, dishes, and coat hangers skewed about. A red quilt with herringbone stitch was pulled up over her bed, by way of making it. She was an auxiliary nurse but training to be a true nurse because that was her calling, to serve mankind. She was a Martha. There were Marys and Marthas, but Marys got all the limelight because of being Christ's handmaiden, but Marthas were far more sincere. Because it was a special occasion she would allow herself a little toddy. She wanted me to know that she was not a drinker but now and then had a drink as a pick-me-up. From a small bottle she poured some into a mug, kicked her shoes off, then threw off her glasses, and her eyes without them looked dopey and sheepish. Tears gushed out of her when I gave her the porter cake my mother sent and she hugged me. After that it was all "gee whiz." Gee whiz, I was out of the bogs now, I was in the beautiful borough, starting a new life. We would go to Coney in the summer. I didn't know what Coney was but imagined it a place full of rabbits. She laughed at that. Coney was the last word in thrills, roller-skating, love rides, stunts such as being sucked into the mouth of a giant tobacco pipe and slid out through the bowl at the other end. She'd gone there in the summer with a beau, a beau that worked in construction but announced one day he had to move on. That was the thing about America, people always moving on, so that a girl had to snap up a beau as fast as she could. She recalled the day, the petting, dancing cheek to cheek in the open air with the ocean breezes drifting in and she believing that she was hitched up.

The bathroom was on the other side of the bedroom where the couple with the baby slept. It meant disturbing them. The first two times she came with me and showed me a knack of pulling the chain so that it made the least amount of noise. By the third time she was furious. What was wrong with me. Did I have a tapeworm or what. She raised the sash of the window as far up as it would go and lifted me out onto the stone ledge, then pulled the window down to teach me a lesson. I could hear the rumble of cars in the street beyond. Perched there, terrified and certain that I would fall or jump, she laughing at the joke, I saw again the sign in the examination hall that had said CRIPPLES NOT WANTED and began to batter on the window.

Later in bed she said that people at home, her people, my people, believed that America was a land of riches but that nothing could be further from the truth. America was a land of bluff and blighted dreams and I would be lucky if I got a job as a maid in a big house. I would be a Biddy, a kitchen canary.

A Blind Man

ONE OF THE LODGERS worked odd hours and when she came in I bolted, without even a coat. The wind was at my back and I sped down the series of hills to get to the city, but it was not like a city at all, not like the city I'd seen on a calendar with ladies in fur coats, stepping out of a carriage, snowflakes on their fur collars and their cloche hats. It was higgledy-piggledy, trolley buses and horse-drawn carts, a fish wagon, a coal wagon, an oyster wagon, and men with pickaxes hitting stones to make a road where the road ran out. Noise poured out of the saloons and boys in long overalls were running hither and thither to deliver jugs of foaming beer, and in an alley children in rags and tatters were chasing young pigs with cabbage stalks and bits of stick.

There was music coming out of the saloons and different music that the organ grinder played, a monkey on his shoulder with a collection mug in the crook of its paw. Hardly had I stopped to look and to listen when a row broke out, the monkey and the organ grinder on one side and on the opposite a blind man in a belted coat that was too small for him and a white stick that needed scouring. He was in their patch and they were telling him to scoot it, that he was a bum, a clunk, to move on. The monkey was yapping away, as cross as his master, and the blind man refusing to budge. Then it was name-calling and the blind man's pencils, which he was hoping to sell, tossed in the air and rolling over the pavement. I ran to retrieve a few, but most of them had

43

rolled out onto the street where there were the cars and the carts trundling by.

He thanked me, said I was a nice girl, a clean girl, the only person to show a bit of kindness to the blind man who was jostled and robbed and kicked and called a bum and called a clunk.

He leaned on me as we crossed the street, because they were still shouting and haranguing him, and we walked lopsided, but once on the other side he would not let go of me. I knew he was mad, he had to be mad, the way he raved: Walt Whitman, the city's poet, Walt Whitman's masts of Manhattan and tall hills of Brooklyn, Walt Whitman, who had fallen, just like the blind man, into the mire, as had Horace who succumbed to the lures of a perfume seller. I was a clean girl in a city of vice, ancient Egypt or ancient Babylon no more wicked or no more corrupt. He had been a player once, in the saloons, at the trotting races, chancing his arm, scoring, and even the reverent fathers had singled him out. Sold religious articles, up in the silk stocking district, going from door to door, his valise crammed with holy statues, books, leaflets, novenas, miniature altars, miraculous medals, could put the sales over with a real punch, sold more in a day than the peanut man or the hot dog man. Flying it. Long-lashed Lenny as he was known. Face to face with the ladies and their nice drawl, in their morning coats, with their little lap dogs nested in their laps, time on their hands, their husbands making the loot. Yes, the swank ladies in their swank houses. One in particular. A doll. Wanted for nothing but her cup was never full. He knew the cup she meant. He filled the cup. Sweet as butter grass. Blonds, brunettes, redheads. One played him false or maybe more than one. Went from being a player to a human cockroach. Wakened one morning in some dive to know the game was up. Nausea, the shivers, the disease that bums, stevedores, poets, and the city elders all fell foul to. The syph. Had to be burned out of him. Oh man, the mercury that cured also took away, a descent into blindness. "I have sewed sackcloth upon my skin and defiled my horn in the dust."

We were by the trough where the horses drank and a few of the drivers sat with their heads down, dozing. A woman he knew who ran a little food stall gave us two minute cups of black coffee and when he drank it he slugged it down, just like the horses.

He must have sensed that I wanted to get away, because he said that I was his guardian angel who had been sent to him for that day.

It wasn't yet dark, but I knew it soon would be and that I would have to leave him. His hands searched my face as if they could see, whereas by contrast his eyes were quenched, a yellowish pus caked on the cracks of his eyelids. We would go to Wonderland. Wonderland was a home where little blind girls lived and every so often had a fete, sold cakes and tarts and muffins to rich ladies, to show that they were useful in the community. He'd been told of it, how they stood in their aprons behind a long table, with their sieves and their weighing scales and their baking tins, little blind girls, a credit to the community.

"I'll come tomorrow," I said, wrenching my arm away from him.

"You won't . . . you won't come tomorrow," he said, and he started to curse. How lost he looked there in the belted coat that was too small for him and the dirty white stick, unable to hide the sad truth that no one wanted to listen to him, tears running down his cheeks. God knows where he slept.

Then I was lost. Up streets, down streets, the same streets or different, it was impossible to tell. I couldn't remember where I lived. Near a park. "But which park?" she asked, as there were many. She was a child's nurse in uniform, wheeling a pram, and her mistress would be furious if she was late back. The small shops that sold coal and bundles of timber had their shutters down. Knocking on a brown door and a man in shirtsleeves holding a violin bow answered it then glared, the door in my face within seconds.

Darkness coming on. The lamplighter going from post to post with a ladder, climbing up, the sputter, as the flames took, the light ash-white that made the hurrying faces look consumptive. Holding on to the black iron base to read street names that meant nothing. Flatbush. Pacific. Lafayette. Atlantic.

Then running up a road and crossing to an intersection where there was a statue of a man on an iron horse, the same statue that I'd seen when I was with the blind man. A streetcar going by with passengers on the platform, holding on for dear life and me thinking that Mary Kate might be on it, but she wasn't. All I could remember of the lodging house was the little black man that was on the umbrella stand and his curled hair a chocolate brown.

The chapel commanded half a street and ran around the side of another. Three entrance gates, but the three wooden doors all locked. A vault to one side also locked, but I found a little lychgate that opened in. How they found me I never knew. Maybe they'd gone to all the chapels. I hid at the back of the stone grotto, the picture of Our Lady in front in her niche and a little girl kneeling before her, probably St. Bernadette of Lourdes. I knew it was them, somehow knew, Mary Kate and the lodger, and when I called out they ran to me, our reunion, so glad, so joyous, the goodwill flowing from one to the other, her coat around me going up the hills, the wind in our faces, but safe and united.

It was when she saw the pencil that the blind man had given me that she went berserk.

"Who was the blind man?"

"He didn't say."

"What did he want?"

"Nothing."

"What did he do to you?"

"Nothing."

"Where did he want to take you?"

"To Wonderland."

Wonderland! She went mad at the word. It was the very same

as if he had kidnapped me. *Kidnapped.* She said it three times. One of the lodgers preparing her supper looked on, aghast. Her daughter said, "Mama take dictionary," and they took a dictionary from the dresser but Mary Kate's tirade was too fast for them. She was wording the telegram of condolence that she must send to my mother and father. *"My dear Katherine and James, it is with the deepest regret that I have to inform you that your daughter is missing."* She believed it. She who had vouched for me, she who had hawked all the way to the depot to meet me and had welcomed me was now the one to have to forward the bad news. The woman holding the dictionary threw it down: "She crazy, she get crazier, all the Irish people they go crazy . . . they drunkards . . . they break the tooths."

In bed Mary Kate cried, said she shouldn't have shouted at me but it was for my own good, I could have ended up in a house of shame. Then, and between swigs from the bottle that was under her pillow, she relayed the story of Annie, a girl from Wicklow. She'd met Annie's brother Pol, a broken man, going around to the bars and the dance halls, telling his story, or rather Annie's story. When Annie'd got off the boat aged sixteen there was no one to meet her, the cousins that were to meet her had not shown up. Seeing her all alone and unbefriended, a well-dressed woman came across to her and offered to give her shelter, had papers to vouch for her character. So she went with her, thinking she was going to a convent. Instead she was brought to a big house with a madam, where she was made a prisoner and groomed to be a prostitute. No one heard from her back at home, her poor mother getting more and more anxious as time passed, until eventually they realized that something dreadful had happened to her and they scraped and they scraped to find the money for her brother to come to America, which he did. He went from one borough to the next, went to the priests who referred him to the bishop, paid a detective agency, and finally Annie's whereabouts were discovered. He went one night, wearing a trilby hat, disguised as much as he could, showed up as a customer, sat in a room along with the other men, drinking, waiting their turns to go upstairs, and the madam, realizing it was his first time, showed him photos of her little troupe. He chose his sister. The madam said he would have to wait quite a while as the lady, Vivien she called her, was extremely popular, especially with the regular clients. He drank champagne since that was the thing to do, but kept sober. When he found himself in the room with Vivien, in a gown, with soft lighting and the bed replete with pillows, she calling him "Baby, baby," he nearly died. She asked him his name, was he shy, was it his first time, and so forth and unable to restrain himself a second longer, he tore off his disguises and said, "Annie, Annie," which was her real name. She drew back, thinking maybe that he had a dagger or a gun. He told her not to be frightened, he was her brother and loved her as a brother and had come to get her out of there. She hung her head. He thought it was shame. He begged of her to put her clothes on and walk out of that house with him, but she refused. He pleaded. He asked her why. She said for his own sake he'd better leave, as there were toughs on call, who would beat him to a pulp. Finally she said that she had no wish to go. His own sister. "What will I tell our mother?" he asked.

"Tell her I'm dead," she answered.

Mary Kate was crying buckets, for Annie, for herself, and seeing that she had softened a bit I said, "Mary Kate, I want to go home."

"You can't go home," she kept saying, hysterically, and it was like a death sentence.

Dear Dilly

I COULD HEAR my mother talking to me the second I opened her letter, talking and scolding.

I take my pen in my hand twice within a month to say how worried I am about your silence. I have not heard from you in two weeks. I beg you to write to us. Do you not know, do you not recall our situation here? We are barely able to keep a roof over our heads. To make matters worse we had a setback. Things have conspired against us. Your father swore me to secrecy, but I have to tell someone, what with your brother hardly ever here. With the money he got for the corn that he brought to the mill, he decided to treat himself to a pair of boots and unfortunately got the shopkeeper to grease them in order to wear them on the ten-mile walk home. That was his mistake. He was crippled in them but could not return them because of having been seen to wear them. They're no good to anyone. You say you are looking for a post and I pray that you have secured it by now. It seems your cousin is not as friendly to you as she could be. That's sincerity for you. I will say nothing to her mother about it as there would only be a coolness. I'll be watching for the postman. I now bring this letter to a close, your loving mother,

Bridget

Mass

I COULD NOT write back and tell her how strange and false everything was. My cousin drinking in secret and hiding the empty bottles in a shoebox under the bed. My cousin pretending she was a nurse when it turned out that she washed patients and dressed them, her hands pink and raw-looking from all the washing.

In the lodging house the people kept to themselves, slunk into their rooms, their doors usually locked, and in the kitchen and in the icebox their names printed on their provisions, on the strange foods that they ate, bread that was a brown-black and little cucumbers that tasted vinegary. We stole a few when we were hungry, which was usually at the end of the week when Mary Kate's money ran out. The gold sovereign and the florin my mother gave me was confiscated toward my keep.

Everything hinged on money, the paved street and the parts where the paving ran out and pigs ran wild and were pelted with cabbage stalks.

That first Sunday in the palatial church with its altar and side altars, the priest's sermon centered on the parable of the camel unable to pass through the eye of the needle, no more than the rich man would be able to enter heaven. He was a visiting priest, his skin dark and shining like dark shining mahogany, the folds between his dark fingers were a pale shell-pink and there swam in his eyes such faith, such fervor. The congregation, he said, was indeed lucky to be living in such a leafy borough with its clapboard houses, its stone mansions, and its lines of beautiful trees, but that such comforts had been obtained at a price. The past could not be blotted out. The very site on which we knelt had been stolen from others. He cited the first settlers, mostly Dutch, who had come to the new world, the New Amsterdam, come to the fields of wild blackberries and hickory, where deer, muskrat, and wild turkeys roamed, honest men and women by their own standards and yet prepared to cheat the tribes of Lenape Indians, traded guns and wool for the pelts of animals that they sold for fortunes, gradually acquiring the deeds of those lands so that the native tribes were driven out, the great open tracts cut up in lots, to make houses, to make streets, to make progress, to make the colossal wealth that some, but not all, enjoyed. And what, he asked, did the newspapers and the politicians do? They colluded in their corruption, in their greed, backroom politics, and party patronage, ensuring that the cunning few reaped the fat of the land.

People coughed and fidgeted to show their disapproval, a few even walked out and afterward he was shunned when he stood outside the chapel door in his gold vestments to greet them. Mary Kate shook his hand and lingered because he was so good looking and on the way home said that it was all right to shake hands with a priest because a priest was made in the image of Christ, it was not like kissing a beau in one of the rides, at Coney.

Mr. and Mrs. McCormack

A DIFFERENT PRIEST brought me to my first job. His car was chocolate-colored with a hooded top, the smell of the leather seats so clean, so cleansing, and he put on motor gloves before we set out.

He kept impressing on me how eminent my new employers were, esteemed in the parish, the husband high up in a bank, his wife so musical that she paid to have the choir trained because she liked a sung Mass. He reckoned I was lucky to be placed in such a select neighborhood, what with the park opposite with its meadows and waterfalls, and moreover I wouldn't feel lonesome as there were sheep in it and I could hear them bleating at night.

It was a big stone house with stone figures on the gable ends and a foot scraper at the top of the flight of steps. The double glass doors were fronted with wrought iron so that nobody could see in, but the woman inside who was waiting for us was tapping irritably on the glass. Mrs. McCormack, my future boss. "What an hour of night to come," she said to him, then throwing me a sarcastic look she asked, "Is she from Roscommon, one of the sheep stealers?" The priest tried to smooth matters, said he had had a sick call and hence the inconsiderate hour.

It was the husband, Pascal, who led me to my sleeping quarters. Two flights of carpeted stairs with brass rods and then linoleum the higher we went. The last bit of stairs was so narrow that we had to walk sideways and my bag that had crossed the seas kept bumping into him. He opened a bedroom door and sent me in. There were two narrow beds with a girl in one of them. In the light from the landing I could see she was blond, nearly an albino, and wore a nightgown that buttoned up to her throat. She was like a weasel.

"You are in my sleeping room," she said as she sat up and thrashed her arms to get rid of me. I forget how I undressed in the dark, but I must have and I must have slept because I wakened with her pulling me out of the bed because the missus was calling for her breakfast. The missus shouted her orders from three floors down, shouted them into a pipe, and we heard them through a hole in the wall that had a brass shield over it. The girl, her name was Solveig, tore to the kitchen, with me trailing her. That morning, as with all the mornings, it was the missus's breakfast, her husband's breakfast, then running her bath and her footbath and laying out her clothes for the day. She had such a rich assortment of corsets, frilly drawers, and morning coats and her day jewelry was kept separate from the jewelry down in the safe.

She had a down on me from day one, remarking on the way I clumped, my flat arches, my brogue, my unkempt crop of hair.

Nothing but rules. Rule the first: no callers at the front door. Rule the second: no callers at the back door. Rule the third: no going out after dark. The six dusters had to be washed each evening and accounted for. She took me on a tour of the house, blowing about everything, Chesterfield this and Chesterfield that, the grand piano that was never played in all the time I was there, the Ormolu clock, the terracotta busts, the jasper veinings in the marble fireplace, a cellarette with decanters of port and sherry and, most prized of all, her secretaire, a Napoleon III desk, full of nooks and crannies and pigeonholes, where she and I and Mr. would have our battle one day.

After that it was into the dining room to point to the dinner set, to have me count it, white plates with birds on swinging boughs, soup plates, starter plates, dinner plates, gravy boats, platters, her saying that if one got broken there would be hell to pay. She said maids were notorious for breaking things. She read from a newspaper clipping that she kept in the cutlery box: *"Does your maid waste food spilling and dropping, do mop and broom in her hands do their task slightingly, does your treasured china slip through her fingers, is she a genius at chipping the edges of your beautiful cut glasses?"*

By the time I was finished I had furniture and ornaments coming out of my ears, rosewood, tulip wood, apple wood, burnt elm, the swan neck pediment, the foliate dragon, and a brass eagle that I must remember to dust religiously.

Boasting and bluffing and still she counted the biscuits in the tin in case Solveig and I touched one.

Solveig was higher up than me. She had a white apron. She was the cook. Sieving and singing hymns that her pastor in Sweden had taught her. Her eyes were the beautiful twinkling blue of a sleeping doll. She had a wooden box for her shoes and her shoe polish and was allowed out to a language school three afternoons a week. She cooked dishes I'd never heard of, lobster in aspic and shoestring potatoes for the lunch parties that the missus had for her girlfriends. Mamie and Gertie and Peg and Eunice. They were forever saying each other's names. Mamie and Gertie and Peg and Eunice, all the size of her, boasting about the presents their husbands gave them for their birthdays and their anniversaries. The missus would point to the big white box of flowers on the hall table that her husband had sent, every single flower in a snood of tissue paper, the box left there for them to see and for her to say, "Oh, how he spoils me, that man of mine."

After the lunch the card table would be moved closer to the fire for their bridge game. They nibbled bonbons and truffles and sometimes they bickered over the cards.

My work was rougher than Solveig's, cleaning the ashes, laying the three fires, polishing the grates, then the silver, then all the dusting, the cornices, the moldings, the legs and paws of the several chairs and her heaps of ornaments: shepherds, shepherdesses, jugs, vases, rose bowls, powder bowls, and the big brass eagle that had a venomous look.

The carpet in the sitting room was gorgeous. It was like sand, the various colors that sand can be, sand that water had seeped into and sand that water had drained out of, patterns of roses and rose blood, spatters where a rose had bled and elsewhere clusters of rosebuds, dangling.

About a month after I began, I was down on my knees with a nailbrush, getting the stains out of it, when Mr. came in, gave me the fright of my life. Was I saying the Angelus he wondered and knelt down beside me.

"Your hair, your hair," he kept saying, asking did other people remark on my hair, the red-gold halo all around it, asking how long it took to brush, morning and night, said what a ray of sunshine I was to the house.

.   .   .

Dear Dilly,

A reign of terror has started up. Once more our fields are Calvary. On the day of the annual horse fair it was decided to attack RIC enemy barracks in the old jail in Ennis. It was a well-known fact that the changing of the guard took place at six P.M. and that was the hour when the volunteers struck, others all along the street in case of mishap, the buying and selling of horses continuing as if all was normal, which of course it wasn't. When the whistle blew they opened fire, English soldiers running it seems like red shanks, three captured and brought to Daly's stables, relieved of their ammunition and taken away. There were twenty local men in the raid, which did not include our Michael, whom we believe is training others in the woods beyond Cratlow. Searches all over. Your father was searched on his way to the common land up the mountain. Finding a bottle of milk in his pocket, the British officer tried to make out that he was bringing it to his son or another bastard volunteer.

"I'm bringing it to drink," he told them. They did not let him go for over an hour. All this and you not here to help us.

Your poor mother,
Bridget

Solveig

SOLVEIG WOULD PUT small knobs of dough on top of the bread, baby loaves, for our clandestine feasts in our bedroom at night.

> Come butter come
> Come butter come
> Little Johnny's at the gate
> Waiting for his buttered cake.

She learned that rhyme from me and would say it, though it clashed with the hymns. It was no longer her sleeping room, it was our sleeping room now. We made friends the night it thundered, big claps of it and forked lightning flared then sizzled inside the room, she cowering under my bed, terrified that Eric Eric, the man with the clapper who broke up the big ships in the harbor in Malmo, was coming for her.

Ever after we were friends, we put paper curls in each other's hair, and I helped her with her English compositions:

Snow is frozen moisture that comes away from the clouds.
Snow falls in feathery flakes.
Boys make snowballs to pelt at one another.
Snow crystals are a beautiful sight.
The whole world falls asleep when snow settles.

How we scoured the magazines and the newspapers that the missus threw out.

A great-grandpa cut a tooth and a Mrs. White who lost a silver mesh bag with a pair of glasses and money was offering a substantial reward. A hostess, we learned, took poison at her own party and her husband was trying to hush it up. The Harts would be remaining at Huntingdon for the season but the Hammonds had gone to Connecticut and a Mrs. Harding had offered her beautiful home in Southampton to the president and was awaiting a favorable reply. A flighty Mrs. Stillman had formed an intimacy with her Indian servant while her financier husband was in a romance with a revue girl, and Mrs. Stillman's substantial alimony was only because of a baby just born, but, as the judge said, she would carry a stain that could never be erased. Houdini, who lived only a few streets away from us and who could do amazing stunts, such as escape from a barred prison cell, or a first-class straitjacket, met his Waterloo on a crowded streetcar at rush hour, realizing he was going in the wrong direction. Houdini tried to get out, had to wriggle, squirm, twist, and elbow his way and when by dint of sheer muscle he did escape, he fainted on the platform with nerves.

We had yet to get on a streetcar.

Up there in our attic room, dreaming of crush-proof blouses and coatees and capes and stoles and muffs, we were happy, because we had each other.

"For your Mademoiselle a symphony in toiletries," Solveig would read, puzzling over the words. Two pools of limpid beauty could be ours, hers and mine, by just cutting a coupon and sending off for Dr. Isaac Thompson's eye water that silvered the eyes to a diamond glitter and brought snowy whiteness to the cornea. Everything was just a matter of cutting a coupon and enclosing ten cents before stocks ran out, oriental creams in white, flesh, and rachel, the colors decreed by Paris, Princess-pat powders from Biarritz with almond base and for those hands red and rough from scrubbing, a hand cream rich and lubricating to rule out any possibility of offense. Cosmetics alone were not enough to draw out the impurities of the skin, to bring color, fineness, firmness, and rose complexion, we needed a plasmic pack. Moreover a Mrs. Edna Wallace Hopper had priceless secrets to impart, her wave and sheen perm ideal with our airy frocks for those starlit evenings, for motoring and dancing, either afternoon or night.

When we went to the races it was a *must* that we pay attention to our nail coloring—natural with bright frocks, rose with a blue or black gown, and coral with beige and gray. At the races we were likely to meet Hank or Elliott, but we must remember that there were five million marriageable young women, all seeking, that life moved quickly, a few hastening years and a Hank or an Elliott would be turning his attentions to a younger girl.

An ideal trousseau consisted of sixty pairs of the sheerest silk stockings, twenty-one nightgowns, three pajamas, fifty-four pieces of lingerie, handkerchiefs, and tucked in an inner secret drawer away from a husband's searching gaze might be the baby dresses, baby coats, and napkins for when the stork came. Once married we might permit ourselves a cigarette of an evening. A Mrs. P. Cabot did not enjoy a flat cigarette, much preferring a stronger, richer taste but we need not be so sophisticated. The picture showed Mrs. Cabot in her drawing room, in satin, with a big jug of roses beside her and a squat ball of ridged glass on which to strike matches, groomed for the arrival of her husband and possibly some guests, Mrs. Cabot's cook toiling in the kitchen.

Two hundred and forty brides from eleven cities, Detroit, Chicago, St. Paul, Cleveland, Pittsburgh, Philadelphia, Brooklyn, Providence, Denver, Cincinnati, and St. Louis, all brilliant homemakers who did not sacrifice their charms or their good looks and why, because of that certain soap powder that they all used.

Nevertheless, some of those brides were troubled by doubts and, living in a distant city as they did, were without a confidante to turn to. Then, the sorry saga of Leonard and Beth. Blissfully happy until misfortune struck, Beth was unable to confide in her dear darling mother, so as not to show her husband in a bad light. He was a salesman for office furniture, a job that entailed traveling great distances. Beth loved her new home, cuddled her new baby, and Leonard was an exemplary husband who at weekends got up at night if the baby cried. They had never had squabbles, never disagreed over money matters, their marriage ideal until a rival stepped in and Beth learned of it. Her friend Mary Jo who had just come from Cleveland had bumped into Leonard walking down a street with a girl, the pair of them linked, laughing. Not long after a letter came for Leonard in a feminine hand and though Beth was tempted to open it, she remained stoical, handing Leonard the letter when he came back, which he reluctantly opened and then put away. Brushing her hair before her mirror that night, Beth broke down and upon being questioned, Leonard said yes, he had met Flora, an old friend who did all she could to vamp him. He tried, oh how he tried to fend her off, even depositing her on her own doorstep after a dinner out, but sadly she returned to his hotel and the inevitable happened. He swore that he loved Beth but Beth could no longer believe in that love, her trust had been quashed, sinking deeper and deeper into the dark grotto of her despair.

We waited on tenterhooks for the next installment, wondering what the outcome would be.

Photographic Studio

"BRING YOUR DREAMS TO LIFE." Bring our dreams to life.
We saved up.

The photographic studio itself was up a side stairs with a stool on the landing. There was a couple in mourning, black from head to toe, the black ribbons fluttering on the brim of the husband's hat, and an engaged couple staring down at the ring, the diamond no bigger than a grain of sand. The photographer with his coffee-colored skin and his coffee-colored suit beamed when he saw us, said he would take us last. He walked with a waddle.

The room where he took the photographs was almost dark, the camera on a tripod with a big black cloth over it and an opened black umbrella, which at home was always deemed unlucky. Incense wafted from the nostrils of a bronze Buddha, which, as he said, was for the ambience. Everything was ambience.

We were star material, he saw that at once. Our two faces, Solveig's ivory cheeks and my peaches and cream, would be mounted side by side on a white card, embossed with violets and put in the showcase in the entrance hall. The masculine and feminine world of passersby would be set agog at the sight of us. We were lucky to catch him in. Stars of stage and screen were forever vying for his services, often he had to shut shop and dash to snap a famous screen actress during her lunch break. He was number one in his field, his tones, his shadowing, his definitions, unique, his competitors crazy to find out the secret that was his alone. But to us he would reveal it. He grasped the personality, the soul, he looked into the eyes, the windows of the soul, and saw what girls were dreaming of.

Might we step into something dandier, more eye-catching, he wondered. From a trunk he pulled out boas, fox tippets, capes, and frocks and ushered us behind a screen to change, telling us to be as daring as possible.

"I am a little boy now," Solveig said as she appeared in a sailor suit. It thrilled him. Boy and girl. Bride and groom. He ran to get a cigarette case, made her practice opening and shutting it, like a swain. Then he stood her on a box to be taller and put me sitting, made me cross and uncross my legs several times to show to advantage the green silk shoes that matched the peppermint-green satin dress.

When I sent the photograph home my mother wrote back, aghast, asked was it a streetwalker I had become and who was the insolent boy with me.

The photographer urged us to think of our sweethearts. We were bound to have sweethearts, what with our skins and our complexions, oodles of sweethearts. Solveig raved about her grandparents, their cottage in the countryside where she spent her holidays and the small lake and the small boat, her grandmother reading her stories of princesses, reading only nice stories, not wanting to scare her, her grandmother combing her hair, and telling her there was *gund* in it, and *gund* signified gold, which meant that she would marry a very rich prince. Her grandma, her mother, and herself at Christmastime carrying a small sheep or a small cow to the pastor, to give to baby Jesus and the shepherds, then home for the feast, meatballs, tiny sausages, sliced potatoes with anchovies, and then the big treat that her papa handed out, marzipan pigs with red ribbons on their bellies that would make people richer in the year to come.

He wanted us to kiss. He said it wasn't like kissing him, it was just two young girls on the brink of stardom. He saw only riches, our names in lights, "It" girls, snapped up by some Hollywood agency and heading for Tinseltown. On the cusp of being discovered, but still we wouldn't kiss.

He said if Hollywood seemed too far afield, too outré, he could find us attractive work in our spare time, as he had contacts with the advertising people, all crying out for new faces, fresh faces to model soaps and face creams, or even lingerie in private homes, a tempting nest egg, as he put it.

"You are a little bit of a scoundrel," Solveig said. God knows where she had heard the word. He was fuming. He pulled down his shirtsleeves, pulled up the blind, pointed to a photograph of his wife, a sallow woman with a child in her arms. Then he got very businesslike and demanded the deposit, which earlier he had promised to forgo.

Walking up the hill toward home, the lamplights roosting in the trees that skirted the park, we'd stop and laugh and go over every bit of it, his lips puce as if he'd painted them, his coffee-colored suit, his waddle, the Turkish Delight he fed us on a wooden spatula, wiping the sherbet off our lips, and the sudden umbrage in him at being called a scoundrel.

. . .

Dear Dilly,

I yet again take my pen in my hand since we have not heard from you in four weeks. Are you sick or what? We understood that people have good health in America. Making and trimming bonnets or having yourself photographed cannot take up all of your time. We are crazy with worry over your brother. He is a wanted man because of an ambush in a graveyard beyond Moynoe two weeks ago in which a British soldier died. A thousand pounds on his head. His picture on posters nailed to trees with three other suspects who are also on the run. He called once in the night, stole in while your father and I were asleep and took a pike that was in the thatch. He lives in bog holes and potato pits. If the army don't get him then pneumonia will as the weather is wretched. Raining, raining, raining. With the last money you sent us we repaid one set of cousins, the Duracks, for their contribution toward your passage. I keep seeing you in my dreams. If only you knew how I miss you, especially on Sundays when I sit in the plantation for a rest. I enclose a prayer. Tuck it into the cavity in the back of the amber brooch that I gave you.

> The days grow longer
> The nights grow shorter
> The headstones thicken along the way
> Life grows shorter and love grows longer
> For Him who is with us night and day

I hope your silence does not denote anything serious. I bring this scribble to a close.

Your worried mother,
Bridget

Bless This House

IT BEGAN GREAT.

"Bless this house, O Lord, we pray. Keep it safe by night and day," played over and over again on the gramophone. It poured down the steps to where Solveig and I were working helter-skelter. The singer was a favorite of Pascal's and he kept clippings and photographs of him coming out of concert halls in cities all over Europe.

"Bless the people here within. Keep them pure and free from sin."

Earlier when she came from Mass, the missus was in a foul mood, yelling at Solveig and me because one of the fires smoked, the logs were not properly stacked in their brass boxes, the goose not pierced of excessive fat, the napkins not folded into miter shape, which she had particularly requested, in order to show off the monogrammed *M* in blood-red silk needlework. *M* for Matilda.

It was all bustle. A ham with cloves and crusts of brown sugar lay on a platter, a white paper frill around it, dishes and chafing dishes being kept hot, boats for different gravies, and the sizzle sound of the goose when Solveig basted it. The trifle, jellies, and a blancmange dyed green for the patriot effect were on the pantry floor to be kept cool. In small bowls of carnival glass the bonbons, the crystallized violets, and the maraschino cherries for when they would have their liqueurs.

Mr. and Mrs. McCormack's annual Christmas "at home."

The rooms were decorated differently for the contrast, the drawing room all light and blaze with two roaring fires and the fobs and pendants of the chandeliers that I'd washed in sudsy water and rinsed, twinkling as if to say, "We're here . . . we're here." The cushions and velveteen sofa had to be re-covered because the chimney sweep being so absent-minded, he only put the dust sheets down in half of the room. An impertinent little squirt, with his brooms and his brushes and his set of rods, ordering Solveig and me about as if he owned the place.

A man had done the hall, spent days doing it, dressing the tree that was as tall as the house and decking it with the small penny candles like the ones in the chapel because the missus wanted a woodland effect. Along with the candles, there were yellow fleece birds that chirruped a song every so often, nearly lifelike. There was holly twined and wreathed on several banisters of the stairs and the door outside framed with myrtle and the heads of hydrangeas that had been bronzed, so that it was like entering a castle.

The dining room was a "little Ireland" with fat red candles in scooped-out turnips and glass harps, as a gift, at each place setting. They had come from a foundry in Italy.

Chrissie was the first to arrive, craned to take a bite out of the satin apples and satin pears that hung from the tree, said they reminded her of the days when she played snap-apple at home, on Halloween. She had a limp, one of her boots with a heel higher than the other, effusive, kissing Mr., kissing the missus, and then having to be hoisted up to kiss the big sprig of mistletoe that was above the drawing room door. She asked if there was any nice fellow come that would walk her home and Mr. told her that there was Kevin, as per usual. She scoffed, said, "Ah, sugar, he tells the same ghost story every year, about the girl with the consumption."

There were eleven guests in all and twelve if the congressman came. Everything hinged on the congressman's coming except that it must be kept secret, in case at the last minute, as Mr. said, he had a more pressing engagement.

"Answer it, answer it," the missus barking for me to get to the hall door posthaste, taking their coats and the presents, the presents in gorgeous paper with yards of different colored ribbon, left on the hall table for etiquette, the fur coats up to the bedroom for minding.

There was Mr. and Mrs. Keating, Mr. Keating with a black ebony cane and Mrs. Keating keeping her ermine wrap on although the room was boiling. Next came Felim and Mrs. Felim, then two bachelors, Eamonn and Kevin, to correspond to Chrissie and Jenny, who were both unmarried, and Father Bob, the missus's private confessor, who came once a fortnight from Long Island to hear her confession in the morning room and afterward sat by the fire for a high tea that had to include apple fritters because he had a fad for them.

A punch cup to start, Mr. ladling it into silver mugs that had a gold lining, like little chalices. The visitors were in raptures, the missus showered with compliments, her hair, her crushed velvet, the ruby necklace that lay on her chest, so dazzling, so scintillating, so unusual and priceless.

"She has me broke," Pascal said and held up the ornamental alms plate to get a laugh.

"Is that Rococo, Pascal?" Chrissie said as she stood by the missus's desk, peering into the nests of pigeonholes and cubbies.

"Oh, don't touch there or you'll be shot," Pascal said, because it was where the missus kept her souvenirs, love letters from men before him, locks of hair, dried shamrock, and the words of songs that she rehearsed for her parties. Her family was musical, always boasting about it, her father could make a tune out of a blade of grass.

Chrissie tried all the chairs, the armchairs, the high chairs, the spindle-back chairs, "Is that apple wood, is that tulip wood, is that rosewood, Pascal?" People pitying her with her limp, in a yellow summery dress with a wide green sash as if she was entering a dance competition. Remarking on the holly to be so rich with berries, she said a good crop of berries always meant an addition to the family, a babbie, and the missus gave her a glare.

But as the others arrived she went all soft and unctuous, shrieks of delight at each newcomer, marveling that they had ventured out on such a rotten day, freezing cold and slippery to boot, could break their necks on the steps even though she'd got Pascal to sprinkle the coarse salt. She was in her element, offering her hand to be kissed by the men and her powdered cheek to be brushed by the ladies, every so often scolding her husband on account of a glass being empty, or a sod fallen onto the tiled fireplace, or Jenny all alone in a corner, like a wallflower.

"Jenny is super duper" was the answer back. Jenny knew how to humor the missus, calling her a slip of a girl and drawing attention to every feature of her attire, down to the velvet shoes, that would you believe it were called mules, mules with a field of flowers and medallions on them, like a carpet.

"Sure, it's only home . . . it's only home," the missus kept saying.

The punch was getting to them, their faces redder and small tiffs between couples, Finoola taking the silver cup from her husband, reminding him he was on the pledge, and he grabbing it back and slugging it down in one gulp, then crossing to Matilda to kiss her hand again, "Oh, deathless Leda." She told all and sundry that Felim had taken a bite off the Blarney Stone, hence the flattery.

Chrissie kept kissing a dark brown painting of a poor man and his poor wife in a potato field, leaving off from their toil to say the Angelus. Written underneath was "Mary and Manus are saying the Angelus," and she said that to hang that picture amidst all the treasures was a sure sign that Matilda had not forgotten her roots, had not let the rosewood or the Rococo go to her head.

"Now where on earth is that man of mine?" the missus would call out, consulting her bracelet watch, saying Father Bob had promised to be first, to give her Dutch courage.

"It's the buses, my sweet . . . they're always slow in from the Island on a Sunday," Pascal said and told the guests that if he had to be jealous of any man for his wife's favors, it was Father Bob, who had taken Holy Orders.

Solveig was in the doorway beckoning to me like mad.

The roast goose lay in a heap on the flagged floor, a pitiable sight, potato stuffing oozing out of one end of her and chestnut stuffing out of her craw, the brown legs falling away from the flesh, which was over-crisped. We tried picking it up but were tiddly from having helped ourselves to the sherry from the bottle that the missus left behind after she had laced the trifle. Mr. nearly fainted. He'd come in to fill the decanters, his earlobes a foolish red compared with his pasty face, and began blessing himself, saying, "She'll kill us, she'll kill us all." So it was down on our knees, three sets of hands and three sets of implements trying to maneuver the bird onto a platter, then separating the various pieces, the brown meat, the white meat, the legs, the wings, the pope's nose, all of it garnished with parsley and chestnuts to cover up for the mishap.

"Ladies and gintlemin, would yous be so kind as to come and be sated and take a crust from me humble table," the missus said, ringing a little glass bell after Father Bob had arrived profuse with apologies. They trooped in to the dining room, rapturous once again over the beautiful linen, the array of crystal at each place setting, and the red candle in a scooped-out turnip for a rustic effect.

Mr. Keating read aloud from the table d'hôte that the missus had written on a sheet of parchment.

Green Turtle Soup
Roast Goose
Stuffing Ensemble
Pig's Crubeens and Cabbage
Battered Eggplant
Spuds
Vegetables Galore
Sauces Galore
Plum Pudding, Trifles, Jellies
Napoleons with Fluffy Strawberry Sauce

No hotel in the city could better it. The gourmet touch and the human touch. The napoleons, she reminded them, were so named because of Napoleon getting indigestion from the pastry and thereby losing the Battle of Waterloo. They all laughed and said Bony had it coming to him. Seeing us, Solveig and me, in our black shoes and our black stockings, like nuns with our white lace overalls and caps, Mr. said that the little girlies must get some credit too.

"Oh, I have to watch them," the missus said and snapped her fingers for us to start passing the turtle soup around.

Unfolding her napkin and seeing the *M* in red silk, Finoola said it brought tears to her eyes, it was like seeing the fuchsia flower on the hedges in Kerry long ago. They vied with each other over memories and the talk then went to the vaudeville shows that were all the rage, the home life of Paddy the drunken Irishman and Mrs. Paddy his half-drunken wife, fighting it out, he with the leg of a chair and she with a flatiron, in their hovel of a kitchen. Scandalous altogether. A bloody slur on the race, on the Paddies, depicted with ape lips and grass hair, pick and shovel in the hands. Kevin then put it to them if there was a man or a woman who could do justice to the history of their country, their dear Dark Rosaleen, their Kathleen ni Houlihan. One said Yeats, at which Kevin shook his head but Eamonn, who had not spoken a word, piped up to recite the line "Said Pearce to Connolly there's nothing but our own red blood can make a right rose tree." From Yeats it gravitated toward Maud Gonne, his muse, some praising her, some saying she was a firebrand, exhorting young men to put dynamite in bags of coal bound for England and before long there was a slanging match, Felim and Mr. Keating, haranguing each other, both at opposite political poles. A flood of accusation and counter-accusation, rebellions, botched rebellions, informers, Robert Emmet's speech from the dock, and Mr. Keating going too far by claiming that the men of 1916 were nothing but boy scouts, laughed at when they surrendered and were led out of the post office. Felim rose, the pieces of goose crumbling on his fork, his neck muscles bunched and gathered, said no doubt it was cowardly to die for your country, cowardly to face the firing squad, his wife clutching and reclutching her cameo pendant out of shame and Eamonn egging him on, shouting, "Keep it up, Felim, keep it up." Felim was there to tell his right honorable friend Mr. Keating, an English lackey, that no Irishman had ever done a dishonorable deed in his life. It was too much. Mr. Keating exploded, cited the savage murder of the English lord lieutenant and his secretary on their way to the Viceregal Lodge in Phoenix Park, minding their own business but stabbed to death with surgical knives by the said honorable Irishmen.

"Political necessity," Felim thundered back.

"Political necessity, my arse," Mr. Keating said, and Matilda pleaded with Father Bob to reason with them, to put a stop to this appalling language and appalling behavior. He stood with his arms out as if to embrace the gathering, his voice muted: "Friends, we're all fellow Irishmen and Irishwomen, our country in the cradle of her independence . . . we are here to heal wounds, not to open them," to which Mr. followed with a toast — "To the freedom of Ireland, to the freedom of Ireland" — and they all stood to respond. Sitting down, Father Bob asked the good people did they realize that Irish scroll work, Irish symbols, Irish illuminations, torques, knots, and crosses were copied in Egyptian halls and later adopted for their beauty in the schools of Charlemagne.

"Excuse my Dutch, Father Bob," Felim said, still seething. "But it's an effing disgrace when people who have never set foot in Ireland feel nothing for her, only insult and disdain."

"And what did you ever do for Ireland?" Mr. Keating said, his mouth full of food, eating with hard vexed jaws, his wife tugging at him to sit down.

"I'll tell you what I did for Ireland," Felim replied and rolled up his sleeve to show the knife wounds he had incurred from a bastard who simply could not stomach the fact that Christopher Columbus was not the first man to discover America, that an Irishman, Patrick McGuire, was the first to step on American soil. Mr. was by his side, praising him for his patriotism, saying to put politics aside for one day, and begging him not to get the hump up. Felim sulked, turned his chair to one side, and Mr. Keating, feeling victorious, asked Father Bob if he might regale them concerning the rocky courtship of Pascal and Matilda and he, having played gooseberry, party to it all. Father Bob thought it a capital idea and with a braggart air Mr. Keating began: "Pascal and myself would go dancing to the Hibernian on a Saturday night and before many moons Pascal and Matilda had clicked, except that the good lady began to play tricks on us, began to vanish. She would promise to meet us but come Saturday night, our eyes peeling the hall, there would be no sign of Matilda. We asked around. It turned out that she had signed up for dancing lessons with a Parisian woman. We tracked her down and one evening after a class I confronted her. I said, 'Whatever you do, Matilda, don't go over to the Hibernian anymore.' That shook her. She went wild altogether when I told her about the Mayo girl that had set her cap on Pascal and what brilliant partners they were—Charleston, Velincia, Black Bottom, Caledonian. She could have put a knife through me. A Mayo girl! Mayo, God help us! Galway was where kings, queens, and chieftains sprung from. Following Saturday she arrives, dressed to the nines, taps him on the shoulder and said, 'Hello, stranger,' and the denouement, well, the denouement is right here at this gathering with hosts whose generosity and hospitality is a byword in the parish."

After the clapping, Kevin stood up, his yellow paper hat askew on his head, and asked Mr. if it was time for his ghost story.

"Cripes, I hate ghost stories. They give me the runs," Chrissie said.

"Will someone rap her knuckles," the missus called and Chrissie limped off, said she knew where she was not wanted, Father Bob having to follow her and bring her back with his "Chrissie Asthor, Chrissie Mavourneen, Chrissie Macrae."

Kevin stood by the sideboard, so as to be in view of all.

"There was this girl at home, Dotey was her name. She had only months to live, consumption eating her, neighbors stopped coming in case it was contagious. No appetite, a spoon of jelly or blancmange and to make matters worse her father and mother were not hitting it off. Her father left for Scotland to get work picking the potatoes, gone six months and never wrote a line home. Her poor mother seeing her child wasting away, five younger children half hungry, and the hour came when Dotey opened her eyes for the last time and the death rattle started and I tell you this, her father beyond in Scotland saw her in her bed gasping for her life. She appeared to him and said, 'Come home, Dad, come home,' so he ran from that field and got a lift on a cattle boat and when he came into the room in his own house the women were all crying; he walked through them and Dotey sat up and kissed him, kissed him fondly, and from that day on he was a model father and a model husband. You see, Dotey had been dead twelve hours before he got there . . . it was her ghost that sat up and pleaded with him beyond in Scotland."

The talk was of ghosts that prowled the city, the Bowery, Hell's Kitchen, the Five Points, Harlem, soldiers from the Civil War appearing to their mothers and their sweethearts, because they had died too young.

"Goodness gracious, we are getting very morbid," Father Bob

said and decided that the moment had come for Matilda to give them a song in her inimitable soprano. Everyone knew that the missus's aria was the highlight of the party and she knew it too, but she made much of declining, said she couldn't, she simply couldn't, her throat, her larynx, asking to be excused, citing the lovely records that she had ordered specially, songs that would far surpass her little repertoire: "Where the Shannon River Meets the Sea," "Little Brown Jug," "May I Sleep in Your Barn Tonight."

She started out very hesitant, like she was singing to herself, and then her voice got high and coaxing, just as Solveig and I had heard every morning when she practiced in the bath for this performance. She had one hand on the rung of the chair and the other extended, her chest rising, swelling, so that the rubies palpitated and the perfumed sachet in her bosom jutted out:

> There's a bridle hanging on the wall
> There's a saddle in a lonely stall
> No more I answer to your call
> For that bridle's hanging on the wall.

Bravo. Brava. Calls for an encore. Nellie Melba wasn't in it. Matilda could knock spots out of the Caucasian or Russian ladies, could be in Carnegie Hall, the star attraction under the baton of a great conductor. In the commotion, the congressman glided in, like he had materialized out of nowhere, in a long fawn coat, a deputy behind him.

"The hall door was open," he said with an easy smile and the missus brimmed over with welcome and fluster, getting three people up as if he required three chairs, then as he sat next to her, introducing him to the faces down both sides of the table, all of whom were enrapt except for Chrissie, who was drooping, her head on Kevin's shoulder.

Whereas it was Father Bob this and Father Bob that, now it was congressman this and congressman that and he took her compliments with aplomb. Everything about him spoke of assurance—his smile, his gold-capped teeth, the gold ring with the wax seal on his little finger, and the abandon with which he allowed the coat to slip off his shoulders and slide on the floor. He repeated everyone's name and tried to guess from the accents what county they had come from, smiting himself when he got it wrong. When Mr. Keating tried to engage him about some marshal involved in a scandal and getting a licking in the newspapers, the congressman sidestepped it and said, "I can promise you it will all blow over."

If he hadn't asked me to sing and if afterward he hadn't come over, all pie, and said, "Thank God that there are girls like you" it mightn't have happened, except that it did. "The Castle of Dromore." October winds. The emptied lofty halls. Afterward such a rush of compliments, Mr. and he surpassing each other, what a voice, what purity, what feeling, and the missus taking it all into her heaving outraged heart. He asked our names, Solveig's and mine, and said we would never be true Yanks until we came to Jersey City and promised that he would send a car to fetch us one day.

Then he was gone.

The gift he had brought them was opened. It was a chocolate cake in the shape of a log with her name and Mr.'s name piped in cream icing and the message on the card read "Cherish the traditions but embrace the newfound liberty." What a beautiful message, so edifying. What a great man and what a great Irishman, on a par with Boss Tweed, John Kelly, the folk heroes, starting from nowhere, his father dying young, eleven children, up the ladder in the district, learning the ropes, no job too big or too little, the loyalty to his own, an Irishman drowned on the fleets up in the Cape and the congressman was there, an Irishman crushed by a beam on the railways and the congressman was there, an Irishman suffocated in the mines and the congressman was pressing for compensation for wife and children.

"Wasn't there some other lady, Louella?" Chrissie said.

"She was never a factor in the marriage," Pascal said, chastisingly.

"Oh, I don't know . . . he has a reputation for the ladies," Eamonn interrupted, because he had read that she followed him to a big party and he was with the wife and she threw down the fur coat he had bought her, told him to take it back.

"He's the coming man . . . rumor hath it that he might even be president one day," Father Bob said, in nearly sacred tones.

"God . . . and he came here," Pascal said, amazed.

"And he liked the little lassie . . . the little linnet," Felim said and looked at me and wondered when I'd be summoned to Jersey City. It was too much for Matilda. She barked at them, told the men to get out on the porch for their pipes and cigars and the women to go to the drawing room where the coffee would be served.

Mr. quenched the candles, some with a snuffer and the one in the turnip with his fingers, then tiptoed out. The yellowish smoke fogged the room. The missus had not got up, she was sitting, her breathing pronounced and her cousin Jenny leaning in over her, comforting her. Only her lips moved.

"Did you see the way he looked at her . . . the pair of them . . . I don't know which of them was the biggest ape, Pascal or him."

"Ah, that's men all over . . . pay no heed to them," Jenny said, kissing her.

Realizing that I was by the sideboard, she shunted the dishes in my direction and roared at me to go to the pantry and serve the sweetmeats.

It was the party but not the party. I was in a jaunting car at home, the posh table out in the field, the visitors with the paper hats that they'd pulled out of the crackers and Father Bob giving me the dime that he'd got from the plum pudding. Then it was not a dream. The missus shouting at us, "Get up, get up," and half asleep, rubbing our eyes, not knowing what had happened, Solveig and I staggered out of bed and clung to one another.

"Thieves, thieves," she was screaming it. Her sapphire ring was missing. I was nervy because secretly I loved that ring, the blue of it so various, so varying, seas of blue in the square nugget with its two shoulders of diamond, the two shoulders of diamond alone worth a fortune. I remembered the day that I'd cleaned it, dipped it in the ammonia water, then scrubbed it delicately with a toothbrush, rinsed and placed it on a soap dish to dry. She had supervised me, but when she was called downstairs to the telephone I tried it on and twirled it round and round, admiring it on my finger. Her fingers were fatter than mine.

Our drawers were ransacked, our mattresses turned over, and the letters my mother wrote me tossed to one side.

Mr. was holding a hand lamp and she was shouting at him to hold it higher as the paraffin was dripping. She was in her quilted dressing gown, metal curlers above her ears, and she looked like a big, fat doll gone mad.

Solveig's autograph book was opened, all her secrets disclosed, the hand-pressed flowers from Malmo and the motto her friend Greta had written: *For Solveig, this is my farewell present to her, forever.*

Next it was the scapulars belonging to my brother and feeling the relic inside the cloth the missus decided that undoubtedly it was her ring. With a glee she cut it open and when she found that it was not the ring, she swung the legs of the scissors in a chopping movement close to my eyes.

"It is not nice what you are doing to her," Solveig said.

Then it was back downstairs to their room. Cushions and pillows strewn about, drawers pulled open, drawers with his socks and his underwear and the gifts she had been brought for the party, the perfumes and soaps and frosted bottles of talc, discarded, as if they were useless.

"It must be somewhere, Matilda," Mr. kept saying, stooping to search in the carpet and the pile of the new rugs and she shrieking back at him, "Find it, find it."

My tin box with the picture of a glen in Scotland where they malted whiskey was the next thing to arouse her suspicion. She shook it and listened. The shopkeeper at home had had a little padlock made, for safekeeping on the passage over.

"Open it," she said.

I defied her. I would not open it. I defied her for as long as I could.

When she lifted the lid she was triumphant because inside lay the evidence of my thievery. A scarf of hers that was in flitters and the ends of bars of soap that smelled of lavender and rose water, then worst of all there was a white pompom that had fallen off Solveig's knitted cap. That did it. The missus exulted, told her husband that the proof was there in that very box, and struck a division between Solveig and me by dispatching her to the guest room until she was called.

My nightgown lay in a heap, bagging around my ankles, where I'd had to pull it down for her to inspect me. Her eyes went up and down my body, a violence in them, as if she would kill me for being thin and young and a favorite with her husband.

I thought I would be left there forever. It was a cupboard under the attic stairs, filled with suitcases, quilts, bolsters, pillows that smelled of dust and feathers, a dungeon, where I was quartered until I owned up.

She would come up from time to time and rap on the door. No words were said. The three or four raps were simply to know if I was ready to confess. Then I would hear the thud of her footsteps going back down the stairs.

It was dark by the time Mr. came up and shone the lamp in over me, tearing through the thick skin of cobweb. He just leaned in blinking and his voice was hoarse and wearied.

"Give it back and we won't tell the fathers," he said.

"I don't have it to give back."

"Is that true, Dilly?"

"That's true . . . I'll swing for it if I have to."

He beat his head against a wall, again and again, as if he wanted to dash his brains out, dash his memory out, and dash every piece of jewelry to smithereens.

"Come on," he said, and I crawled out.

The missus was still in her dressing gown, her feet inside the fender warming herself, and yet she shivered all over. There was a tray with food that she had not touched.

"You haven't had your tea, Matilda," he said.

"The fecking milk is gone off," she said and turning with a victorious expression said, "So she has confessed."

"She didn't steal it," he said.

"She didn't steal it," she almost spat at him and then laughed and asked if he had taken leave of his senses. When he said that it could be anyone, any of the guests who had gone up and down the stairs throughout the day, it could have been her cousin Jenny or Chrissie, she slapped him, fiercely, and a rush of blood to one of his cheeks contrasted with the other, which was deathly pale. He smarted at the humiliation, began walking around, his fists clenched, and then he looked across at the writing desk and it was as if he had been guided to it. He sprang but she was ahead of him, sprawled on it, her arms spread out like a wading bird. He tried pulling back the roll-top lid but she thwarted him.

"It's locked," he said.

"Yes, it's locked," she said.

"It's not usually locked," he said, and they faced each other with a submerged world of wrongs and then he knew and she knew that he knew.

"And I'm not doing anything about the fecking milk either," he said as he stormed to the door.

I was given a quarter of an hour to pack my things.

Exile

IT WOULD BE A ROW over a biscuit or a comb that was missing. The truth was they did not want me there. I was an extra person and an extra body in the bed. In return for my lodgings I did the laundry and ironing, all the cleaning and sewing for Betty, who was mad for style. Betty was boss, a big girl with big feet and big hands, always making novenas because her hair was falling out and she feared that no man would want to marry a bald woman.

Nan was the most money-minded. One evening she came home jubilant because a workman carrying a ladder had hit her by accident, struck her close to her eye, and she had insisted there and then on compensation. It was a dollar. It was put under an ink bottle to be smoothed out because it had been folded many times inside his pocket. I never knew what to expect. Sometimes they were friendly and sometimes not. All four of us slept in the one bed, two at the bottom and two at the top. All of us tossed and turned and raved in our sleep.

They would drop hints for my benefit about the landlady threatening to raise the rent, on account of an extra person, the extra person being me. Other times they would be all pie. Nan gave me a cardigan, a purple cardigan with knitted violets that served as buttons, said the buttons got on her nerves because of the way they never stayed shut. A week later she asked for it back. It was nothing but moods, moods.

Then one evening when I got back from the convent where I

worked part-time my clothes were in a bundle on the step, my name in big print on a label on top. At first I thought it was a joke, but when I examined it I saw that every stitch I owned was in there, my pleated skirt, my good shoes, laddered stockings, my brush and comb, my prayer book, everything. They were telling me to go. It was the month of May and there was a magnolia tree in bloom in the garden. The blinds inside the house were drawn, all the blinds, the way they are when someone has died. I reckoned they had conferred with other lodgers and had done it as a team. It did something to me. I stood there and called up, thinking that one of them would come down and, seeing I had no one to turn to, would take pity on me and let me back. No one came.

In the waxen flower of the magnolia that was wide as a saucer, a tawny bee fed itself on the saffron threads and I thought, *I'll never forget this moment, the hum of the bee, the saffron threads of the flower, the drawn blinds, nature's assiduousness and human cruelty.*

. . .

Dear Dilly,

Black and Tans and their elite brothers in terror called here two nights back, they burst in with blackened faces, seven or eight of them and I had to make a dive for my life. Your father had his hands and feet bound while they searched. Having failed to find your brother I had to act as candle bearer, going around the house while they rooted in drawers and presses, everything skiving out and then one said to the gang leader, a big tall fellow with a military cast, said, "C'mon, Reg, there's nothing here," and the leader struck him and used the most terrible language because of his name being said. They do not want their names known for fear of reprisal, but it is creatures like us that the reprisals are vented on, hay and crops burned, animals slaughtered, taking revenge on families that they suspect have housed the volunteers. Shops and business premises have been set fire to. Even a doctor that rendered medical aid to a wounded volunteer had his automobile burned and he is frightened for his life. A man beyond Tulla that was a known sympathizer was taken out of his house along with his wife and children, then the house set fire to and the man thrown back into it, his wife and children looking on and the gang shouting, "Let him fry, let him fry." They were drunk as they so often are.

Write to me, in God's name, write to me.

Bridget

Coney Island

THE SUN WAS a bowl of fire above us. There was no escaping it. It poured onto the sea, the ranges of color blue and blue-green and turquoise that stretched all the way to home and back again, the same waves but in different colors, different tumblings, home that I wanted to forget and both could and couldn't.

Jugglers, sword swallowers, men in turbans and togas, young boys in every kind of uniform, tugging at our sleeves: "Step right up, ladies, step right up, ladies, everybody wins."

There was Mary Kate and Kitty and Noreen and me. Kitty was the fashion plate in a pale buttercup muslin dress with leg-of-mutton sleeves, her eyes the color of snuff, needly and inquisitive. She was Mary Kate's friend. And Noreen, with flat feet, in her flat shoes and long black streelish skirt, stopping to gape at the sights, the domes and palaces painted the white of wedding cake, the roller coaster, the cannon coaster, the bamboo slide, the barrel of love, saying the same thing over and over again: "Aaragh, shure, isn't it all marvelous."

The smells of frying oil and sugared doughnuts made us ravenous, but Kitty was in charge of the money that we'd pooled. People were dancing cheek to cheek in broad daylight, different bands clashing, German and Cuban and Mexican, an oriental woman dancing by herself, an array of silver coins clunking on her chest, her arms bangled and with the writhe of a serpent, men around her, staring, her smile for everyone and for no one, a faraway smile. Two dwarfs in neat suits shook hands with passersby to entice them into the Hall of Freaks. They were either brother and sister or husband and wife, because they had the same name. Above a booth, the letters in scarlet, twinkling on and off, MADAM CASSANDRA, and an assistant assuring us that if we went in, we would come out knowing who our husbands would be, because Madam could predict the very moment when we set eyes on him. We were all for it but Kitty intervened, said hordes of people were rooked, taken in by that bluff.

He stood out because of being so very tall and the fact of his wearing a heavy overcoat in the boiling heat. He looked aloof, like a preacher, his lean bearded face tilted, looking up at the figures on the Ferris wheel, going skywards, screaming with terror, their hands clutching the side chains, then dipping down and those that had been below sent up to face the music. Kitty tapped him from behind — "If it isn't the Angel Gabriel himself" — and he turned and smiled, taking us all in, a bearded man with searching brownish eyes that seemed to listen as intently as to see.

"Are you afraid you'll catch cold?" she said.

"I was just on my way," he said, that bit awkward.

"Sure, you're always on your way and here's four lovely lassies for you to dance with."

They bantered. Was he married yet? No. Was she married yet? No. Maybe he was married on the sly to some wild woman, an octoroon, out there in Minnesota or Wisconsin or wherever, with not even a priest to hear the vows. What happened to the words of the song that she was to send him? What happened to the dance he failed to show up at on St. Patrick's night? The two of them scolding one another and Noreen, feeling the nap of his coat: "Aaragh, shure, isn't it all marvelous."

"Can I get ye a cup of tea?" he asked.

"We'd rather ices," Kitty said, speaking for us all.

She linked his arm and they walked ahead, us lagging behind, the crowds milling, as the next train and the next arrived, the ice cream sweet and thick like a custard deliciously cold and the biscuit taste of the cone.

It was from that to the open-air shooting gallery, men shooting like billy-o, some with caps, some without, their eyes looking down the barrels of the guns, so intent as if they were in a war.

The spare guns were tethered to the counter for anyone to join in, and Gabriel paid for us all to have a round. How we laughed, how we protested, him teaching us how to hold it, swivel it, and how to sight the targets, which were tiers of unflurried white ducks.

"Don't forget to breathe," he said laughing, and we were off.

The atmosphere so heady, what with us shooting and the spectators, mostly women egging on their husbands or their boyfriends, the muzzles of other guns maneuvering this way and that across the counter, the music from the carousel nearby, various bands and the slight *ping* as the bullets hit the wings of the falling ducks, so fast and furious, then a faint after-smell as of something having been singed.

"She's a good shot," I heard Gabriel say after I hit the target three times, flabbergasted that I had done it, and Mary Kate said tartly that it was because of my brother, one of the mad Fenian men.

Gabriel and another man a few guns away were such crack shots that the official called for an impromptu competition, knowing it would draw a crowd, and it did. That was the first time that I noticed he had a finger missing and only a stump for a thumb.

Such a sense of thrill, ducks on three levels came cascading down, their falls fast and free, that and the booming as one or other hit the gong that hung from a long swaying pendulum, spectators taking sides, caps thrown into the air, people jostling for a better look and sparring.

Yet the two men shook hands cordially when it was over.

Gabriel was given a cranberry jug as a prize, the gallery owner's name in gold lettering swimming inside the rich crimson waves of the blown glass.

"It's for ye all," he said, and Kitty took it and began to polish it with the swag of her dipping sleeve.

It was she who proposed getting in the water for a paddle. I didn't want him to see my white legs, which was why I volunteered to mind the things, the shoes and stockings, his overcoat and the jug. Sitting there on a knoll of scorching sand, people all around so carefree and loud, men in awful flannel swimsuits smoking pipes and women in knickerbockers lifting their backsides to be photographed, not minding how foolish they looked, yet the whole world when I looked at it through the waves within the jug seemed rose-colored.

When they came back, so glowing, he said I wouldn't be able to say I had been to Coney Island unless I got in. I was alone with him then, the water so silken over the ankles, but my footing unsteady because of the shifting sand and seaweed tangled in the toes. Across the bay was a jut of land suspended in sunshine that he said was named after a flock of sheep that once grazed there. Then he asked where I came from and if I missed it. Was I homesick for Ireland? No. His mother and father had been youngsters when they left, meeting up on the boat, sweethearts from then on, but they had died young, too young, and so it was in his bones. He knew the locality, which was near a mountain named after a warrior. He asked me to repeat the names of the townlands where I came from, as they were poetry to him, which they weren't to me and yet as I recited them I could see drills of cabbage in our bit of garden at home, slugs on the green and blue-green outer leaves, and into my head came the bawling of stray cattle on a road.

Torick
Derry Gnaw
Kilratera

Coppaghbaun
Pollagoona
Bohatch
Derrygoolin
Glenwanish
Alenwanish
Knockbeha
Sliabh Bearnagh
Sliabh Aughty

We'd waded far out. I saw the breakers vault up and head toward us and I knew that I was falling and so was he. Inside the water he held me. I held him. Swaying like dancers but clumsier and that wild happiness, hoots of laughter all around, people getting drenched, keeling over, a woman's shout, "Pick her up, Dwight, pick her up," the child hoisted up, the waves like big barrels rolling in over us, the foam in our faces and he saying, having to shout, "You're all right, we're all right," borne back in, half swept, half cresting, without ever letting go of one another.

They were raging. Mary Kate ran to squeeze the water out of the tail of my dress, saying I'd catch pneumonia, and Kitty remarking that a person could be excused for thinking we'd got engaged out there. He laughed it off and sat to put on his shoes, half smiling, already gone, thousands of miles distant, to the untamed world of the bush, to the wilds where he worked as a lumberjack, far from us and the hurly-burly and the cheek-to-cheek dancing on the open marquee.

Only by a sort of hidden smile when he stood in front of me to say goodbye could I tell that it was not nothing out there in the ocean, that it was something. How I longed to be alone, to relive every second of it, the swoop of the waves, the way he held me, the spume over our faces, my wet clothes wetting my ribs, clinging to each other and the water trying to suck us down.

"I bet he's not going out west . . . it's too early for logging," Kitty said, reckoning that he would be somewhere in the city that night, seeing some old flame or going to a dance, whereupon she and Mary Kate sparred over the different girlfriends he'd had, a Rita Thing-um-bob who'd given him Irish lessons, a barmaid the time he worked in a bar, a nurse from Roscommon, different girls, different Gabriels, and guessing at my elation, Mary Kate thumped me and said, "Don't you go getting soft on him, he breaks hearts he does," as poor Noreen hailed some drunken passersby to say, "Aaragh, shure, isn't Gabriel a love barrel all to himself."

A Ghost

THE TWO OTHER GIRLS in the room, Mabel and Deirdre, said I imagined it. But they were wrong. My brother appeared to me there. A beam of light from the streetlamp lay in a crooked zigzag along the floor, toward the bed, and my brother stepped onto it, his face pensive but not crying, dressed as he might be for a wedding, his good suit, his collar and tie, and not a mark on him, no bloodstain, yet I knew it was not as a bridegroom he had appeared. He was dead and he had come to tell me so. After the first shock of seeing him I spoke, I said, "Michael, Michael," but he did not answer. I asked him what was wrong, was it dead he was, but he did not answer. Then he was gone. The next day came the telegram from my mother, saying that her darling son had been shot by enemy fire and that a letter would follow.

August

Dear Dilly,

You got my wire. My Michael is gone. A bullet from an enemy transport lodged in his chest, which in less than an hour occasioned his death. He lay in the market square, people too afraid to come out to him for fear of more gunshot. It was a boiling day. The blood caking into him. He had gone into the town to get medicine for a comrade when a member of the garrison recognized him as being part of the ambush. He was just let lie there in the hot sun. Even the sparrow finds a place to die, even the swallow wherein to find his rest, but not my

89

son Michael, my darling light. Be sure to have Masses said for the repose of his soul and for us.

Your loving mother,
Bridget

September 15

Dear Dilly,

We went to the military barracks in Tipperary town. We asked to see the officer in charge and had to wait all day. A tall standoffish fellow came out and led us into an office. He opened a big ledger, then read it out to us — cause of death hemorrhaging. Cause of death Murder. He said the incident was looked into and the army were in their complete rights as our son, your brother, was a felon and execution was what felons were dealt. We came out of there broken and dumb.

A man wheeling a bicycle walked behind us for a good bit, so as not to arouse suspicion, and then told us that he would bring us to the house of the woman that had run to succor our darling Michael, at the very end. She was too frightened to show her face in the town ever since it happened, in case she would be arrested as a conspirator. She hid in her own house and the man with the bicycle brought her a sup of milk or a bit of bread every three or four days. She was a washerwoman, she took in washing. She told us how she had been walking up the market square, taking washing back to a hotel, when she heard a human cry. She heard him before she came on him. The square was empty, people having fled into their houses once they had heard the shots. She knelt and saw that it was a dying man and listened to his last words, his last words asking God to accept him in the final resting place and asking his mother to forgive him the suffering he had caused her. She saw that he was ebbing and then he said he would like her to remove his miraculous medal and give it to his beloved mother. It's all I have of him. Sweet Jesus, was not the blood of the Savior enough to turn mankind away from slaughter.

Your broken mother,
Bridget

Ma Sullivan

I HAD SECURED a place in a big store as apprentice seamstress, thirty or forty of us down in a basement, the whir of the sewing machines all day long, so brisk and businesslike, baking hot in the summer with the steam from the irons and the windows never allowed open in case dirt or grime got on the precious bales of silk or satin, pelts of chamois like little carcasses, their edges brown and shriveled and curled up. A supervisor like a spitfire, walking around, making sure we didn't idle or make mistakes with our sewing and not allowing us to go to the bathroom, only when we clocked in and before we clocked out. My specialty was sleeves, collars, and bastings, along with buttonholes, cross-eyed from doing silk buttonholes, doing them in my sleep, the stitch slanting, the little knot, then down, then up again, in matching threads for ladies' outfits. Every morning I set out with my thimble, my spools of thread, my big scissors, and the bread for my lunch, but it mattered not, because I had Ma Sullivan to come home to.

God shone on me the day I knocked on Ma Sullivan's door. "You've come to the right house anyhow," she said and brought me in. She needed a girl, part-time, to help with the dinners when her boys, as she called them, came home in the evening. She kept eight lodgers, her wild geese, all from home and ravenous when they got back from the building sites and the railway lines where they worked, often miles outside the city. She was mother, landlady, nurse, and banker to every single one of them. She hid their wages so's that they could save to go home, got them up for Mass of a Sunday, and saw to it that they were in bed early weeknights. Whatever ailment they had, she dosed them with castor oil, castor oil was the cure for everything, including, as I was to discover, a broken heart.

She and I slept in the same room, a room with twin beds, a big brown wardrobe, and a tin washstand with a china basin and ewer. She had had a son that got drowned up in Long Island and though he was never mentioned below stairs, she and me prayed for him every night, each at the end of our own beds, praying for our departed. He was a Michael too, same as my brother.

Her dances one Saturday a month were famous all over. The big kitchen would be turned into a dancehall, chairs and stools pushed back, the long table with a white cloth for a buffet supper that was either bacon and cabbage or mutton stew, the entrance charge half a dollar per head. Christy, a famous concertina player, provided the music. His concertina was kept in its folded box on the mantelpiece as she did not trust him to take it away, in case he pawned it for drink or left it in some dive.

Then one night Gabriel was there, the same long coat, the same reserve, and Ma Sullivan rushing to welcome him and sit him down for a drink. Several girls knew him and before long he was dragged up for the set dance, four men and four women facing each other, Christy's face bent over his instrument as if it was part of him, the atmosphere so pent up, lighted lanterns at either end of the kitchen floor, and the men that were not dancing already tapping their feet to mark time with the music. The dancers faced each other and though they did not speak, they had already communed with their eyes. The music transformed them, gave them license to be wild, wilder, the hard high heels and the hard low heels stamping the flagged floor, girls looping in and out under the arms of their partners, sliding away but not before they had made some sort of pact with them and Gabriel the favorite. All wanted to be in his radius, smiling up at him.

At the end of a round Christy would play something quiet, eerie, eking notes out of the concertina that summoned bits of home, rocky land, fields, that limestone landscape with Cromwell's curse: "No timber to hang a man, no water to drown a man, nor no earth to bury a man."

Gabriel had come across to sympathize with me as Ma Sullivan had told him why I was not dancing and why I was in black. It was clear that he had not remembered me, not remembered Coney Island and the big waves and the place names, and reading it in my eyes, the slight disappointment, he just flinched and turned away.

When he left I thought it would be the best part of a year before we laid eyes on him again and I imagined the train covering those great distances, the Great Lakes, then the wheat fields, then the long and lonely stretches of prairie, and into the bush that Gussie said was a savage place and made men savage. Gussie had been there, had spent fifteen years of his boyhood and youth there, apprentice to a blacksmith, pulling off old horseshoes, digging the dirt from the hooves, paring the calluses but, as he said, he never got the promotion, never got to shoe a horse in his life. Gussie used to help around the house, fix lights and fuses, do a bit of plastering or painting in return for his dinner, and afterward he would sit by the stove drafting a letter to a widow woman in Longford who had gone home and had built a house on a hill, a big house that overlooked all the others. He kept hoping that she would send for him, but there was nothing in her letters to suggest it. Me mooning over Gabriel and Gussie over the Longford woman, and she boasting of the fine herd of sucklers and dairy cows that she owned.

Courtship

THE STAMP WAS GREEN with red-coated cavalry in a misted wood, their spears flying, the front legs of the horses charging and buckling in the frenzied air. I thought it was some cousin who had tracked me down, but it was Gabriel. The letter was short. *"I am sorry you lost your brother. He put his country before himself and you can be proud of him. If you feel like sending me more place names or any bit of news, it would be appreciated. Thanks anyhow. Gabriel."*

They were not love letters; if anything they were letters determined to dampen any notion of love. They could have been letters to a man and yet they would arrive every three or four weeks, the envelope often damp and cold from being in a mailbag for so long, and mostly they were written on greaseproof paper. Where a word would have soaked in, I'd search for it on the other side with the beam of a candle, so as not to miss anything. They were snatches of his life, and through his eyes I could see the tracks of the wolves in the snow in the early morning, he and the men off, before sunrise in their hide boots, their socks tied up over their knee pants to keep out the slush. A lonely freezing place with clumps of green alder burning for a bit of warmth, the rasping of the saws all day long, pairs of men whose lives depended on one another, chopping, limbing, loading, and skedding, weary when evening came and they and the dogs glad to be going back for their suppers.

He would describe the forests and the different trees, pine and cedar and hemlock, trees two hundred feet high, tall and proud, like tall proud ships, and the fight that they put up against the hackings of the cross saw, the long battle, then the waver before the big crash, the long low hiss as it fell, a smell of wet sap, sap as alive as blood, as true as blood and the stumps sulky and lonely-looking, then the cut planks loaded onto the horse-drawn sleighs, down to the rapids to end up in the sawmills, for various items of furniture.

He and the cook were hoping, he said, to make a vegetable garden, to plant potatoes and onions, anything to make a change from the dreary diet of beans and pork soused in saltpeter, and he added that he might be asking Gussie to forward him a sack of seed potatoes.

One night they had a stag party that ended in a drunken brawl. He painted a picture of it, the vast forest, wild venison on slats over an open fire, the entrails left in for flavor but emptied halfway through, and juniper leaves or juniper berries put into the cavity, a makeshift dance place on a raised platform, the music hammered out on kettles or tin washboards, the one Indian woman with her baubles and paint, wife to none and temptation to many. Finns and Swedes and Canadians and Scots and Irish and South Americans getting blind drunk because they refused to water the rum, singing rival songs, shouting each other down concerning their country's woes and their country's injustices. A Finn and a Scotsman had gone a distance away to fight, had stripped to the waist, ready to kill each other, the lit pine branches held up, as in Roman times, men reveling in it, until the superintendent had to be brought to separate them, dousing them with bucket after bucket of water, both men rolling around in the snow, cursing but claiming victory.

Then it came, the letter that unknown even to myself I was waiting for. He couldn't get to sleep, what with the lads snoring, the straw in the ticking itching his face, the wool blanket itching his feet, finding himself outside under a roof of frozen stars, he sat down and realized how he kept thinking of Dilly and wondering if it was too much to ask, to suppose that Dilly might be thinking of him. And she was.

And she was.

The first time that we kissed was in Ma Sullivan's after a dance when he came up to the bedroom to get his coat. His coat, like himself, was made an exception of, other coats were kept on the floor of the back kitchen, and picking his up he bumped into me and kissed me even before he knew he had. Then he looked at me with such a baleful look and said, "It couldn't be helped, could it."

"She'll be coming up," I said. Ma Sullivan was very strict about boys.

"Come outside," he said, and after he'd gone I climbed out the window and into the garden and stood with him and we did not kiss then, just stood there, just looking, just drinking one another in.

It was snowing in the vast cemetery in Brooklyn, big bulky overcoats of snow on the tall tombs, draping the headstones and the flat tablets with their long loving recitations. Not a soul about. The paths cleared for visitors to walk on: the Ravine Path, the Cedar Path, the Waterside Path, the Sunset Path. We walked and walked. On the heads of the marble angels and archangels caps and skullcaps of snow, so jaunty, so jocular, and the silence so immense and Gabriel and me. We came upon a little house, a little vault with steps down to it and an entrance door with a woman's face carved on the outside, a woman with a mourning expression and strands of long marble hair that fell down onto her shoulders.

"She looks a bit like you," he said, and then he touched my arm with such a gravity and asked was I ready to be engaged.

There in the ravine path or the sunset path or the waterside path, I forget which, the angels and archangels with their jaunty head-gear, the blanketed tombs, he and me became engaged, without having to utter a word. Then he dug the end of a branch into the white earth and wrote our names — *Dilly Kildea and Gabriel Gilchriest October 6th* — and we looked down at them, so settled, as if they would never be effaced, the snowflakes like little morsels falling into the dark grooves of the lettering he had transcribed.

Betrayal

A THIN FALL of snow had turned to sludge and the wooden boards of the bridge were skiddy. Crowds were hurrying in both directions, some like us crossing into the city and some going back home, children with rosy cheeks holding magic packages to their chests, packages that could not be opened until Christmas, which was three weeks away.

The same Christmas that I'd lived for. I was making Gabriel a satin waistcoat. His measurements were taken by the cook and forwarded on bits of darning wool. All else about it was to be a surprise.

I'd never set foot on Brooklyn Bridge before, never had cause to. It was like a ship, the sides all steel and might, steel railings, steel cables, steel ropes, steel girders, and big steel pipes like crocodiles dipping down into the river.

In the distance lay Manhattan with its lit windows, a vast honeycomb of lit windows, behind one of which, as they maintained, he was lurking.

The way they broke it to me was vile because try as they might, there was gloating in their eyes. I'd come out just after six, along with all the other girls, into the fresh air, to window-shop and then walk the mile or so up the hill and home to Ma Sullivan's.

The main window had only one item of clothing, a beaded satin dance dress across a chaise that rested on a floor of artificial snow that was strewn with snow-laden branches of silk fir trees and little toy silver motorcars. Santa Claus was ringing his big brass bell for money and the gifts for the poor were in a big heap, like the heap for a bonfire, the air biting cold and the singing from the choir reaching up into the heavens from where more snow was forecast.

The way they broke it to me: "You tell her. No. You tell her. No, you tell her. I don't know how to break it to her, poor girl . . . poor Delia . . . poor Dilly."

False sympathy oozing out of them, their eyes brimming with it, and then Kitty opening the sheet of folded ruled paper for me to read it myself by the light from the shop window: *"Dilly Kildea will not be seeing Gabriel Gilchriest again but she doesn't know it yet."* The words swam before my eyes like a mirage, like something there and then not there. It could not be true. He had promised. I knew the hour he was coming. I was making the waistcoat. It had a scarlet lining. He had a piece of jewelry for me that an Indian had specially made. I would have to keep guessing what it might be.

They were plying me with questions. Questions. "What had he promised?" *Nothing.* "What was between us?" *Nothing.* "Had he behaved dishonorably?" *Nothing.* My nothings infuriated them even more. Somehow they had got wind of the engagement. I wrote it once with white flour on the oven in Ma Sullivan's, when I was making a pie, then rubbed it out.

The anonymous letter, they said, had come to Kitty's lodgings, and she could swear who was behind it. Rita Thing-um-bob was behind it, an old flame of Gabriel's, the girl that had taught him Irish and Irish dancing and still had a yen for him, had told the priest in her parish that she could wind him around her little finger and it seems she could. He was a ruthless man they said, false-hearted, like the false-hearted lover in the forester's song.

My heart broke at what they had to tell me next. I had asked him once about his missing finger and he'd said the accident had happened very early one morning, before sunrise, the saw jamming in a tree, his comrade trying to undo it too fast and the saw flying up and backward, like a jackknife, taking one entire finger and the mound of his thumb. I'd asked him what he did with the finger and he said that he'd put it in his pocket, put a rag around the thumb, and that night in the camp, the blacksmith who doubled as doctor sewed the wound up, but as for the finger he forgot, it must have been thrown away. But it hadn't. He had given it to Rita Thing-um-bob. A keepsake of him that, as she told the priest, was priceless, worth more than any engagement ring.

On the far side were the skyscrapers, reaching nearly to the stars, and that unbroken vista of lit windows that seemed to be spying on us who were heading to spy on him. We passed under the two tall arches, like the arches in an ancient church, and set foot in Manhattan, which he had said we would explore one day.

Twice on the bridge I had rebelled and said I would go no farther. They vacillated between sympathy and threats. A bronze plaque in the side wall had engravings of the many who had toiled and the many who had lost their lives in the twenty years of building it. Farther along, another plaque of clasped hands, signifying the clasped hands of the two cities, and I felt for a second the warmth of Gabriel's hand, the splay and the safety of it.

Kitty had business with the priest who knew Rita Thing-um-bob and his church was just at the end of the bridge, in a backwater all to itself. No cars, no traffic, just one old Chinese woman in her slippers, pushing a barrow and holding a black umbrella that was broken. The rectory, as it was termed, was around the side, and she went across a little garden with steppingstones bedded into the clay, overgrown plants and fallen fruit bushes, like a cottage garden at home.

Mary Kate said that as the church was new to us we would go in and make three wishes for our special intentions. My three wishes were all rolled into one, which was that we would not find him. The inside of the church was a somber brown and gave off a smell of polish, brown pews, a brown gallery, a brown wooden crucifixion, brown pillars guarding the altar, and brown confessionals with thick brown curtains. The only bit of light was a gold shimmer from the edging of a huge missal, where the candle rays had caught it. She lit a candle for us both and whispered to me that probably oodles of girls had crushes on him.

Kitty came back beaming, like she had won money. The priest was so kind, so obliging, and had given her a holy medal that she allowed me to kiss.

We walked through crowded, rundown streets, losing our way more than once, they full of bravado, mouthing the home truths they would tell him, yet Kitty unloosening her black hair from its thick slide, quivering as she had quivered that day in Coney Island when she spoke to him, and Mary Kate squeezing me for courage.

It was a squalid street of tenement houses, children playing, drunk people, bicycles, lame people on crutches, arguments, a laundry, and a foul smell from the river. They rang the doorbell several times before anyone appeared, then a woman stuck her head out an upper window, the cord broken so that she had to hold up the frame with one hand as she shone a bit of candle down. They asked to see Rita Thing-um-bob and were told that we had no business coming to that address. They asked if she was home and were told to scoot it. They asked if they could pass a note through the letterbox and have it read, which maddened her even more.

"You sure stick your noses into other people's business," she shouted, and a big spurt of hot candle grease was flung in our direction.

We stood there like three apes, a fresh fall of snow swirling down, and I knew the way one knows in one's gut that I would not ever see Gabriel again.

. . .

Yet all the way up to Christmas I kept listening for him, listening for his whistle along the street, the way a dog listens and can hear its master, except that he did not come. Christmas Day was the worst. After the dinner the lodgers played hide and seek, up and down the stairs, into the garden, into the basements, anywhere and everywhere, and at times I had to escape to Ma Sullivan's bedroom to cry my eyes out.

It was her idea that I go home. This pining was no good, I was like a scarecrow, but the fresh air and my own people would console me. She gave me the fare, said I could pay it back in installments, and arranged with my supervisor that I would get my job back when I returned.

Why I brought my scissors I will never know. My big scissors, cumbersome as shears, that traveled home with me on the boat. To cut clothes, to cut their hair, or maybe to cut something out of myself?

Homecoming

AT FIRST GLANCE in our kitchen I mistook the oxtail for trifle, a pinkish mass on a plate with white streaks in it, which I thought to be trifle and whipped cream. The lamp on the settle bed threw out such a feeble light that everything else was in semidarkness, the neighbors so shy, and my mother all in black, shrunken and weeping. There was the smell of turf smoke and milk going off and cold potato skins on the dresser, high up where the dog could not snatch them. My mother stared at me and squeezed my hands while the others admired my brown trunk with its brass latches and my name painted in bold letters.

"At long last, at long last," they kept saying, as though it were a dirge.

Keepsakes of my brother everywhere, a photo of him in uniform, his leggings, his revolver, and a letter in a frame that a priest—who had risked coming into that square to give him absolution—copied out in those last moments, in broiling heat.

My father was upstairs bed-bound and they sent me up with a cup of tea so full that it sloshed onto the saucer. Since he had taken to his bed he ate almost nothing, only currant-top biscuits, which he dipped in his tea. His teeth didn't fit, so he couldn't chew. My poor father, too proud to let me see him without his false teeth, his stubble white and raw and sharp as thorn, saying that he meant to shave for me, that he should have shaved in my honor but that he would do so next day, I would bring up the mirror, a bowl of water, his shaving brush, and his cutthroat razor and guide his hand while he did it. He was so thankful that I had come. He said I had grown to be quite a swank but there was no sarcasm in his voice or his saying it.

At the supper it was nothing but questions. Questions. Was New York full of gangsters, how wide were the streets, what friends had I made, what foods did people eat, and did the different races live in ghettos and come out to challenge one another? A child under the table kept on tying and untying the shoelaces of my brown high-heeled shoes, then its mother, Josie, smarted at the fact that I didn't realize whose child it was, it was hers and Ned's, Ned that I'd driven cattle with and forked manure with before I went off and forgot them all. My mother kept urging me to eat up and not to be so standoffish. How long was I staying? They both asked and answered for me. I would not leave a mother alone in her plight. They described how she had kept the news of my brother's death from our ailing father and on the evening that he was brought home, chapel bells rang out and kept ringing in honor of him, his valor, and my father kept asking if it was a bishop or something that was visiting the parish, not knowing that it was his own son. He was not told of it until the day of the funeral itself, because they believed that if they had told him earlier he would insist that the lid be lifted and it would be too much for him to see a son with half of him blasted off.

The neighbors were at great pains to remark on the spread my mother had got ready for me, the oxtail that she had ordered weeks before, fearing that either it or I would arrive too soon. Noni described how it had to be left to simmer for hours, then taken out and my mother having to remove the root and the gristly bits, the broth half-jellied and my mother thickening it with a corn flour for flavor. So why was I not eating it? The overstrong smell of the country butter that I had not smelled since I left had made me nauseous. They remarked on how different

I was from the good-natured girl who had left with the oilskin bag and her few treasures in the tin box that Dinnie had padlocked.

My mother fed the crusts of dry bread that she had soaked in cold tea to the dog at her feet. It was a new dog, the spitting image of the old one, black with white splotches on her forehead and mismatching eyes. Princess she was called, on account of the other dog being called Prince.

They were eager as they stood around the open trunk while I took out the presents, my mother instantly saying that my father would have no use for fur-lined gloves, nor she for a black coat with a turquoise clasp, but the others grateful, over-grateful, for the things I had given them: a rope of artificial pearls, a glitterish bracelet, a nightdress case, and a box of handkerchiefs with lace borders and embroidered mottoes.

The rain wakened me, the mountain through the back window lost in gray drizzle, the few cattle and our one horse huddled under a wall but not lowing, just standing there shivering, because they were soaked wet.

My mother was crisp with me for coming down in my style and would not hear of me going out to the yard with her to do the jobs. I was a lady now. There was a gulf between us, she knowing I had already gone and I not knowing how soon I could break it to her. After she went out, I did something rebellious. I emptied the contents of the cutlery drawer onto the floor and poured a kettle of boiling water over them to clean the stains, egg yolk and meal and cod-liver oil, wanting to throw away everything that was sad and poor and stale and musty and rancid.

Silverfish

IT WAS TESS who told me about the crowd going to the all-night dance. We'd been school friends. We'd picked mushrooms and pretended to have seen a big ship. She had got married since I went away; it was a made match, a man from the midlands, a Donal, who had worked in a garage but took to farming, out all day, draining fields and callows so that he could till them and sow corn. It was Tess that put the keepsake in my hand, saying it would bring good luck. It was a silverfish with gold-threaded scales and when she put it in the palm of my hand, I felt it spring backward as if it was a real fish, something telling in it. Their new house, built on the grounds next to the old thatched cottage, was ugly, it felt like a barracks, the walls only recently plastered and damp coming up from the cement floor. We were in the good room and at first she had been shy, remarking on the change in me, my clothes, and even a bit of a twang. The wedding presents, even after a year, still lay on the dining room table, a tea set, sheets, pillowcases, small blue glasses, and a blue decanter with a silver chain hanging on its throttle that read CLARET. Among them the silverfish that she made me take. She was happy I was home, I would come often, I would be company, Donal was the best man, the kindest man, but men were not company. On the floor there was a cradle, a low cradle like a little boat, padded and lined with white linen, and she was praying for it to be filled, for a baby to fill the days. Then all of a sudden she ran out and I could hear her mounting the stairs as I looked at the one picture on the wall, a petrol-blue sea, the waves moiling but the ship with its sails and rigging bellied out, ready to go. She came back with what remained of her wedding cake. It was in a white cake box with a doily and the icing had to be hammered with the handle of a knife before we could crack our teeth on it.

She said lads would be going to the dance-cum-card party the following Sunday, and telling it she blushed scarlet as if she harbored a secret yearning to go.

Revel

THE LORRY TO COLLECT me hooted and I ran down to the stile in my silver-crusted shoes, my long velvet coat trailing in the grass.

There were six men, all in their good suits, and they gabbled their names as I mounted the high step and a hand helped me in. I was squeezed between Iggy the driver and a man named Cornelius, a chain-smoker, his brown hair flopping over the side of his lean face, the others all beholden to him and Iggy telling me to watch out for that man, that he was Mr. Coaxyoram himself and many a young girl soft on him, but oh, what a gentleman and from a scion of gentlemen. I learned that it was his horse, Red River, that would be played for. He had given it to his friend Jacksie who had lost his all gambling, and the lady he'd been engaged to had jilted him and had not even returned the engagement ring that was his mother's, which was an heirloom.

Careering along the country road and then onto byroads that were wet and icy, there was such jocularity, their telling me I might be out for a week or more.

Carts and sidecars had pulled up in the big courtyard of Jacksie's house, horses feeding out of oat bags and a fiddler ignoring the rain, coming out to usher us in. Jacksie was dressed as a bandit, had a patch over one eye, and ran to Cornelius to tell him that twelve tables had been taken, six players per table at five quid a head, packs of cards and grog donated by publicans far and wide, and Red River, as he whispered, in a barn miles away, because with a crowd like that and maybe a bit of jealousy, a horse could get stolen or poisoned or nobbled or anything.

Greyhounds rushed and yelped around the hall where there were pots and pans put down to take the rain that came pouring in.

"Have a tour, have a tour," Jacksie said to me and regretted the fact that since his poor dear mother died, the rooms lacked a woman's warmth, a woman's touch. In the kitchen two big women in cooks' outfits were carving legs of ham and beef for the sandwiches that would be served all through the game, then a big breakfast at dawn.

The players were mostly seated, itching to begin, impatient men shuffling the packs of cards, a center lamp on each table, and a hail of welcome as Cornelius entered. From the moment they started, everything quieted, the faces serious and concentrated, except for two men who were drunk and skittish asking if Red River had been covered by Man O' War himself.

The players were mostly men, with only two women, a Mrs. Hynes, who kept shouting to her partner to remember more of the red and less of the black — "Remember more o' the red and less o' the black, Timmy" — and a Miss Gleason, who had kept her hat on, a pearled hatpin skewering the cloth, the pearling a sickly yellow.

Nobody danced but the fiddle squeaked in fits and starts and the greyhounds slipped in and out under the tables that wobbled as fists were banged in recrimination. Disputes after each round as to how many tricks this person or that person had got, and muting when Miss Gleason got flustered, first reneged on herself, then played her best card, which she needn't have, and her partner, a gruff man, jumping up, calling her a mad Irish eejit and telling everyone, "She can't count, she can't blasted count, she doesn't even know that a five is better than a knave." Poor Miss Gleason mortified, her cheeks the same vermilion as the walls, asking him in a screechy voice to take that remark back and people next to her pulling her to sit down, then Jacksie standing on a chair and in a thunderous voice declared her a liability in any game. She sat frail and sulking, her cheeks scalding, vowing that she would never darken his doorstep again, some hushing her and others sniggering at her disgrace.

Cornelius and Iggy were in the final round and their opponents, who were from the city, displeased and spiteful, not a sound in that room until, at the very zenith, cries of disbelief as it turned out that Cornelius had the knave, the ace, and the king, each of which he threw down with a braggart air and Iggy pooled the winning cards onto his lap. They were the joint winners. They agreed to toss for it and one of the women from the kitchen, being thought to be impartial, was called in to throw a half crown into the air. She flipped it up with such vigor and the excitement was contagious as we watched and saw it spin through the air, almost invisible to the eyes in its dizzy descent. And then the whirl and rewhirl before it made up its mind to land. She stood with her arms kilted out so that nobody could trespass, her arms the two boundaries around the spot where the coin had fallen, and shouted "harp," which meant Cornelius had won the toss.

"Don't worry, lads . . . I'll give her back . . . we'll play for Red River another night," and a sudden tide of happiness poured into that room as they lifted him onto their shoulders, four men carrying him to the supper room, tears of pride and joy springing not just from his eyes but from his whole being, and he saying over and over again, "I was afraid I'd win her . . . I was afraid of that."

It was daylight when we set out for home, all of them merry, too merry, piling into the lorry, branches and fallen boughs down the avenue and along the main road, but far from being daunted they laughed and replayed the fractious moments of the game, the enmity and poor Miss Gleason like a little bantam, flaring up, not even realizing that hearts were trumps at the time. The rivers we passed were swollen, either a mud brown or a mud green and the lake water a gunmetal color, the reeds all along the shoreline slanted and flattened, and then a sudden shout and a hail of Jaysuses as the lorry swerved on a bend and Iggy pulled on the brake to avoid crashing into a fallen tree.

They spoke all at once, what a narrow escape and what an expert driver Iggy was, kept the head and didn't lose control of the wheel. We climbed out and stood to look at the tree; it was the width of the road, bits splintered off and scattered everywhere, and a few new greens furled shoots, like small birds about to take flight.

"She's gone," Cornelius said.

"Lucky we weren't gone with her," another said, but their mood was ebullient; they raced after their caps that had blown off in the wind, two soaring over a high bank of hedging, forever lost, yet their spirits undampened as they returned to survey the tree in her fallen pride, Dessie tracing her age by the number of circles in the trunk, declaring her to be well over the hundred, a sorry sight, the base caked with damp clay, the torn roots, scrawny and maggoty and by the curl in them wanting to get back into the earth. Nothing for it, as Iggy said, but to get a pair of workhorses with the chains and the traces and pull the lorry that was on its hind wheels, like a balked animal, stuck.

"Keep the home fires burning" was their password as we marched down the road toward a public house that they knew of. The gold lettering that read FINE ALES AND WINES SINCE 1892 faded and flaked into the black paint that bore the name of the owners. Pebbles were thrown up to the window and a startled man came down, his wife following, rushing to make us refreshments, thanking God that no one had been injured, and telling how her children had cried all night, had got into bed with them, scared that the wind would carry them off to the lake. Two of the younger men, Brud and Dessie, were sent to the yard to get the horses and the chains and go back down to retrieve the lorry.

Cornelius had the woman open the rarest bottle of whiskey on the shelf and they were drinking once again as if it were nightfall, laughing over everything, the missing caps that were probably by now in the Shannon, poor Miss Gleason, a crackaillie, coincidence at the fact that Cornelius had won back Red River, but the gallantry of his giving her back for another game.

The pub adjoined a grocery and hardware, and Con insisted on buying new caps for everyone, shy men, drunk men, walking around, looking in a small mirror that was propped against the windowpane, saying one to the other, "Oh, we're quality now," lifting and lowering the new caps to get themselves used to the size and the feel of them, squeezing their old caps in their hands as if they were dishcloths.

It was late in the morning by the time we reached home, our two cows had been let out, the milk tankard and churn on their sides airing and when it came for me to say goodbye, the others insisted that Cornelius walk me up from the stile.

"Take the girl up home, can't you?" they said.

Finding ourselves alone for the first time there was that shyness, that hesitancy.

"Will I sing for you?" he said and immediately began to sing:

> Come and sit by my side if you love me
> Do not hasten to bid me adieu
> But remember the Red River Valley
> And the cowboy that loved you so true.

The rain had stopped but a low cloud full of water and sunshine was ready to open, to burst asunder.

Fresh Horses

"GO ON ... TOUCH HER ... touch the side of her neck ... she's just a bit nervy ... a nervy lady like yourself," Cornelius said, as one of the mares, a chestnut, recognizing I was a stranger, shied away, then backed into the stall, snorting in jerky rapid snorts. There were five or six mares in all, a roan, a bay, and a piebald, and in the semidarkness, because the shutters were drawn, their eyes were a liquid blue, the big moist sockets navy and brimming with curiosity.

It was in the stables in Rusheen, so clean and snug, like a clean warm kitchen, a fire at the far end and the old groom boiling up pots of barley for their dinners, the tackle and the brasses all beautifully polished, the smell of leather and linseed oil and all the horses now in an agitation as the stallion at the far end began to kick at his partition so as to get to them.

The house across the paddock was a ruin that he'd walked me around, a bit of painted wall still standing, a staircase that dropped down into nowhere, its iron rungs choked with briar, the set of green gongs from the back kitchen still intact in a net of mildew, and starlings flying in and out with bits of twigs in their mouths, making nests in the crimsoned corners of the high rubbled ceiling. He told how it had had to be burned at the height of the Troubles to prevent the English from using it as a headquarters, and many of the big houses around had met with the same fate. He had done it himself along with three other lads, going there in the dead of night with cans of petrol and bags of straw for tinder, took only minutes, a big bonfire lighting up the whole countryside, sucking the cold, the flames seen for miles around, the house exploding as would a paper house, walls and ceilings collapsing onto one another and the chimney pots skiving off. A new house, a stone's throw from the charred ruin, was going to be built and it too would be called Rusheen.

"Sure, a child would touch her . . . would tame her," Cornelius said and drew me in to sniff the fidgety chestnut, to make friends with her, but the moment I got close and saw her mouth damp and black as moleskin I must have shown my nerves because her whinnying got louder as did all the others and the stallion leapt, leapt high above the top of the partition, his arched neck black and ridged, gouts of dung and straw flying up, the neighing now furious and maddened.

Cornelius spoke to them, words and bits of words, and the old groom came across with two wads of tobacco, one for him and one for Cornelius because that was a favorite smell of theirs. Then it was feed time and it all quieted down, only the munching, munching and touching the chestnut mare and the proud sweep of her crest. Con said, "She'll love you . . . she'll love you yet," adding that she would be one of the pair to drive us in a coach on our wedding morning. That was his way of proposing, and the old groom shook his hand and wept with joy at the announcement.

I knew my mother would be happy, because when the pony and trap had come to fetch me, she blessed herself, shook holy water on me, and hoped it would lead to prosperity.

Six weeks was the period of my engagement, six dizzy weeks, plans and purchases, gifts for my parents, a new set of false teeth for my father specially fitted by a dentist in Limerick and for my mother a bog-oak sideboard that she sat down in front of each evening, as if it was an altar. I would be fetched each day in order to go over to discuss with Alphonsus the groom plans for the new house that was to be a replica of the old house, rooms, bedrooms, bathrooms, tap rooms, bay windows, and even a rose window dividing the vestibule from the hall. Because I had hankered to go back to America, my husband-to-be agreed that we could go there for a year, while the building work was being done.

My parents were too shy and unsure to make the journey to the church on the quays in Dublin where we were to be married. Only a handful of guests — Cornelius's friends, unshaven and rough from the previous night's binge, who had not gone to bed at all, merely splashed water on themselves and fortified themselves with coffee and spirits. Cornelius met me at the altar because I had gone alone, since it was deemed unlucky for the groom to see the bride beforehand. I had not wanted a white wedding, it may be that I had not wanted a wedding at all, because in the nights previous I had written Gabriel's full name again and again in the hot ashes with the legs of the tongs. My mother, seeing that I was in two minds, made speech after speech of famine times and times when our forebears were evicted. I had a plum suit and matching hat, the veiling dotted with little bruised berries that looked edible.

When the moment came for the ring to be put on there was a hitch, the stocky priest standing on the altar steps scanned the faces swiftly and with mounting irritation, his gills getting redder and redder, the three altar boys sniggering, knowing the eruption that was to follow. Frank, the best man, had mislaid the ring. He tried all his pockets, then retried them, and for a moment I believed that I was free, standing there in a rapt and joyous suspense, the men, especially Cornelius, bashful and confused until a sacristan emerged, wormy and thin in a long frock coat, and cocked his head toward a side altar, beckoning to the best man to follow him. A long casket beside a statue of St. Anthony was filled with keepsakes, gold chains, necklaces, rosary beads, springs of coral flower, and unlocking it, he picked out a wedding ring, then between them there followed a bit of whispering that no doubt was about money and my fate was sealed.

Opening my locked fingers for the ring to be put on, the thought came to me that it had belonged to someone who had died and who had possibly asked for it to be put in that casket for the repose of her soul. The vows were spoken at a gallop and by the time we filed out, the bell ringer was already at his task, the bells jubilant, and soon other bells, bells from all the steeples up along the quays, a convoy, their peals so clean and crystalline in that clean and crystalline air and when an altar boy threw a packet of rice over us, my husband and I exchanged our first married kiss in the view of the Liffey water, which was pewterish, with chunks of ice, some ungainly, others minute, rinsed and re-rinsed, scattering bursts of diamond light, like jewels, like so many rings, thousands of rings slicked in the water's wetness.

Part III

Nolan

A MULTITUDE OF SMALL BELLS, followed by bigger bells, are ringing inside Dilly's head, chimes half a century apart, bringing her gradually awake, her mind clogged with memories and with muddle. She sees a strapping young girl pushing a tea trolley with a flourish, coasting it down the ward as if she is in an open field, having a tournament, gouts of tea splashing from the spout of the metal urn, laughing as she throws a word to this patient or that.

"Mornin' . . . mornin', all . . . mornin', all," she says with a jocularity.

Then she is standing over Dilly, smiling broadly, her eyes flecked with amber motes, her hand with its puce tattoo thrust out to introduce herself — "I'm Nolan . . . I brought your breakfast" — and goes on to say how Sister Consolata left a note with strict instructions for there to be no milk, no butter, no boiled egg, just black tea with bread and jam.

"You're a gas woman," she says, though she cannot understand how a country woman used to hens and chickens and cows and calves could be so pernickety about her diet.

"Is Sister Consolata the nice nun I met at the top of the stairs?"

"The very one . . . a nice craytur, but off the wall . . . woman brings anemones in here for a patient and Consolata says the reason they're red and purply is that they grew at the foot of the

cross in Calvary and got splashed with the blood of Christ . . .
woman can't believe her ears . . . looks at me . . . thinks to herself am I in a regular hospital or am I in the John O' Gods with
the loonies and the alchies . . . still there's no bad in Consolata . . . only daft . . . ready to float up at any minute to heaven
. . . meet her boyfriend St. Augustine . . . 'late have I loved thee,
O beauty so ancient and so true' . . . off the wall and that's the
holy alls of it."

"I was drugged up with tablets," Dilly says.

"Oh, the bitch, Flaherty," Nolan answers, overfilling the tea-
cup.

It only takes moments for them to be united in their griev-
ance over Nurse Flaherty; Nolan deems her as only a step above
buttermilk and kinda mad. Barely pausing for breath she raves
on: "Frustrated bitch, right cow . . . not married . . . who'd have
her . . . if there's a plate missing she's up to ninety . . . the likelihood of her hooking anyone is thin . . . don't pay any heed to
her . . . she's off today . . . wishes she had a fella . . . good-looking
young house-surgeon on his rounds and she tries to impress . . .
'Shake that mat,' she says to me. 'Shake it yourself,' says I back.
She went every color. Red brown beetroot. Fit to kill me. 'You
do as I say. You do as I say.' Shouting it. I stood my ground. I
could see that she was effing and blinding inside but of course
she couldn't freak out altogether with him listening. Beads of
sweat on her and the hairs on her chin like a man's. She'll have
a beard, I'll lay a bet on it. Them old maids always get beards.
'You don't expect the surgeon to walk on that mat,' she says.
He has to go out of the ward for laughing. I told her to go to
Matron and report me. That shut her up. If you ask me people
want to make life hell for others. It's either that or the boasting. Some of them in here, big shots . . . the rose window at
Chartres, life changing. Marcel Proust, whoever he is when he's
at home, life changing. Pure baloney. If you've got kids and no
nappies nothing is life changing, only nappies. That's how I feel.

Who's going to look after me and the kid, Larry I hope, unless he does a bunk. We've a lovely house an' all . . . I got the money after this truck hit me . . . took ages to get it . . . my granny put it away for me and soon as she knew there was a baby coming she hands me over three thousand pounds and says, 'You'll need this, Nolan, for baby things.' Straightaway Larry and me go down to the furniture mart in Castleknock . . . got a pine bed and a chest of drawers . . . people ask me what I see in him, I know what I see in him . . . when we're alone together, we have a right laugh . . . he's no car now . . . a lunatic wrote off his car on a roundabout on the Naas Road . . . we're in no hurry marrying, we're free-thinkers. My mother dying to make up, to get pally with me . . . jealous because I'm having the baby . . . dumped me and my sister . . . put us into foster homes . . . I wrote her poems . . . if you ask me poems are instead of going straight up to a person and having it out . . . didn't give a damn for us . . . only worried about her figure . . . you see me now . . . you see the size of me . . . well my clothes would fall off my mother . . . she's all on her ownio since she lost the looks . . . I hung up on her . . . my child won't hang up on me because I'll know how to mind it . . . I'll know how to love it . . . we're in no hurry marrying . . . it's a mug's game. The baby will be all right . . . I have this Sacred Heart lamp that's always lit . . . day and night . . . that'll do us" and for the first time she looks at the face on the pillow, wan and homesick.

"Could I have my cardigan?" Dilly asks.

Nolan takes the cardigan from the chair and eases the two arms through it, then buttons the lower buttons, her touch so soft and gentle in contrast with her tirade.

"Ah, missus, don't mind me, I'm a blatherer," she says and waits because Dilly has a question.

"What will happen to me?"

"What will happen to you is this . . . a nurse will wash you and then you'll have a little stroll up and down the corridor . . .

Mary's Lane they call it . . . you'll meet others . . . most of them dopes . . . the gamey fellas . . . sex mad . . . but before that you'll receive Holy Communion . . . everyone does . . . a nun coming ahead of the priest with a candle and bell, her head bowed . . . all the heads bowed . . . the priest following with the chalice and you'll close your eyes and say Ah-men."

Sister Consolata

"IS IT THAT we're both countrywomen and from the west?" Sister Consolata says, clapping her hands in jubilance, her eyes ink-dark and shining.

A friendship has sprung up between Dilly and herself. She has taken on the task of bathing her in the private bathroom, of seeing to it that the shingles are retreating, and, against hospital rules, applying a putty-colored ointment that Dilly had secured from some quack down at home. She has lent courage on the mornings that Dilly went for her tests, linking her, saying how they would spring-clean all the sluggish cells and make her like new again. Dilly believed it, yet as the rubber strap was put on her upper arm for a blood test, her fears returned and her own blood in the little glass vial looked treacherous to her.

Then at night, the ritual of their little "conflabs" as the Sister has called them, the curtain drawn around the bed and oftener than not a slice of cake or a bun from the nuns' pantry. Sister regales her new friend with the stories that she has gleaned from history—Cuchulainn of the shining delg, fated to slay his own son whom he did not recognize because of a mist that lay in the willows, killing his own son, deranged from it, then at the very end strapping himself to a pillar in order to die standing; Cuchulainn opening his tunic to allow the otters to come and drink from the flow of that proud blood. And poor Grace Gifford, as Sister says, given ten minutes in the dead of night to say goodbye to Joseph Mary Plunkett, the man she had married only an hour previous, and writing some secret message on the timbers of his cell in Kilmainham jail. Joseph Mary with his paeans to Christ — "I see His blood upon the rose and in the stars the glory of His being" — poets and martyrs all. They are her friends she says, as are the saints, especially her pets, Anthony and Jude and Padre Pio, and other astonishing beings ripe for beatitude: Iron Curtain Paul who risked the wrath of the Communists to live underground and preach the faith to thirsty Russian souls; Therese Neumann, with the wounds of Christ all over her body, her clothing bloodstained, abstaining from food and drink for thirty years, receiving only the Host, but happy, happy as Sister says, her full-throated birds chorusing all around her.

As the days unfold the friendship deepens, the little secrets and the bigger secrets made known. Sister getting to know Dilly's house, the setting, the two avenues, the old and the new, the two sets of gates, the marvelous trees, the palm tree that wasn't a palm tree, then the inside, going from room to room, curtains with pictures of peacocks, big mirrors, the box room where Dilly kept apples and crab apples that when ripened gave off a cidery smell, the flowering plant on the tallboy that shed its little husks that dropped like hay onto the carpet, the little plant possibly dying of thirst since neither Con nor Crotty would remember to water it.

But for Dilly the crux of her thinking is her family, her children, disentangling the hurts they have caused her. Take Terence, her son, once her white-haired boy, until he came under the influence of a grasping wife and became as hard and as grasping as she.

"It was like this," she says, her voice dropping as she recalls the night the treachery commenced. Terence arrived late, overwrought because his wife, Cindy, had left him, his darling wife had vanished without even a note, had not got in touch with her own family or her one friend, Alice, the dressmaker. Five days and five nights and for all Terence knew she could have gone to the cliffs, something she had previously threatened to do, the cliffs where unfortunate people, even young people, threw themselves off and Terence's father sick of hearing this saga made some cutting remark about Cindy, a row ensuing, father and son almost coming to blows, Terence storming out, saying his own life was finished and he too would drive to the cliffs. Yet he returned in due course. His wife had got in touch with him from a hotel in Dublin and the couple were reconciled. But ever after, there were only flying visits from them and even at Christmastime his wife would not deign to spend a night under their roof. Eventually Terence broke it to them, that the reason for his wife's unhappiness and her disappearance was on account of not being accepted with open arms by them, of being made to feel an outcast, and the only consolation would be for Rusheen and all the lands to be signed over to them. Eventually he wore them down. She describes the chicanery of his driving them to the solicitors, the stiffness in the office, a big desk laden with papers and ledgers, a canvas blind on which the firm's name was indented in black lettering, her husband sitting next to her, her son and his wife on the seats behind, having to state her wishes, her enforced wishes, then the solicitor reading it back to her and even as she took up the pen to sign, regretting what she was doing and realizing that she had omitted her daughter completely, had not even willed her daughter the kitchen garden that she had been promised and that a surveyor had been enlisted to measure it up.

"And I'm still reeling from it," she says tearfully, and Sister agrees that it was quite a hardhearted way to behave.

But her daughter, as she says, is trapped in a life of vice, beyond in England, her young sons in a Quaker school that Dilly was not consulted about, and her books that have scandalized the country, though as Sister is quick to say and a priest remarked to her, the nature sections so beautiful, so radiant, if only she had excised the flagrant bits. Yes, Eleanora in peril, evidence of which she, Dilly, had on her one visit smelled a rat, as she put it, when Eleanora gave a party in her honor, though she did not know a single guest, wines and spirits galore, oysters, prawns, wild salmon, and a married man, her paramour, taking the pendant that had slipped inside her see-through blouse, lifting it out to kiss it, saying, "I've wanted to do this since I got here." Dilly recounts the ingratitudes regarding gifts that she had sent over the years, the bawneen cushion covers that she had embroidered so painstakingly with ancient motifs that she found in a press, the mauve and indigo dyes having run into the white material, where they had been washed and only half dried, stuffed in there, not good enough for the illustrious guests and the married men. Holding the metal crucifix between them, Sister says they will pray, they will storm heaven, and just as hares become white by eating snow, so do the souls of humans by availing of the spiritual food meted out to them.

Later, Sister recalls having read about Eleanora, seen photographs of her, an unhappy divorce, and a husband most handsome but much older than she.

Dilly writhes at the mere mention of him, a man so odd, so godless, an autocrat, a man who to her knowledge never sat down to dinner with his own family and from whom his wife, her unfortunate daughter, had to borrow her own earnings back from him to buy shoes and clothing for her children.

"Why, oh why, oh why," she asks, still angry, still grieving, still flabbergasted that such a marriage should ever have taken place.

Part IV

SCENES FROM A
MARRIAGE

Scene One

ELEANORA'S HUSBAND, HERMANN, would always contend that she had married him under the guise of love to better her ambitions. Her mother believed that by choosing this madman, this infidel, her daughter had wanted to drive a last nail in her mother's coffin. Eleanora herself thought that perhaps literature had had its vertiginous effect upon her. Literature was either a route out of life or into life and she could never be certain which, except that she had succumbed to it. There was Samuel Richardson's Clarissa, with fastenings on doors and windows to bar the ruffiany Mr. Lovelace, who said he did not know whether her frost be real frost but who succeeded, much to her downfall, in making Clarissa yield and pass as his wife. Then there was Jane Eyre, in thrall to the inscrutable Mr. Rochester, and Jane Eyre's creator, Charlotte Brontë, falling in love with Monsieur Heger, a married man, the iniquity discovered and she and her sister Emily dispatched from Brussels back to the moors, later on, their forlorn lives transmuted into visions of shattered love.

Then there was Charlotte's unchristened daughter, who had died in her mother's womb and whom Eleanora believed as haunting those selfsame moors, wailing her circumstances, neither fully dead nor fully alive, perpetually waiting to be.

She thought as well and often of John Clare in a lunatic asylum in Northampton, looking at the vowels and consonants that he was convinced the authorities had filched out of his head and consequently the poem he had written about a Daisy was not to his liking. His last couplet on the inadequacy of the word to pierce the hidden soul of love filled her with both exultation and terror.

How could her future husband, Hermann, have guessed at such irrational ruminations, no more than her mother could or would. Her mother, abjuring the seaminess of the written word and once, in an outburst, declaring that "paper never refused ink." Yet she was in bondage to both, doing her best to please both, dreading their strictures but smarting under them, an impostor carrying on her secret subversive life.

There was her night self who would come to sin with him, her morning self who would atone for it, her evening self when she laid the table, lit candles, the little geisha as he called her, and the child self, not fully dead, not fully alive, waiting, through the alchemy of words, to crystallize into life.

The first journey to his house had in it a host of enchantments. An avenue, the lines of beech trees, a rusted green wrought-iron gate, and daffodils, daffodils around the roots of the trees, stray ones forking out from the grayish bouclé barks, huddles of them in the grassy glades, their brazen yellow muted by the high damp green grass and sheep that to his chagrin had broken in, rising clumsily, then thumping their haunches against the loose stone wall, being too hefty to scale it.

As the car came to a stop outside the long low house, plastered white and chinked with shards of blue glass and china, set down in a dip under a horseshoe of woodland, she half-expected to see a curtain be drawn apart and Mrs. Rochester appear and stick her tongue out at them, then retreat back into her ravings. He had been married before as Merlin, the friend who introduced them, had told her, to someone exotic and much traveled.

She wrote an account of the first day in her diary, which years later he would throw back at her as an example of her cretinous attempts at composition: "*A spring day with everything agog.*

The birds cheeky and spry, swooping everywhere, clouds like great lazy liners roaming across the rinsed blue heavens, the gorse bushes flecked yellow and the spring trees with their immemorial flow of sap."

Hearing her recite — "Beside the lake, beneath the trees" — he smiled a slightly scornful yet indulgent smile. His friend Merlin, so he told her, had christened her a literary Bessie Bunter, on account of her spouting passages from poems and books. She smarted at the insult, her eyes brimming with scalded tears.

She had known him only a few days, had been in his company a few hours, this handsome austere man with carved features, a sallow complexion, deep-set eyes, and beautifully telling hands that moved as if they were about to deliver something unique into life, a child perhaps. It was a spontaneous meeting, a chance telephone call; Merlin had rung to ask if by any chance she was at a loose end. She was. She borrowed a red muff from a girl in their digs to disguise the shabbiness of her coat, which, though once a jet-black, was black-green and mottled with holes. Sitting in a pub in Henry Street, mesmerized by his urbane conversation and by the way the other men deferred to him, she felt that she had stepped into a book, breaking from her tedious life of working in a pharmacy and bicycling to lectures at night.

His downstairs rooms had an unlived feeling, slightly dark because of the shutters half drawn, leather sofas, leather chairs, a black lacquered cabinet with two pink china slates on little easels, the word *menu* engraved on both. There were paintings stacked, waiting to be hung, one wall white, another terracotta, an unfinished quality as if someone, maybe him, had given up in the middle. There was a portrait of him, which, when she stood before it, made her come to the conclusion that the painter disliked him. His skin had a greenish tint and his deep-set dark eyes smote with a consuming anger. When her mother and family in pursuit of her saw that portrait, her mother claimed to have become so frightened, so stricken, that it was as if she had seen a portrait of Lucifer himself. But that was not for some time yet.

First there was courtship, a tour of the house that he was so touchingly proud of. He took her hand and led her into his study, the stacks of books, some leather-bound like ecclesiastical books, a barometer on which the weather forecast was inking itself on a graphed sheet of paper. To amuse her he wrote out the expected week's rainfall and propped it on the mantelpiece. The bedrooms, although furnished, had a gauntness, waiting as it were for footsteps, some beds made, others stripped and in one room a pink crib without either mattress or blanket, telling of another time. He said yes, he had had a son and was now without a wife and without a son, which made him disconsolate but in the eyes of the local people branded him as a rake and a reprobate.

They walked in the woods, the breeze so soft, so gentle, branches in a sway, to and fro, last year's birds nests fraying in the upper reaches of the trees and swarms of flies in dazed drifts as if they had just wakened from their winter slumbers. In the far field the gorse bushes in thick sullen clumps, a few already in flower and some newborn lambs crying with an infant's plaint. They stood on a wall to look down at the lake, his telling her that he would take her out on his boat for a picnic, that being his way of saying he intended to see her again. He pointed to the small white cottage on the far side of the lake and said that a woman lived there all alone and had become such a recluse that she did not even greet the postman, who rowed up once a month to deliver a letter or a circular; instead she hid in the room off the kitchen telling him to be off, as he was not wanted. She shivered at the thought of such isolation, as if that would be her destiny one day.

"You've never been lonely," he said, quizzical.

"I was . . . I talked to trees when I was young," she said.

"You talked to trees," he said, deeming it daft and lovable.

In the evening they ate off a card table, close to the fire, they drank red wine and told each other engaging stories, that repertoire of stories that people tell each other when they have first met and are on the brink of falling in love. When a hairpin fell out of her hair, he picked it up, studied it, said, "My house is not used to finding a woman's hairpin," and with tenderness put it in his shirt pocket as a keepsake. It was a plaid shirt with bold patches of red and yellow, one that she would appropriate in due course, coming as she did, penniless and in the clothes she stood up in.

Later that week he drove to the city and took her to the cinema, where they saw *Ballad of a Soldier*, a Russian film about a soldier being given leave to go home to see his mother, bearing a gift of a bar of soap, but because of many hazards and the soldier's kindness at helping others, he arrived at his mother's house only minutes before the twenty-four-hour leave had expired and he had to return immediately. Her husband-to-be could not understand why she cried so much, cried in the cinema, then cried out in the street, cried in the restaurant where he had taken her, tears that neither he nor she could assuage.

Scene Two

THEIR ELOPEMENT HAD in it some of the perilousness and subterfuge of Natasha Rostov's fling, but with no rustling dresses, no gems on bare flesh, no troika or sable cloak, no whistles at midnight by a wicker gate, instead a flurried trip to a rocky island off the coast of England, where they went to hide until, as he said, the hysterics had died down. Her secret had been disclosed. In an anonymous letter her mother had been apprised of her abominable life and hence the family's pursuit of her to the rocky island, asking for her to be handed back to them. Hermann had gone out to confront them. She waited in the hotel room, cowering, never guessing that in the altercation two of the men, her father's adjutants, would strike him, knock him to the ground, and in the scuffle injure him. Police were called, evidence taken, the assailants sent packing, but a disgrace hung over room seventeen.

The manageress, who liked him, said it was true that her boss would much prefer that they departed, but since he had paid for the week, a compromise was reached. They could stay but be served meals in their room, and contrary to hotel rules she supplied them with a kettle and an ironing board. It was that copper kettle now that Eleanora boiled and re-boiled to steam his wounds and when the water ran out and she saw the coils at the bottom, greenish and twisted, they seemed not dissimilar to

134

the knot in her gut, quaking as she was at his cold but seething temper.

Everything she did was wrong.

In the downfalling light of the reading lamp, his trouser rolled up to his knee, she saw the wounds, a purplish black, his shins and insteps grazed, yet refusing to bleed and consequently paining him all the more. Denouncing her kindred — savages, small-town hicks with their caps and their drunken red faces.

Now in the aftermath she was holding the spout of the steaming kettle to these wounds and being held responsible for their barbarities. A gash above his elbow made him wince each time that he attempted to raise his arm but yet he persisted with his irate letter. He rasped when she brought the steam too close, asked if she was so stupid that she could not even tell the difference between near and far, their stupidity having infected her also, something that was not evident in her first girlish gushings. Midges blew in from the garden in random gusts and with the muslin swatter that he had borrowed, he struck, so that soft brown smears muddied the pink china globe.

When he had finished the letter he handed it to her and told her to copy it out in her own hand and then sign it. It was an ugly letter, full of contempt, outlining their ignorance, their quasi-medieval habits, of which she was the consequence.

"I can't," she said and threw it back at him. Infuriated at being disobeyed he thrust a leaking fountain pen into her hand, then swore as the droplets of ink fell onto his incendiary words.

"I'll do anything, but not that," she said, begging him to tear it up, to vent all his anger and spleen on her. Instead he took three sheets of clean paper, told her to sign all three, a precaution lest the first or even the second letter did not have the full fruits of his outrage.

In a strange room full of fear and remorse, sleep does not come. By signing the blank pages, she had become a Judas, sold herself for that mess of pottage, and hearing the clatter of the typewriter, sometimes in a welter, sometimes in almost a pause, she guessed that he was adding more deadly ammunition to his words and she thought, "I don't know him at all . . . don't know how stern, tormented, and unforgiving he is."

All those giddy and high-flown notions of love, learned from books, swept away.

Scene Three

BACK IN HIS HOUSE she learned to cook, studied recipes from the two grandiose cookbooks left by his wife where there were also tips for hostessing: breakfast ideas, brunch ideas, seating and serving, and how the flowers on the table should not have too delectable a scent, must not for instance compete with the aromas of the sauces. She sometimes produced floating confections with egg white and raspberries, but more often than not the exotic dishes failed, both because of her inexperience and the unpredictability of the wood stove, which either smoked or sallied like a bonfire.

One particular bird, a soft dusk-brown in color, a she-blackbird she reckoned, hovered in the folds of the cedar tree, roosted there, scarcely showing herself, yet always present, always on the watch, and she thought it had flown up the hundred or so miles from home. She had dreamed of her mother more than once. In one dream she was with a man, a stranger to her, and was wearing a blue gauze nightgown that he lifted and lowered in play, when quite stealthily her mother slipped into the bed beside them and all three lay rigid like effigies. To make matters more unsettling, a few mornings later there came a brown paper parcel that contained a nightdress identical to the one she had worn in her dream. The stamps were smeared over so that she could not tell the postmark but guessed it was from her mother because it smelled indisputably of home. She would tell herself that if she and her husband, together, saw the pack of red deer come closer to the house at evening time, the marriage or intended marriage would be happy and the rift with her family mended; yet when they walked together, the deer would already have gone in the instant before they were glimpsed, in flowing and almost invisible formation, bouncing off into woodier and more shrouded places.

Sometimes, too, she longed to be back in a street in Dublin, hearing ballroom music, while also having to admit that when she was there, those branched fairy lights and swooning love songs did not satisfy her at all. Once she had been walked home from just such a dance by a man who worked for a bakery company, delivered breads to towns down the country, and he had told her that if ever she wanted a lift home, he was her man. He wrote his number on a torn-off end of a cigarette packet. That was the extent of her gallivanting.

She loved her husband, or believed she loved him, but she was afraid of his dark moods, of the way he retreated into himself, estranged from her. He had had a nomadic childhood, his father a foreigner, at loggerheads with his mother, many homes and no homes, then later on a wife, the exotic, much-traveled woman who had absconded and of whom Eleanora was jealous. In her prowls, in which she felt more interloper than wife, Eleanora would find traces of her predecessor, a silver-backed mirror, a powder bowl, and copied in an ornate hand the words of a song: *I dreamed I saw Joe Hill last night, alive as you and me.* In his photo album, a dazzling photograph of her in the plaid shirt that he now sometimes wore. How they must have loved each other to wear each other's clothes.

He had made her a gift of a subscription to a special library and once a week when they went to the city for the special "outing" she returned one stack and collected another, opening them there and then in the street, for a foretaste of them.

It was a little room off the kitchen where she sat, a box room that she had fitted out with a lamp, a table with a red chenille cloth, an easy chair, and again and again she would ask herself which story was the more beautiful, by which she also had to concede the more wrenching, poor Hans Castorp, with his tuberculosis, in the mountains for the cure, sitting out-of-doors with his cousin, camelhair rugs on their knees, poor Hans, with his unrequited love for the little Russian, Claudia Chauchat, persecuting himself with thoughts of her knee, her back, her neck bone, knowing her body to be as diseased as his own, yet waiting for that one moment in the dining room when she would sweep past him and either give or withhold a look. Which was worse, that or Emma Bovary, with a husband, two clandestine lovers, and eventually nothing but that fistful of white powder that she stole from the apothecary to poison herself. Which was worse. Both were worse. War did for Hans what a broken heart did for Emma. Hans, a soldier in his hobnailed boots, marching over cold, plowed, treacherous mire, flinging himself down as the enemy shells exploded and discharged fountains of mud, fire, iron, molten metal, the pitiful fragments of his fallen comrades all around. Emma in her last throes, ice cold creeping from her feet to her heart, Emma raising herself up like a galvanized corpse to hear the drone of the blind man and then letting out an atrocious frantic despairing laugh.

To some of the authors, to those that were living, she wrote letters. They were not letters that she ever intended to send. She also wrote to Scott Fitzgerald about his summer nights, his blue gardens, women like moths, the pale magic of Daisy's face in a window as Gatsby kept his vigil. She wrote out of loneliness. Her gardens were not blue, her woods were green and greener still from downpours, and moths ate into the sumptuous folds of the bedroom curtains, something that Hermann remarked on, dismayed at her making such a poor fist at housekeeping.

She missed things, clothes, dance music pouring from a dance hall as she and other girls approached the entrance, that excitement, quiffing their hair up, although oftener than not they were not asked up to dance because girls were in the majority. And a Goray skirt that she loved, tartan, with warm yellows and warm terracottas, lost or left somewhere. Sometimes she wrote to her mother, letters that she knew she would not, must not, send.

Dear Mother,
Your clothes were exquisite, though faded, though flittered, though lamentably out of fashion. There was too that time when we both believed we had run away forever, run from the shades of Rusheen. To your mother's for your long-awaited dowry. Oh what fools. She flew at you, your poor startled mother. If only I could talk to you. If only I could confide in you. This husband-to-be is an enigma in many ways. His father's people, he says, hailed from Armenia, way, way back. Sometimes I see such a dark look on him, not aimed at me or not always aimed at me, a scowl that seems a summoning of treacheries he cannot remember because they run deep in his blood. Love was something you put your foot down over. You have won in your way. So many promises of love that I envisaged, here, there, and everywhere, along with the heady stuff that the traveling players provided, consumptive heroines drawn to cads, wretched farewells, prefiguring the cold star of doomed love. In my life here I often go up into the woods to think. My thoughts go round and round in circles. If I think ahead, to say, twenty or thirty or forty years I cannot see this liaison continuing and I so recently betrothed! I make jam when the medlar trees and the damson trees bear fruit. He likes when I make jam. We have it in a sago pudding. There are things he does not approve of. High heels for instance. He says they are bad for the feet, later on. Many things about him are solicitous but yet when I think of those twenty or thirty or forty years I shudder. Just as I used to when you questioned me about sin, sinning. That time when

I declined Holy Communion at the altar rails and on the way home your asking why, why, my young lady. I can still hear you and hear our feet on the grass, the high frosted spears of grass that rasped and your determining to chastise me.

As the weeks and months went by she began to write. Nothings or next to nothings. Nettles, hens laying out, or the cackle of geese and their glee at being allowed into the stubble and gorging themselves on the leavings of wheat and barley. Her mother came into everything she wrote and she remembered once in a guesthouse an unspoken covenant that passed between them. It was a guesthouse due to be opened and the owner, Cecilia, had asked them as a great favor to come so that she could rehearse her skills. In a newly papered parlor with gilt chairs, a pot of tea with a strainer, and a china slop bowl, Cissy, eager to serve, was practicing her etiquette, her *Sir* and her *Madam*, pressing on them scones and sandwiches and a fresh sponge cake, still warm and from which the raspberry jam oozed out of the two sandwiched halves, debating aloud how much she should charge for high teas.

At one point when Cissy ran to get some other dainty, they looked at the intricate crimson needlework of Christ with a motto embroidered on it in looped lettering and her mother asked her, like a good girl, to read the verse aloud — *"Christ is the unseen guest at every table, the silent listener to every conversation"* — her mother thereby inferring that she too would be the unseen guest and the silent listener to every conversation.

Scene Four

IT WAS AS THOUGH just beneath the surface something dangerous and unsettling lurked. She and Hermann did not mesh. What it wanted was for them to be more equal, not to be master and slave because already she was ceasing to be that slave, finding in the books she read not only riches but also rebellion and in some though as yet convoluted way, she knew she was being unfaithful to him and he saw it, sensed it. She had eloped in a trance, in haste, her docility a mask, a thousand hers revolting within herself and toward him. Yet coexisting with her flounder was the hope that one evening he would call her into his study and they would talk openly, talk of the things that had kept them apart and from their candor there would be born a real love, a lasting love that they had both envisaged.

The news of her pregnancy elated him. Upon hearing it he wrote in celebration on the several windowpanes. He would have a son. He cradled her and went around the room, marveling at the fact that he would be a father again; the theft and the treachery wreaked upon him would be undone. They drank Madeira wine and he said that one day he would take her to Madeira, all three would go to sunny Madeira, a triptych.

Once in her convent she had been given a holy picture of the Virgin, in a dimly lit interior, with a line of cypresses outside, beautifully symmetric and the Virgin herself emanating a harmony, realizing she was pregnant. She did not feel like that at all, she felt terror, but she could not tell him so. They sat, quiet, united, the wine sweet and viscous, an intimacy in what would become the most cherished moments of their history.

She wrote to her mother knowing she would not send it:

Dear Mother,
When my child is born, you may perhaps forgive me and we will be close again. Or is that wishful thinking. Between you and I, I am scared. Your labor pains have got mixed up with mine. God grant I don't scream when the time comes. Hermann is most kind to me. In the evenings by the fire I see the nicer side of him, the side of him that you also would like. The way he listens and has a tender expression and perhaps everyone is tender at bottom but it gets buried. Flaubert claimed that we each have a royal room in our hearts into which only very few are admitted. Yet his mother said his love of words had hardened his heart, had shut her out. There are mornings when I waken and see the sun coming through the curtains and I am not in my bedroom here by the lake with him, but in your bedroom, which was also mine. How it poured in and picked out the emblems and the tweeny birds perched on roses and rosebuds, so adroit and so mischievous on their background of cream cretonne. By the way, I don't seem to be able to get the stains out of the linen tablecloths and napkins the way you could. Was it those Reckett's cubes that you used that made everything snow white again with a tinge of blue.

And so it was that their thoughts conjoined. The blotched and rained-upon postmark of home. The letter in a pink envelope. Treasa, her mother's friend, has gone to expense with the notepaper or maybe her mother has supplied it. A missive outlining the many months since she eloped, a mother's tears and gnashing, a father's tears, an entire parish reeling from the shock, and moreover the blow to her poor mother's heart, who had collapsed up in the yard but luckily was found by a passerby. After much prayer and deliberation her mother is proposing that they meet. A hotel in Limerick is suggested and two possible dates, one immediately and one in four weeks' time. She thought it better to get it over, to look at last into her mother's eyes and not flinch.

On the long train journey she put her fret to one side, immersed herself in the book she had brought. Not once did she look up from it to see the passing landscape, which she knew anyhow, suburbs, small allotments, wild ponies, cattle trampling in the ruins of fallen castles, wet fields, and bog land unyieldingly black. She was reading Virginia Woolf's *The Common Reader,* was with Dean Swift in those splendid rooms in London, silver plate, a galaxy of guests, vivaciousness, the Dean leaving to go home and by the light of a wax candle to fill page after page, recounting it to Stella, who guessed his greatness, the handwriting illegible, since a bad scrawl ensured secrecy. The formidable Swift telling Stella the events of the day, the talk at dinner, conversing in nonsense language to her in the house in Moor Park, she on one side of the Irish Sea and he on the other, yet in no hurry to exchange the rarefied circles of London for the trout streams of County Meath, Stella thirty years his junior, living frugally with a chaperone, Mrs. Rebecca Dingley, to whom he sometimes sent a gift of tobacco. Stella was privy to all his movements, the pamphlets he wrote, the Tories he harangued on behalf of the Irish, the twenty guineas he gave to a sick poet in a garret, the duchesses he scolded or befriended, and on and on, until one day Stella began to see traces of something less open, less confiding, in short the specter of a rival. Swift bridled. What was so wrong with visiting Mrs. Vanhomrigh, recently widowed, and her daughter Esther, why shouldn't he have supper with them if he boarded nearby, what harm was there in leaving his gown or his periwig in their keeping, and who could accuse him for joining in a game of whist? Yet in time Esther, who had not Stella's reserve, nor Stella's forbearance, threw down the gauntlet, writing in vehement tones, demanding to know the exact nature of her relationship with the Dean. Upon learning of it he went to Esther, flung her letter down, then rode off, leaving her, as she put it, with his killing killing looks, which were prophetic because soon she was dead and Stella left in the shallows.

From that it was to Dorothy Wordsworth and Brother William, Dorothy's eye so acute, jotting down all that she saw to be of use to William, the raised ridge on the backs of sheep, a cow giving over eating, to stare at them, the sloe tree in blossom, the varnished beams of her bedroom that in the light of the fire looked like melted gems, Dorothy controlling and repressing her own impulses for the sake of William.

A moment of vindication when she read of Christina Rossetti, Christina Rossetti dressed in black at a tea party of Mrs. Virtue Tebbs, having to listen to banality, social nothings, suddenly standing up in the middle of that room, holding a green volume of her poems and saying to the frivolous group, "I am Christina Rossetti. 'Bring me poppies brimmed with sleepy death.'" Yes, she would be Christina Rossetti when she confronted her mother.

The train had stopped. There was no knowing how long. She got up and walked, or rather ran, down the short length of street to the hotel where her mother stood outside under an awning crestfallen, with a look of bewilderment, fearing she was not coming.

Her mother is kind, soft-spoken, a small drip like a tear on the end of her nose. She is also nervous, as Eleanora can tell by the strain in her voice, a timidity on account of all the reproaches, their pursuit of her, the assault on her husband, the insulting solicitors' letters from one party to another, and the unfinished state of affairs. They order soup to start with, pea soup, followed by lamb cutlets and roast potatoes. While they wait, her mother places her hand on the table and then gradually inches closer to Eleanora's by way of saying, "I forgive you." The soup is too salty, pickled with bacon, the cutlets somewhat greasy, in short she is unable to eat and her mother with an uncanny clairvoyance says in shock, "A baby." The word seemed to hover in that constraining dining room with its smell of fried onions and gravy.

"You're having a baby."

"I'm not sure."

"I'm sure." Her mother seeing into her and to the child in her and she said yes, she was having a baby. She must now marry the man with the Rasputin features, the man Treasa had christened the anti-Christ.

A few days following her husband received a letter saying that considering recent and significant developments, the family was giving their consent to the marriage.

He resented being told what to do, but marry they did, the ceremony proving to be somewhat joyless, in the sacristy of a Catholic church, two workmen acting as witnesses. She wore a fawn crêpe de Chine dress with a hidden pleat down the front and hidden zip fasteners that could be released as the child inside her kicked, making its presence known.

In the dark, a few nights before it was due to be born, a pearled, full moon shining in and along the bedroom floor, she confessed to her husband that she was afraid the child would be deformed because of her many macabre thoughts and the fact of its being conceived out of wedlock. He saw how inexperienced, how frightened she was and wiping her eyes said, "Now there are two children that I will have to take care of."

Yet the birth was not so awful. It was as if something came free in her and though howling as the pain gripped and encircled her belly, she felt her body to be obeying some instinct older than her, older than her mother, older than time; she felt a freedom. The nurse coming at intervals, telling her to push, then going off to tend to another woman in labor, alone with it and yet not alone, this tournament as it were between her and it and in the last ferocious half-hour her whole self seeming to be carried by it, then the great burst of water as the infant came hurtling into the world. A son, her son, their son, red and raw but sinuous as a wrestler and roaring its lungs out, a protest at being ejected into a cold, boundaryless world. His father chose its name and arranged for it to be circumcised. After the operation, two mornings later, it lay in its basket like a little snowman, a sheaf, pale, mute, chastened inside a white lace shawl and on a greeting card she wrote, *"In the bag of your napkin a berry, fresh from the morning's blood and your tippet raw from the morning's knife."*

She dressed him in new dresses and the pale blue matinee coats that her mother's friends had sent her. Blue for a boy and pink for a girl. If she had another child it would be a girl, one of each, a little clan. At times he laughed and gurgled with a glee, then burped back the milk he had swallowed that was already solid and at other times there was a gravity to him, the little seer that knew, that comprehended, as though from the well of bygone memory. Then he was crawling, reaching for the gravel in the front drive, to put up his nose or pelt at the sight of strangers, whom he resented. Then he was talking. In his own world, in his own crib, gabbling away. The words myriad and full of fascination, sound and color, sense and non-sense, his smell so particular and so affectionate and the silk skin silkier than the sheerest flower. Her son and in some way her shield. His father too showered love on him, tossed him up in the air to catch him on the way down, his little arms the two branches going to her, going to his father, a candelabra bringing them together.

Her next child came into the world differently, stole in, no big breach of the waters, just finding his way through. Enormous navy-blue eyes, drinking in his surroundings. She thought he would be a girl but he wasn't, he was a boy, and his brother poured the bath of water that was on the bedside over him, say-

147

ing *nice babbie, nice babbie,* while dispatching him to his end. In time they sparred. They sparred over the rocking horse and over the mashed blackberries and sugar that they loved, their hands and their mouths all purpled, two painted faces and two painted warriors. They enjoyed their battles but were also comrades. The day her elder son tripped over a hosepipe and split his forehead, her younger son attempting to mop the blood and called out *geth the dhoctor, geth the dhoctor.* He had a lisp.

The peace that she and her husband had made was tenuous. He knew that she wrote and tucked it away in folders and between blotting paper so as not to be discovered. But he found it, made notes on it, sometimes quite caustic notes — *"There is no such thing as a blue road,"* he wrote with a red pen on one of the pages. He worked at night. A light in his window and a light in hers is what a traveler would chance on, two disparate lights signaling a divided house.

It was in his study, which had become his habitat; it was where he took his meals, listened to music, did his exercises with dumbbells that he had sent away for, and wrote as he said but always put those writings in a strongbox, lest she read them. The fire was lit and a stack of logs lay in a wheelbarrow that he had just wheeled in.

The book he held was covered in the same ocher wallpaper as that in their bedroom. He read aloud and with conviction. The story concerned a man with fever, in the hold of a ship, visited by a woman and presently declaring his passion for her, saying that if she were but a savage maid and he a strong hunter, they could fly to the wilderness where there were great trees and bunchy grapes. Throwing protocol aside, the man confessed of a warm love to come, a life of blood and heart such as she had not had with her husband.

He asked her what she thought of it. It was not for her.

"Why was it not for her?"

"It has no life," she said awkwardly.

"In what way?"

"It's too generalized . . . great trees and bunchy grapes . . . that's not how . . ."

"You mean that's not Hans Castorp," he snapped back.

"I mean it's not Hans Castorp," she said, and with infinite meticulousness he removed the wallpaper and there on the dust jacket was his name in handsome lettering and a photograph of him as a much younger man, so earnest and studious, a young man filled with great and poetic endeavor and she looked from the photograph to him and back again, saying the same inept thing, "God help us . . . oh, God help us," and he stood, not stirring, not moving a muscle as she tried to undo her mistake, the very attempt so cringing, so cretinous, his eyes seething with murderous grief.

Shadow and half-shadow as they walked between the line of trees, moonlight spilling down and slashes of it on the path, silvering the tree trunk and path where they walked and halted, each surprised to find the other abroad at so late an hour. She had gone out by the back kitchen door and he, as she reckoned, must have left by the door that led to the potting shed. Then passing on, as strangers might. If ever there was a moment for reconciliation it was there, it was then, the softness of the night, the trees in their spring vesture and the sighing of the leaves, not like winter's brawl.

She carried on up to the fence, climbed it, and looked beneath to where the sheep lay in their shifting slumbers, a stream from somewhere trilling happily along and seeming to say the same thing — Irrawaddy, Irrawaddy . . . Irrawaddy.

Scene Five

A LOVE AFFAIR.

It happened that she had come across a small advertisement in the back pages of a magazine, in which readers were invited to apply for the job of reading manuscripts. To her surprise she was accepted and so began her working life, a connection to the outside world, the world of letters, through which she now sought deliverance.

How she flung herself into her new endeavor, the excitement of opening the envelope, counting the pages, expecting the self-same transports and mesmerization as she had found in the great Russian novels, intrigues, masked balls, thunderous skies, irresolute love, duels, but mostly they were tales of forlorn, lack-luster lives not dissimilar to her own and as a consequence her reports were a little crisp, sometimes even condescending.

Then one morning, enclosed with her check there was a short note from the managing director of the publishing house, saying that going through the warrens of his office and his endless dreary correspondence he had chanced on a few of her reports and what a breath of fresh air they were—a new sharp intelligence, nervous, feminine, strangely personal, and yet not afraid to get out the chisel. For two guineas a time she was giving the company more than their money's worth and he simply had to thank her. She did not reply, sensing in it some attraction.

He wrote again, said his curiosity was aroused as to who

this person could be and before many months an intimacy had started up.

It's evening and I've come back to the office, all the corridors dark and deserted, tons of manuscripts, tons of torn-up paper and the stale smell of the scent of the secretaries. I drove down through a shower and then came out of Albany Street across a clean line drawn straight across the road where it had not rained at all. I stopped and got out to see what direction the wind was blowing in. It was coming from your country and I thought of the mist on the mountain, the clouds so big, so roaming, reluctant to cross the Irish Sea and come and hang over this great wide blotch of a city of London and hang over me. I thought of you, whom I have never met.

So he had left home in order to go to his office to think of her, just as she went up into the woods with his letters to be alone with them. She kept telling herself it was all harmless, they could be Swift and Stella, corresponding on different sides of the Irish Sea. By writing to her he said he was finding relief from the ifs and buts and strains of editorial life, he was also asking for little glancing descriptions of her own life, not that he intended to pry.

In one letter he wondered if she had ever written anything apart from her insightful reports and if so might he be allowed to read them. She sent some pieces, apologizing for the rambling in them, yet his letter back was the transfusion she had been waiting for. Despite certain awkwardnesses he saw a new voice, a new slant, a girl revealing to him that the angels were on her side. Stories poured out of her, small things, bigger things, her father's eczema that always came on after he had taken the pledge and the way it itched and crazed him, her mother squeezing oranges that they could not afford to humor him and giving her the pulp with a sugar loaf in it to suck from; then that winter night when a man in a leather coat and leather gloves, possibly a doctor, came to their house to examine a neighbor, screams from the dining room, and next day the girl sent away and not heard of again. There was Drue, the workman, always asking her for a kiss, a birdie, but warning her not to tell. All this under her husband's roof and without his knowing it, her friend meanwhile delighting in them. He would interlace his praises with talk of meetings and committees, describe the people who worked for him, a highly strung secretary, a voluble Scotsman reciting the poems of Iain Lom, who had fought with Montrose and thanked God that after the battle of Inverlochy that the plains and the hillside would be green and fertile in times to come because of the great enrichment they had from the bodies of the Campbells, left piled in the field.

To think that just two months ago he did not know her and now while fighting off art editors, advertising managers, and production directors, he was searching for her handwriting, searching among the stacks of mail for her reports, her stories that brought him from stoical begrudgery, from the hard carapace of money and budgets to his true self. In one letter he said she reminded him of a certain day in his youth when he too had discovered literature, the way she was discovering it and perhaps, perhaps, in time they would meet and they would talk about it and much else. He could feel and respond to some inward pressure in her and wanted to save her from the harshness of the world because he knew the world had already taken its knife to her.

He knew her husband's name and her children's names and would always conclude his letters with greetings to them. Then came the incriminating letter. He was on a business trip in New York and he described the evening before, going to a theater, going to dinner, then to a club, bushels of whiskey, then the dream of her that with the distance of an ocean gave him license to tell her that she had him by the hair of his head, for now, for then, forever. In the dream he saw her, the sun on the lake, or rather her husband's lake, the leaves in their wood patterning the light, the blue distance and the blue her, opening her slender arms to life. She was wearing a blue dress, white knitted stockings, and black suede shoes, the wind stirring her hair. She had asked him in the dream which direction was uptown and which was downtown and they got on one of those jaunting cars and told the driver to take them to Central Park. There, a frozen reservoir came into sight, it lay in green and silver shimmeriness, like a dance pavilion under a whey-green moon, and at the instant of asking her to dance he wakened up.

Her dream did not correspond to his.

When her husband announced that he was selling up and that they would move to London she could barely conceal her excitement. There began the flurry of departure, taking down curtains, rolling carpets, wrapping china and glasses, labeling the crates of books, almost too nervous to believe in it. In her dream life a white swan attached itself to her so that she was ferried to where she imagined to be London, standing on a bridge with its chain of lampposts, when a stranger, a robed man, held up card after card of ancient Hebrew lettering, telling her that she must discover the hidden meaning of the word. In another dream she was still in what she believed to be London, a fog-ridden milieu, a silver-gray motorcar, similar to the one her husband had, careening recklessly into a decrepit and shuttered dwelling.

Not Thackeray and not Dickens either. No high-ceilinged salons in which there lurked the trapped laughter of Lord Steyne and Becky Sharp and no Miss Flite with her twenty cages of birds and her daily pilgrimage to listen to the interminable wrangles at Chancery.

Their house was in a suburb that looked out onto a common, dismal and misted, a sluggish bottle-green pond and on the wooden hoarding nailed to the bridge in blotched and fading lettering a list of the fish it had been stocked with. It was a semidetached house with mock Tudor windows and gabling, a small front garden with straggling rosebushes, identical to all the houses that ran either up or down the hill. There was a hatch in the small kitchen where dishes could be passed through, the linoleum, left by the previous owner, of black-and-white squares, which the children stamped on, asking plaintively when the family was going home.

She did not hurry to meet her friend, fearing the outcome, and kept offering lame excuses about settling in and fetching children to and from their new school. Yet she would make tentative journeys in anticipation of it. In the bright evenings after the children had gone to bed she would walk a mile or so down to the main road where the bus to the station ran every twenty minutes. She read the timetable, imagined getting on the bus, getting off the bus and onto a train, getting out at Waterloo Station and onto an underground train and the noisy venue where he would be waiting. What would he make of her? What would she make of him? Sometimes on those aimless walks she saluted a neighbor, an elocution teacher who lived three doors down and had handed her a card in case her sons wished to take lessons. A Miss P. Trevelyan, a timid woman, her white ermine collar and white pigskin gloves testifying to better days, yet rhapsodic at recounting the names of two famous actors that she had helped onto the London stage.

In the window of a newsagent there were handwritten signs, people looking for work, looking for love, looking for furniture, and one that struck her as being especially pitiful: "*Widower wishes to dispose of recently deceased wife's clothing, as good as new, call evening.*"

At the supper table her husband would resort to doggerel or rhyme so that *fife* and *strife* rhymed with *wife,* wife who bribed children with sweets and toy guns to unseat father, to steal their love away from father so that he would be disliked and associated with duties such as taking their cod-liver oil, brushing their teeth, and doing their homework. Children were being sucked daily into the emotional incubator of mother, which rhymed with *smother*. The children were not deaf to these barbs but dealt with them in their childish ways, either laughing uncontrollably, making funny faces, or staring into the distance as if they had floated off. They asked the same riddles that they knew the answers of—"What bow can't you tie—a rainbow, tee hee hee"—and when one answered precipitately the other threatened him with extinction: "My gang is bigger than your gang and will get you." Her younger son read the essay he'd been given a gold-foil star for:

> I was playing in a small enclosed space surrounded with young apple trees that the boys were using as goalposts, they were blossoming into color and it seemed a pity to see them being continuously pummeled by the hard leather ball. For some reason I had a magnifying glass in my hand and a girl ran away with it and I chased after her, but by the time I got it back the lunch bell rang and I had to go in. The girl started to throw apples at me so I threw some back at her.

His brother named the girl as Eustace and there followed the picturesque names of girls, who graced the playground like so many nascent ballerinas.

Puddle Dock. Blackfriars. Threadneedle. Throgmorton. Cripplegate. Cheapside. Camomile. Names redolent of the toil, the trades, and the hardships that had gone on. Ancient brick walls veined with ivy and smothered in weeds, elsewhere warm brick abutting onto stone and onto newer, blondish brick, a bustle so in contrast to the humdrum tedium of their suburb.

Her friend recognized her at once, hale, welcoming, so lavish were his gestures that his arm succeeded in overturning plates of luncheon that a waitress was carrying with great caution. In those flustering moments as they met, Eleanora felt a little lurch, gone the mystery they had constructed around each other, she saw a man with a near-scraped mustache, amberish, his bearing so cavalier that he reminded her of those officers in Chekhov's plays, full of romantic but unfulfillable longings.

"At last. At last." How could there have been a time when he did not know her—"Oh ye Gods, oh ye jealous prevaricating Gods."

They are in a booth all to themselves, a wooden panel between them and their neighbors, a vista of wooden kegs, wooden hammers, wooden baskets, and photographs of maidens blithe and barefooted who had harvested grapes in Kent. He pointed out to her the regulars, the man in a black beret who claimed to be Marc Chagall's nephew and who would presently ask to do a portrait of her for a reasonable sum. A second man, who was a cadger with a flowing red beard, instantly tried his luck with her and as she shook her head called her a bog-trotting bitch. He had, as her friend told her, published a slim volume of verse twenty years previous and lived in a permanent state of poverty and bile.

She didn't dare talk of home life, instead she told how she had arrived very early and had gone to a small museum. There, from photographs and drawings in red-brown ink, she had learned that in A.D. fifty-one Emperor Claudius needed a victory and invaded England, brought elephants to frighten the Britons but lost thousands of his legionnaires in the marshes. Everything in those times, she told him, was iron, the weapons, the spears, the catapults, even the pens and words, as she said, were carved with the sharp snout of an iron pen onto wooden tablets and what severe words they must have been. He looked at her with compassion and said, "We are not iron . . . far from it . . . we are we . . . and we are here." Then he ordered a wine that was so expensive it had to be decanted, and while they waited he insisted that they each drink a dram of malt whiskey.

Two dishes of steak-and-kidney pudding, with inverted egg-cups to keep the pastry from sagging, lay in front of them untouched. The wine was fuzzing her. Cigarette smoke wreathed the room and gave to the reddish yeomen's faces the gloom of the sepulcher.

Out on the street they let taxi after taxi go by, each knowing there was something that needed to be said, but it was not said. She apologized for the fact that she would not be able to meet him often and it was decided that she would ring him from the sweetshop near her house the Monday of each week. He paid the taxi driver overgenerously, said to bring the lady to her doorstep because she was precious cargo indeed. She walked the last bit home to avoid the suspicion of her husband and she seemed to be levitating, the ground rising and falling under her feet, the common no longer a maze of gloom but a stage with wanderish blue footlights. The elation that she should have felt in his company she was feeling now, reliving every moment.

His letter arrived a few mornings later, the postman handing it to her on her way back from having left her children at school. She stood by the bridge to read it, to revel in it:

It was wonderful and it was hideous. You, whom all the great bards would depict, but oh, the awful pantomime of us not being able to talk to one another apart from yes and no and would it be the rib steak or the fish pie. Yet how close we became in that cramped corner with folks envying us our rapture. I did not want to let you go. You did not want to go. Back at my office I discovered I had taken the wrong coat and the wrong briefcase. So back to the restaurant. The owner of the coat was still boozing at the bar and remarked that his cashmere was much superior to mine, old chap. And my briefcase was in the charge of the nice waitress who remarked that she wasn't surprised at my confusion as there were stars in my eyes. There were. The stars were the eyes of the girl sitting opposite me. So what do we do. Work work work — Thomas Carlyle's recipe for melancholy. I have never met anyone so, so . . . but what's the point . . . you know how I feel.

They would come faithfully, though faithless, two, three, four letters a week, the amorous words, the utterances of his heart, as he put it, brimming over. She put them in an old lizard bag that hung on a peg in the hall behind a trench coat and yet when they were discovered she had to ask herself why had she been so careless, why had she not hidden them?

It was close to Christmas and the stamp that she would never forget carried a picture of Santa Claus floundering in a snowstorm.

The letter began *My living angel* and already she felt that catastrophe had struck. She read on:

Your husband has written to me. It was delivered by hand and this hand shook as it read and re-read the contents, right down to the last cadence. Understandably he is very annoyed, says he will knock out the few remaining front teeth that I have left. It would appear that on our very first rendezvous you were followed to the restaurant, because he knew where we sat and the wines I had chosen. What a bitch life is. We get our happiness in inches and our despair in miles. It was blind and intemperate of me not to have foreseen. I am full of anguish for any harm I have done you and my gut is twisted into a knot when I think of the damage to your life at home. This must be set right. I shall write to him and tell him frankly what he knows already — that I am fond of you, good God who isn't, that we corresponded and that I offered my services to you as an editor. We must learn to lock up our affections, to sit on it, to control it, to keep it from flaring into the open. It all happened too unexpectedly. We seem to have been on the very edge of a volcano, we shall always be in some sense on that edge but we must not fall into the crater. Sad myself, I writhe to think of your sadness and the shadow that has fallen over your family but that will be lifted. Write your novel. Do that for me. It shall be the bridge between us and I shall be a happy man because of it.

· · ·

That evening she left it on her husband's side plate as they sat down to dinner, thereby saying *Confront me*. It was rissoles, which were oversalted, and a cauliflower cheese that had got burned, the good enamel saucepan in the sink, soaking. The children, sensing a storm, felt emboldened enough to ridicule it and leave the table, going as they said to continue the list they were making for Christmas, both wanting a watch with stopwatch and a telescope to study stars and shooting stars from a balcony.

Her husband did not look at her once, merely read the letter, then crossed to the fire grate and she followed.

They stood as in a frieze. They watched wordless as the tiny show of petrol-blue flames veered over the steel bars of the grate. Then for an instant it flared and eddied as if he who had penned those words was voicing an objection, yet soon it petered out, a smear of ash, gray and silver-gray, like a bird dropping on the mossed branches of apple wood that the children had lugged in from the garden after the tree had fallen.

Scene Six

HER MOTHER had been promising to come. She missed seeing the children and their little letters were a fillip to her, but as she said she missed seeing the faces of the little princes.

She came laden with gifts, cakes, jams, chutneys, Fair Isle sweaters in sea colors for the children, and cushion covers embroidered with Celtic motifs in the purple and indigo that served as the inks of old. Her husband was given a bottle of dry sherry that he did not unseal. It was put on the mantelpiece and in time different colored rubber bands hung from its neck.

Her mother found London strange, not as friendly as Brooklyn and she missed the American twang, yet she loved the shops and for three days in a row they trudged up and down a busy and barbarous street, her mother debating on whether the gift that Eleanora insisted she have should be a fawn camelhair coat, which would be serviceable, or a gray astrakhan with a bulky collar, which was swankier.

One evening they ate, just the two of them, in a restaurant so dimly lit that her mother said it was a pure Aladdin's cave. She became youthful, expansive, and made no comment at the fact that her daughter drank a cocktail with a flower in it. She marveled at the decorative plates that were set down before the dinner plates, admiring the painted flowers, and claimed she felt reluctant to part with them. Likewise feeling the warm cloche that came with her spiced lamb, she said what a feature, what a feature, and then swapped recipes with the waiter, who could not understand a word she said, but who was courtesy incarnate. The Powder Room, as it was named, smelled of gardenia and she wondered if there was anyone they could ask what it had been sprayed with. In the taxi on the way home she deemed it the highlight of her life and yet she cut her visit short by several days, not long after. Everyone was most polite and plans were made for visits to and fro across the sea and just before leaving she handed Eleanora a bottle of holy water to sprinkle on the unbaptized children.

Waving to her mother on the platform, Eleanora thought how much was left unsaid, how she had held her mother at a distance for the very simple reason that she feared she would break down completely if she confessed to how unhappy she was.

Scene Seven

THE LILAC in their garden and laburnum in the neighboring garden, tapers of pale purple and yellow, quietly, unostentatiously, bobbing away. Mrs. Humphries, her next-door neighbor, called over the fence to ask if they might have a word. Eleanora went, fearing that the children's ball had been kicked over yet again and had done damage to her borders of pink and orange begonias. But instead it was a friendly encounter. Mrs. Humphries had a surprise. There it was tucked into a circular marbled hatbox, a hairpiece of reddish gold, so lifelike that there might have been a little skull resting beneath it, Mrs. Humphries' own narrow skull. Her crowning glory that her husband had adored so much and when against his will she had it cut off, he insisted that it be made into a copious wig so that he could continue to gaze on it. It was quite a cynosure at the annual Christmas dinner when other wives flaunted their gowns and their jewelry, she with her crowning glory and now seeing it in the lambent evening light Mrs. Humphries ruminated on how it brought it all back for her, memories flooding in, her girlhood in north Yorkshire, making her way to London, finding service as a chambermaid in a hotel in Marble Arch, the good fortune at meeting Hubert, who came twice monthly from a vintners in St. James's to take the wine orders, and there in a passage he had met her, his Durham lass. He called her lark and she called him lark. Their first train journey to meet her parents, their jitters, their first kiss on the return journey as the train stalled and eeled its way into Liverpool Street, the engagement ring that though small was priceless, the wedding plans, the dither, the expenses alleviated somewhat because Mr. Humphries was allowed to bring his own wine, except that the grasping hotelier charged a fee for the corkage. Their honeymoon in Bognor Regis, her hair crinkling after a shower of rain and she ironing it and Mr. Humphries enchanted by her ironing her long head of hair on a bureau and he wishing to God that he was an artist with easel and brush.

Eleanora had to be coaxed to touch it and more than once she felt bound to repeat how lovely it looked, how vibrant. In her thoughtful hours Mrs. Humphries had come to a decision: Brenda, as the piece was called, bore a resemblance to Eleanora's hair, had the same glints and therefore was asking to be appropriated. Eleanora must have her but on no account must she come into the hands of children to malarkey with. Brenda must be kept in her box, her flat strands fluffed up from time to time with a hairpin and when worn Brenda had to be fitted snug, secured to the natural hair or else she would sally off in a gust of wind. Eleanora kept hesitating. Mrs. Humphries was adamant. Brenda would once more take her place amid a galaxy of glittering guests, which Mrs. Humphries assumed to be the pattern of Eleanora's social life.

A friendship burgeoned.

When on Fridays Eleanora made the sponge cakes that her children wolfed, she would cut a segment, wrap it in butter paper, and leave it on the terracotta tiles outside Mrs. Humphries' hall door. She never knocked, deeming it too intrusive. Next day or the day following she would get a thank-you note, saying how delicious the sponge cake was with morning coffee, a ritual that Mrs. Humphries carried on in memory of dear Hubert, always adding that the bottled coffee flavored with chicory was by far the handiest for folk who lived alone. In one letter she asked her new friend on no account to feel sorry for her, she was quite happy, conversant as she was with Hubert twice a week at the séances that she attended.

It was months later that the rift came. The weekly segment of cake was returned and from her upstairs window, Eleanora could see that Mrs. Humphries' garden looked ragged, rose-bushes that had fallen down were not staked up, and the painted bird tray had fallen onto the grass. Mrs. Humphries herself, in a sou'wester, was sometimes to be seen thwacking flowers or bushes, talking to them in an argumentative voice. That same voice was soon to summon Eleanora at an unreasonable hour of morning. The wig must be returned. Something of importance had come up, a reunion with wine merchants, a Saxony silver wine cup to be bestowed on dear Hubert, who, from the netherworld, insisted that she go.

As she took back the box, Mrs. Humphries lifted the lid and saw that she was right, nay vindicated, in her cogitations: Brenda had been in solitary, the tissue paper not even disturbed, Brenda had not been the cynosure of admiration as she should have been. Walking off with it, she smote over the ingratitude of folk, promising Brenda a rousing homecoming.

That small transaction an instance of their small lives in their small houses and their small gardens, their hearts contracting day by day, visiting little malices on one another in lieu of their missed happiness.

Scene Eight

A YEAR HAD GONE BY.

Late May. The plane trees in flower, the pollen dust, a chimera in the air, pink and white peonies, their edges furled, in bunches of five outside the greengrocers, the fat buds plump as an egg.

Her husband was in the doorway of the children's bedroom where she had been writing her novel on the wide windowsill. There it lay, the finished book, a peacock's feather placed across it, ceremoniously.

He stood, pale, haggard, but in contrast his eyes blazed, as if hot coals had been bedded in them and though still in his pajamas, he had donned his brown mohair jacket over the top. She realized that he must have set his clock early and got up in order to go into the room while she was out to confirm his suspicions.

"So you have achieved your aims," he said.

"We don't know yet," she said, resorting to the plural to appease him.

"A work is completed without deference to a husband, an absurd epic of maudlin childhood is about to be sent to a pimp, before a husband is allowed to correct it," he said seething.

"You would only tinker with it," she said fearless, though fearing.

"O pray enlighten me . . ."

"I wrote 'It was a country road tarred very blue' and you deleted it, said there was no such thing as a blue road."

"There isn't," he said savagely.

"There is," she said savagely back.

It was too much, too much altogether. He almost sprinted across the room and was by the windowsill looking down at the evidence of her betrayal, he who had taken such pains to tutor her, who had sacrificed his own gifts to serve hers, he who knew more about grammar, syntax, style, story than she could muster in a million incarnations, he was aghast at the sight of it, now completed.

"Tear it up . . . burn it if that's what you want," she said defiantly.

"Too late to burn it . . . your jackass of a publisher, your pimp, has already seen chapters of it, fawned over it, yours is the voice of your lamenting race, O marvel, O deep diabolic crookedness, he is deceived into thinking that you write like an angel, whereas in fact you could not pen a word when I met you."

"You hate me, don't you?" she said.

"So now we revert to our habit of hysterics, we depict ourselves as the wronged one, the one who is hated . . . the little victim."

"But you do, it seeps out of you."

"I don't call it hate . . . I call it an awakening . . . you were the girl I chose, pure, loyal, untainted, an exemplary wife, and instead I get a schemer, plotting to pursue her own rotten ambition under the rubric of poetry . . . what a mockery, what a marriage."

"So what do we do now?" she asked, daring to meet his eyes.

"He that will eat the kernel must crack the nut," he said.

"Do your own writing . . . stop filleting mine," she said in triumph.

It was too much, something violent and unbalanced was unleashed in him as he stood over the high stack of pages, his hands spread out to eclipse them and almost unknown to himself the words fell out: "You have done it and I will never forgive you."

She left, not even caring if he did tear it up, because in her was a feeling of exhilaration as if she had been waiting all her life for this moment.

She sat by the pond; two fishermen on stools sat a short distance away in utter silence, casting their rods again and again to no avail. It was hot, muggy, scarcely any ripples on the water and swarms of minute insects, the same mustard yellow as the pollen. She began to write it again, the words carrying into the soundless air, the sentences in a ream, like a spool unwinding inside her.

The fishermen paused, poured tea from their flasks, and began to talk. She could hear them, yet she was detached from them, like voices in a dream, not impinging, as she filled one page after another.

"It was in the Blackwater River in southern Ireland," one began.

"In the Blackwater River in southern Ireland," his friend answered lugubriously.

"The longest drag I ever had . . . I let him run . . . and run."

"You let him run," his friend repeated.

"Five hours . . . going on to six . . . when I saw him turn over . . . saw the old white belly . . . I knew the game was up . . . knew he'd had it."

"The old white belly."

"Took over an hour to net him . . . a ten-pounder . . . turned out he was a hen."

"A hen . . . you got the priest on her . . ."

"I did . . . what a night in the pub . . ."

"Big night in the pub was it . . ."

"Big night . . . what they call a ceilidh."

By the time she got up they were silent again, their rods stirring purposelessly on the green, near-luminous slime, under the overhanging willows.

The garage door was propped open and his car was gone. On the oak table in the hall the manuscript lay and beside it a large brown envelope that served as his governance to let her send it.

Scene Nine

SHE HAD TAKEN from him that which was rightly his. He was convinced of it. Aloud he remembered what he had meant to write, what he should have written, what he had not written in his midwifery to her.

The logbook he kept and made no effort to hide had for its title "Little Eleanora."

Besides hating the countryside she wanted to meet more people and so we moved and there she found her lothario, crazed to have something in print, skittish sentimental rubbish, which at night after she had gone to bed I took the trouble to work on, to perfect. I had left my beloved Lake House to come and live in a gray suburb of London for what. Apparently to make it possible for my wife to conduct an affair with her publisher so that he would publish her books. The machinery was in full motion, the greatest publicity charade ever, advance booklets about her, specially appealing photographs taken of her, her name spread far and wide, laudation for work rewritten by me over and over again, whole chapters written from start to finish when her pen petered out or she was too puerile to handle difficult scenes.

Early in our marriage she began to show periods of hysterical jealousy and these states began to take a regular pattern and it was not long before I began to be aware of her personality change, a personality change of a schizophrenic nature, intense depression and quarrelsomeness, feelings of persecution, periodic outbursts, and deciding that her husband was not nice, was not kind, was in fact "cruel." The pattern she set up of compulsive deceit and self-interest, of jealousy and paranoia, naturally began to corrode a relationship that might have been the only saving thing in her life. She was led relentlessly on by sickness and by a sick vanity and ambition. Nothing I could do would stop her. Her name would be in lights. Sooner or later everyone has to face the consequences of her or his action. Seeing her over the years from the girl I first knew or rather did not know to the kind of female monster she has become has been like watching someone slowly die without being able to do anything about it.

I do not even doubt that at times she hates herself, surely she must seeing the harm she is inflicting on others, but these childish pangs of conscience are short-lived, so entrenched is she in her pathological state. She is incapable of working on herself, on digging herself out of the hole of her own emotional slaughter, yet with the peasant cunning that she is weaned on, she hangs on, she chooses to remain married and why, because she would be nobody, the tosh she writes and is determined to write, there being idiots as gullible as herself who want to read it, this tosh is made bearable only by virtue of that husband's honing of it, making it so to speak, intelligible.

There is a saying that we are responsible for our own faces after forty. At twenty-five her face and her whole appearance has cheapened. Whither the bloom. Unloved and unlovable, her whole life has been the crooked using of others. She uses me and no doubt she will use my children in time to come to blacken my name.

Scene Ten

AS THEY FOREGATHERED that summer morning at the coach station and stood in huddles, eyeing each other with a shyness and the wariness of people not accustomed to travel, Eleanora upon hearing a woman say, "I think, Mavis, you'll see big changes in us all before the week is out" could not but feel it was a prophecy of some kind.

Some in the party knew each other as they worked in the same factory in Dundee, joking, bantering: *aye, John, aye, Muriel, aye, Geordie.* Others were from various parts of England, the men somewhat stiff and untalkative in their best suits, women in flowered dresses with straw hats and perms, rummaging in their rush baskets, asking of their baskets if they had forgotten this or that and the evident relief at finding a bottle of pills or a crochet pattern. Two women were thrilled to discover that they were called Violet, lamenting that it had gone out of fashion and deciding that they would be Violet One and Violet Two for the journey. Jesse, a youth in a leather jacket, a gold sleeper in one ear and leather thonging around his neck, shook uncontrollably, bit on his cigarette, and covered up his nervousness with the same salute to all: *no sweat, John, no sweat, Muriel, no sweat, Geordie.*

Standing under the sooted glass roof of the coach station, none could have guessed how stifling the journey, how claustrophobic, how grating the voices, and how for the smallest things tempers would flare then fester, or that the inns along the way would be so nondescript, sunless dining rooms in which they would mutiny over the dishes they were served, poky bedrooms merely partitioned from one another, up at cock-crow for the next leg of the sweltering journey.

Gianni their guide, with jet-black hair and black molasses eyes, busied himself, making himself known to all, helping the stouter ladies up the steps — "For you anything, English lady; after you, English man" — unctuous in his immaculate white suit with the fresh carnation in his lapel. He waxed theatrical in his welcome address, his "wilkommen" as he put it, saying what a privilege it was to be in the company of English and Scottish travelers, with, no doubt, the fabled English and Scottish conquering spirit. How fascinating for him to be the one to awaken them to a new life, new dreams, new sights, art galleries, churches, restaurants, the rugged scenery, the flora and fauna, glaciers and peaks, then rest and relaxation in their alpine castle, clean bracing mountain air, not to mention haute cuisine and tête à têtes by candlelight.

The holiday was her idea, other couples went on holiday, other couples were reconciled on holiday, holidays took the poisons out of everyday life. The children, hearing that they were going to her mother's, were unabashedly happy, believing that their tree house would be unharmed and that all the magic of the previous summers would be restored to them. Her husband had booked the trip and all she knew was that it entailed journeying through several European countries and ending up in a mountain resort in Switzerland, all for a ludicrously small sum.

London suburbia, occasional parks, high streets with funeral parlors and bespoke tailoring, a chip shop, a cinema, another chip shop, ahead of them the continent that few had been in, but one man's father had fought and died at Flanders. Would they visit the fields of Flanders? No one knew.

Her husband had leaned back on the headrest, his handkerchief over his eyes, yet even in sleep flinching when his arm brushed against hers. The driver, determined to discharge them as speedily as possible, drove insanely, the vehicle like some runaway beast, trees on the horizon skidding before their eyes, treacherous roads, treacherous bends, shouts and inducements to slow down wasted on him and once on a swerve almost mowing down a group of cyclists, knights in identical black armor, who, fixed to their gleaming vehicles, hurled fists and torrents of abuse at him.

On and on and sometimes it seemed to Eleanora as if they had reversed their journey, the same hayfields, the same cornfields, poppies in a pink and crimson swoosh, women with kerchiefs around their heads, stooped over their labors, a solitary bird, a hawk or a buzzard, way way up, nearly motionless in the hazed sunlight. The farmhouses so snug, coral roofs set among apple orchards and in the narrow streets of small towns pedestrians ran for cover as the bus tore through, raising swirls of thick fawn dust in its wake.

You drive for one hour. For a lifetime. The little towns shuttered and somnolent. Your one companion Chekhov's "The Steppe." You are with Yegorushka, the knowing boy of nine, looking and listening, with the cheeky coachman Deniska, a wagon party of merchants, and a few holy men, expatiating on life and learning, petrels with their wild joyful cries, bustards either battling or mating in the blue heavens, the endless brown-hued steppe, the parched plains, the windmills like sails, then at night by a fire in the yards of the posting inns, bloodcurdling tales of robbers, everything new and strange, made stranger by mist or by moon or by storm, sky thoughts and grass thoughts, the melancholy and wonder of the little boy seeping into you and suddenly a realization, the botched, subordinate, and puerile instants of your life starting up before you, and turning to the husband who is your enemy, who has come half-awake, who guesses in you the frenzied and futile schemes to leave him, to rob him of his children, to wrap them in the garments of forgetting, you say in a voice that is perhaps theatrical: "To the steppes, for there's dying to be done," and he winks a crooked satyr's wink.

Scene Eleven

ELEANORA HAS DISCOVERED a little private room, the door covered in baize, shutting off all sound and all intrusion. She has gone in there and even helped herself to a pear liqueur that she found after searching in a cupboard.

Georgette, the haughty padrone, has retired with Gianni, up the side stairs, he unpinning her chignon as they climbed.

Eleanora sits for a long time, undone from the day's jangle, the heat, the traipsing through streets, alleyways, and enclosures, the lady guide, a connoisseur as Gianni had described her, enjoining them, she and the few gullible stalwarts who had gone on the history tour, to please observe this fortification, that beautiful portico, that stone escutcheon, stopping at buildings with coats of arms that straddled centuries from Antwerp's golden age onward. Then into galleries, wall after wall of paintings, animal and fruit paintings, dead birds, the vivid greens and russets of their plumage so lifelike and the hunting dogs, unsatiated and bloodthirsty.

It had been a sweltering day. Flight after flight of steps, gasping in the heat, pausing for breath, the men with their handkerchiefs as topnotches to protect themselves from the sun, looking ridiculous, the women swollen and expiring and she herself swollen and expiring; naves, chancels, crypts, an infinity of sacred suffering, the waxen buckled hands of a shrouded martyr in a reliquary, the ravishing reds of the triptychs, Christ carrying the cross, Christ meeting his afflicted mother, Christ nailed to the cross, the ocher trickles of coagulated blood along his loins, Christ down from the cross, weeping women, the cheek and chin of one particular virgin as the guide pointed out, not done by the master but by another hand, as was the right sleeve of Mary Magdalene.

Inside one of the larger churches she struggled with a giddiness that was getting more and more extreme, held on to a pew and just as she thought she had overcome it, the blue-winged angels in the ceiling above her began to totter, began to fall from their perches of cloud as she did, as she came crashing onto the dark, near-invisible tiles, and their running to help her, Violet with the smelling salts, others fanning her, all putting her little tumble down to the heat, to sunstroke, to the strong coffee that she was not accustomed to, whereas she knew it was something other, she knew she would have to go skewey in order to leave him, because they had both strayed too far from the path of reasonableness.

She carried her shoes upstairs and could hear and almost put a name to the various snores.

Her husband was asleep. She lay in the twin bed next to him, bells rang repeatedly from the several churches, thrumming the air, bells metal-hard and vigorous, the stronger peals purposing to drown out the littler peals as from behind the wainscoting rats scurried in what seemed to be delirious glee, their patters light yet menacing, then a scraping sound and she imagined them gnawing their way through, spitting the wooden pulp and the bells even louder, even lustier, jabbering away to herself, and realizing that the avalanche of the day, sights and sounds and heat, were threatening to engulf her, repeating the clichés of the lady guide, merely for something to hang on to:

Chicory is a Belgian endive better cooked blanched since adolescence. Leopold the Second resolved to create a Belgian

174

colony in Africa. The first diamond polisher originated near the central station. At the naval battle of Lepanto, the Ottoman Turks were defeated by the Christian League.

All of a sudden she pictured little dwarf Klara in a niche above that museum, named for the orphans that had been left by their wayward mothers, their coats, caps, and wooden porridge bowls next to the halved playing cards that had been allotted to them, the other halves in the keeping of the mothers who never returned.

She pictures her children, halved, quartered, torn between her husband and herself, her children asleep in her mother's house at that moment, oblivious of the rupture that is to come, and powerless to stop this influx she gets out of bed and kneels and prays, "Oh God, let me not crack, oh please, God, let me not crack in this foreign city with the ghost of the slaughtering King Leopold."

Scene Twelve

THEY CAME AWAY from the lowlands, from the silver flash of the rushing rivers, away from the harvested fields and the wandering drifts of poppies to more rugged terrain, the coach winding through a long narrow defile and gorges down below with rags and tatters of lodged yellowing snow. Mountain peak after mountain peak met them, snow-capped and luminous, while down the sheer slopes fir trees in thickets and elsewhere single ones like inky obelisks in silhouette, black-green monkish figures signaling the way.

As a farewell gesture Gianni read from a guide book, read the height of the various mountain ranges, the characteristics of the plateau, the population of the villages tucked into the valleys, the wines of the various cantons, and an anecdote relating to Protestant peasants who slew a Capuchin monk at the time of the Counter Reformation. Wagner, he told them, had made the region historic because having heard the alphorn on his visit he was inspired to compose the herdsman's air for Tristan.

When the coach lumbered through a gateway that was barely wide enough to allow it to squeeze past, they clapped and cheered, craning with curiosity, the levity of the first morning restored to them, yet before many minutes expired, tempers had flared and indignation ranged all around.

It was a huddle of low wooden buildings of various heights, narrow barred windows that looked onto a sweeping concrete forecourt and a parapet with a few wilting yellow marigolds scattered in a crescent of parched brown grass. At the entrance door a lady with close-cropped hair, who was dressed in a blue smock, kept beckoning and gesticulating to the driver to avoid the flowers and grasses, entreaties that were wasted on him.

"It's a dump."

"It's a shed."

"It's a rat hole."

"Where's the sea, where's the bloody blue sea, Geoffrey?"

"Where's the fucking alphorn?"

"I tell you what . . . they won't get away with this, Dudley."

"You can look out at the mountain, dearie . . . when in Rome," Dudley answered, and his wife huffed and nettled, strode across in her serviceable leather sandals, resolving to have her money refunded, plus compensation.

The woman in the blue smock called out each name or each pair of names, checking them on her notepad, then directed them to be registered, be given room keys and written instructions regarding meal times that, as she said, must be strictly observed.

"Where's the swimming pool?" she was asked.

"*Wie bitte?*"

"The swimming pool, ducky."

"Yoah yoah," she replied.

"Yoah yoah . . . there fucking isn't one."

Their bedroom turned out to be small and stifling, two bunk beds with two massive white quilts folded to suggest two bunched-up corpses. The wooden walls were burning, so that bright blisters of creosote bubbled out of them, reminding her of a fob of amber that she had seen in a shop and longed to buy, a nugget of wettish gold that she imagined would bring her good luck. Her husband had given her an allowance for the journey, enough to cover the cost of postcards and the occasional cup of coffee. It was a curiosity shop that sold braids, buttons, tassels, and thimbles, white china thimbles decorated with posies, which the women asked to be let try on. Slipping them onto their fingers, they played sparring matches with one another in retaliation for irkings along the way. Many of the men, meanwhile, had gone down the cobbled side street, only to be flabbergasted, or so they said, by saucy sights in a window, mannequins with whips in oilskin raincoats, posters of brazen fraus in garter belts and fishnet stockings, ogling for custom.

Flung at last upon each other in that cramped room without the cheer and safety of their children, each waited for the other to charge, yet instead they unpacked and placed their clothes on separate shelves of the built-in plywood wardrobe.

"We'll share them, we'll share them," she said. She was trembling as she stood there in her white slip, in a room too small to hold their despair, purple dark rims under his eyes from lack of sleep, but the eyes themselves on fire, as if he was looking right through her, right into her, and seeing only hollowness within.

"You played fast and loose with me and my children for long enough ... one more deception and you've lost them forever ... forever," and picking up a towel and a clean shirt he fled the room in search of some sanctuary.

The postcards she had bought in the art gallery where they had stopped all seemed inappropriate to send to her mother — Bacchanalian scenes of Pieter Brueghel's, dwarfs and huntsmen under whey-green skies, young debauchees stretched along the floor, broken delph, an eggshell slashed through with a knife, all evidence of a plundered feast. Even the one of the Virgin, sumptuously draped and with her stomach thrust forward to proclaim her pregnancy, seemed too brazen, too corporeal altogether.

She wrote without thinking, because were she to express her plight, her mother would see the outcome:

Dear Mother, we have arrived. I hope the children are behaving themselves and not tiring you too much. The hotel is high up, almost two thousand meters they say, one asthma sufferer has already complained of trouble with his breathing. Otherwise all is well. See you a week from Tuesday.

· · ·

"He trained in Lausanne, you know." It was a running joke concerning the one doddery waiter who shook as he wrote their drinks order in a minuscule notepad, shook as he moved the faded sheet of violet copying paper for the next order and the next and later almost dropped the laden tray as he sought to place each person's order at the correct setting.

They had resolved to make the best of things. The women had dressed as for a gala and the men were freshly shaven and wore clean shirts, mostly white shirts that made them look like a troup of itinerant musicians. Her husband, separate from them as he had been throughout, wore a black polo-neck sweater but she could see that he was animated and even drank a whiskey, animated as he told Mona and her husband about his house by the lake, the vegetables he grew, the marrows and tomatoes under cloches in a kitchen garden.

June got a round of applause when she appeared in swathes of pink tulle and very high heels, tottering like a flamingo, as did the two Violets with their faded satin handbags and almost identical polka-dot dresses.

Eleanora sat next to Jesse, who wore a linen jacket that was both creased and several sizes too large for him. They had become friends since that day crossing a field to fetch water, when wild dogs had descended on them, came bounding out of nowhere, their tails low, their snarls ominous, sniffing them, sniffing her especially, smelling her menstrual blood, and Jesse saying, "Don't run, don't run" and she replying, "I have my period, I have my period" and he telling her to walk backward and she did, the stubble sharp and thorny, walking slowly backward like he said. She saw him fend them off in play, the one huge dog and the two littler ones who soon tired of it, then removing his red bandanna, his cherished red bandanna, he played with the big dog, bull and matador at play, under the scorching sun, the beautiful passes that intrigued the animal, until at last they approached the bus and it saw that it was being bamboozled, then bit into the flesh of Jesse's hand and he hitting back, ugly determined swipes, until the driver came with a jackhammer and the animal had to let go, the thick tongue hanging out in rage and drops of blood on its front molars. Once inside the bus, Jesse fainted, fell flat on the floor and refused to be consoled and refused to have the hand looked at or dressed. He lay there, cradling it, silent, his eyes looking inward and upward, like a boy angel in a fresco. That evening in a restaurant in one of those shady squares, where the party had stopped for a drink, lanterns in the trees, dishes of olives on the several tables, he accepted the silk scarf she had bought for him, simply said, "No sweat, John, no sweat, John" and made himself a new bandanna.

The lettuce was indeed limp, but who cared, and the antipasto of sausage, cut in thick chunks and dyed an unfortunate overrealistic red, was rubbery, but who cared. They swigged their drink and toasted each other — "It's good, it's great, it's the Continent" — all the while laughing at how exceedingly the waiter shook.

The conversation fell to recollection of unforgettable holidays and excursions, June saying there was no place like gay Paree, the Tuileries, the Folies Bergère, Pigalle with its naughty lingerie, Violet One remembering her apprenticeship as a young girl in service, the braces of pheasants that had to be plucked after the shoots in August, sitting by the back kitchen door, she and another girl plucking, plucking, the bustle in the kitchen, while Mavis, who had been a pastry cook in another stately home, recalled how her boss had reserved his own little dining room at

Ascot, whole rows of dining rooms, some far larger than his, rented by the hoi polloi, who clustered onto the balcony between courses to watch the race and guess what, a Royal, a first cousin of the Queen, was on a balcony two down from them.

The main course of pork and sauerkraut met with some disdain, but as Dudley pointed out, "When in Rome . . ." and asked the waiter for second helpings of chips and boiled potatoes.

Dishes of sorbet, spiked with sparklers, were put down and the overhead lights lowered to signal the entertainment.

A dwarf impeccably dressed in black suit with white tuxedo carried a piano accordion onto the stage, placed it on a stool, and bowed. Then, clad in lamé, the singer followed, picking up the accordion, with dapples of mountain daisies painted on the black lacquered panels, opening it slowly, the red pleating coming apart, prefiguring the thrills that were to follow.

"You're the business . . . you can have my knickers to twist any old time," June said, blowing him a series of affected kisses and her husband remarked on the bad breed in her coming out after a few gins.

The first song was clearly about love, he the swain, distraught, pleading with a girl who was not there, crushed by the fact of her rebuffing him, pacing, almost weeping, his sentiments wasted upon an empty world. Love love love. *Liebe liebe liebe.* Then came a selection of Gypsy songs and the singer with his soft and velvety eyes drinking them in, the old waiter placing down the coffee cups and big snifters of brandy, tears in his eyes, either from exhaustion or because the Gypsy songs revived stray memories in him.

For the finale he had chosen a song that he reckoned they would all know and charmingly suggested that they would join in:

> Ae fond kiss and then we sever . . .
> Had we never loved so kindly
> Had we never loved so blindly

Never met or never parted
We had ne'er been broken-hearted.

Afterward he moved among them so amiably, agreed to pose for a photograph with several of the ladies, flirtatious to one or another, young or old it did not matter, June begging to know the words of his first song and he writing it carefully on the dinner menu: "*Mit 17 da hut noch traum.* At seventeen you have sweet dreams." How lovely. How tender. How true. And what was his name. "Konrad." Konrad! they exclaimed, touching the accordion, squeezing and tweaking the keys as if they were tweaking and squeezing him. "It's good, it's great, it's the Continent, it's Konrad," Dudley said, scoffing at them.

After he had done with the courtesies the singer withdrew to a corner of the room where he and the dwarf sat having their supper, deep in mirthful conversation, the old waiter plying them with dishes and pitchers of wine.

Two nights later Eleanora was sitting on a bench in the forecourt, next to the few marigolds that had livened somewhat in the night dew, when he appeared. Moments before there had been consternation on the mountain, the sheep bells, erstwhile so light and intermittent in that crystalline silence, suddenly began to clang and clatter, a united bout of warning rings, as obviously danger stalked up there and the herd ran in confusion.

Konrad came from the side of the building, his attire not nearly so theatrical as on that first night. There had been no sign of him since, as for the two subsequent evenings a lady sang German lieder while the dwarf turned the pages of the sheet music, the applause not nearly so robust as it had been for him.

He seemed surprised to see her, then remembered, ah yes, was she not the lady with the green necklace and the shawl.

"I can't sleep," she said, as if sitting there was a crime.

"It can happen in the mountains . . . the *fuhn* upsets visitors . . . they feel *betruben*," he said, smiling.

"*Betruben* — what is it?"

"I tell you . . . if you come tomorrow to have tea with me in my loge . . . up in the tower."

"I can't."

"*Du bist* so nice," he said snapping off one of the marigolds to give to her and thence from a tangled stack of bicycles he pulled one out and cycled off with a nonchalance.

She sat and studiously plucked the petals, the yes, the no, enquiring if she should or should not go to his loge on the morrow.

The shutters were drawn and he had been lying down as she saw, since the white cotton coverlet was obviously flung back as he jumped up to answer the door.

"Since two hour I am dreaming of this," he said and drew her in, at the same time turning the key in the door.

"I can't stay long," she said, breathless. There had been four flights of stairs — she had not dared take the lift in case of being seen — and then a rickety spiral stairs that led to the tower. In the dusk of that room she met the rush of his kisses, the sweet blast of his muffled words, his hand on the breast that housed her wildly beating heart, and as she was hoisted up she heard one court shoe then a second fall with a tell-tale thud on the wooden floor.

"I love the womans . . . I love the womans," he kept saying, the words lewd and lovely as spoken from his lips.

As he removed her cardigan the shivering got the better of her and he kissed her passionately along the nape of her neck, thinking it would calm her down, except that it didn't. He liked the fact that she was so nervous. Then he crossed to the bed and, like a puppet master, drew a white muslin curtain all around it for them to be enfolded in a bower of secrecy.

She wanted nothing more than to follow him there, yet something stopped her. Without her cardigan she felt naked and asked if they could talk. If they could talk.

He sat her on the wicker chair, he, crouched at her feet, looking at her, musing again and again what color her eyes were, her ever-changing eyes, as he bit on the smooth round disks of her green glass necklace and asked why the word *daydream*.

"Because it's in the day," she whispered back.

"So I daydream and I nightdream of you," he answered and she knew, or rather she guessed, that he would have said it before and yet there was in him such a sincerity and she hesitated at what she would have to tell him. They could be lovers, but not there and not then, up the mountain perhaps in one of the shepherd's huts, or in some other city or resort where he would be singing and where she would arrange to meet him. He shook his head, uncomprehendingly, frowned, puckered, asking why not then, why not there, why not now? She remonstrated with him and saw that his eyes, which she had thought to be brown, were a dark gentian, like the gentian flower.

"I love the womans . . . I love the womans," he kept saying.

"Konrad"—and she blurted it out—"Konrad, could I come away with you . . . can I live with you?"

He looked stunned, looked as if he had not heard correctly, then covered it up with a beautiful smile as he crossed to fetch a packet of cigarettes from the dressing table and lit one for her, without asking if she smoked.

He did not answer at first, he did not know how, but gradually he found himself able to tell her his brief history, his voice soft and considerate and strangely sad. Home was north of Vienna, a small industrial town that was foggy in wintertime. His wife and daughter lived there and yes, they would much prefer to be traveling with him, but it was something hotel managers did not encourage. His wife resented his traveling, resented the fact that he sang for other ladies, and his daughter, Lena, his little Lena, sulked when he returned home after a long absence, went to the window box where his wife had made a small garden and threw pieces of clay and small stones at him, in punishment.

"Your little Lena," she said.

"My little Lena," he answered.

"I also have children," she said, as if to lend respectability to her recklessness at having come up and then his arms came around her, whispering, the whispering that was a presage to the goodbyes. "It could be that we will meet again," he said, but she knew it was merely a courtesy.

"I have been unfaithful in my heart . . . and that is what counts . . . and that is what counts," she kept telling herself as she went down the stairs, exhilarated, emboldened enough to tell her husband how she was no longer subordinate, except and to her utter astonishment he was not there, he had fled, there was not trace nor tiding of him, he had taken his belongings and all that remained was the voucher for her return ticket, tossed on her pillow.

He had gone. It was as if he knew, it was as if he had guessed her transgression and had gone determinedly to collect the children from her mother's house, five days before he was due.

Her mother's letter was post restante where she had asked it to be sent. She read it under a streetlamp, beams of rainbowed fog slanting down on the merciless, turbulent words —

At long last the waited breach has come and it seems like years waiting for it. I must admit it is a terrible blow and I am asking God to help me through it. I am over seventy but wish I were ninety and not much longer for this world. I guessed it was coming and I know it is probably better to live apart when living together proved impossible. I will accept it if you promise me two things, that as you read this, you will kneel down wherever you happen to be and swear that you will never take an alcoholic drink again and never ever have anything to do with any man in body or soul. You are young and temptation will often come your way. Promise me. You owe it to God, to me, and to your children and I know that for my asking you will do as I wish. You chose your own marriage and we made the best of it so do not go on blaming us for your misfortune, as I believe you secretly do. It seems you are quoted as saying that all writers are queer and exempt from the normal mores. They are not, nor should they be. You conquer writing rather than letting it conquer you. It is no good living in the escapism that has been your wont. Look for the faith that you have lost, that you have thrown away. Go back to it. Religion and a belief in the hereafter is what counts and without that life is a sad place. I will write to you faithfully as I always have done, even though I am heartbroken but perhaps my life won't be long. I am seventy-four and wish I was ninety-four. For the rest of my life, long or short, I will be praying for you and yours and asking God to be always beside you, guiding and counseling you. I am very very sad, you will never know how much, but then we are not born for happiness.

• • •

The children were in his house now, captives, and she allowed to speak to them on the telephone each evening at a given time, their voices thin, pinched, the conversations stilted, she telling them that she would call again the next evening at the same time, as if by then something might be resolved and one or other of them ringing off, miffed, and close to breaking.

Part V

Dickie Bird

THE DICKIE BIRD SPINS, without warbling, on his long thin pole in the hospital garden, round and round, sulfur yellow, the two white propellers turning to a gauze transparency in the gusts of wind. Waiting for the wind the way Dilly is waiting. Her daughter. Her tests. Full of forebodings. The hours weighing upon her.

The dickie bird is called Busby. Busby talks to her in his rattle, in his semi-rattle, a gabble. She talks back: "Sister Consolata says we'll get the broom out and sweep the tumor away, but can we, can we, Busby?" and she waits as he does another dizzy circuit.

"I am not a good candidate for death," she says and thinks that Eleanora will answer her phone at last. All her hopes are pinned on Eleanora coming.

Glancing up, she sees the consultant striding down the corridor, the squeak of his rubber-soled shoes so pronounced, a nurse escorting and kowtowing to him.

"Doctor L'Estrange to see you," the nurse says.

Stiff mannered, his gold-rimmed spectacles down below the bridge of his nose, in his white coat, fastidious, she asks herself why he has come on a Sunday morning and at such an ungodly hour. She remembers him so clearly from that very first consultation, remembers the waiting in his office, his leather chair behind the desk, a burgundy leather scored with buttons, the leather crinkled as it ran out from the buttonholes, an imposing chair, the chair of jurisdiction, and the wan handshake when he saw her out.

He stands above the bed, wooden-backed and wooden-faced, a small speck of dried blood on his chin where he has cut himself shaving and she looks up at him, her expression woebegone, asking without the words, "Is it bad news you're bringing me?"

"It's not bad news," he tells her and goes on to describe it as merely a hiccup, saying that the aspiration from her tummy will have to be repeated, and that the registrar has been instructed to do it the very next day. She asks why. All he will say is that there has been a query from the laboratory.

"You mean they lost it?" she says, nettled.

"No, they haven't lost it . . . the diagnosis is inconclusive . . . that's all."

"Well, if it's not bad news, it's certainly not good news," she says, the umbrage rising in her, asking why hers should be inconclusive, out of the dozens sent.

"We have to be clear about matters . . . otherwise we can't proceed."

"I feel like walking out of here," she says, her eyes blazing.

"That would not be a good idea," he says, then consults the chart to read her temperature and her blood pressure and presently he is gone, his right thumb describing a circle in the air, as if that was his way of diagnosing, a departure so abrupt that he has failed to hear the woman halfway down the ward yell out: "Doctor, when is Easter this year?"

Once alone she pulls it from her soap bag, the two-page article that she filched from a magazine in Dr. Fogarty's waiting room, long before he twigged that there was something other than shingles that ailed her. She reads, as she read then, of ovarian cancer, the silent killer, claiming the lives of women, the symptoms almost undetectable, often similar to common, mild, or benign conditions. Nature besting her. And her daughter not come.

Between them once such nearness, breathing in tandem where they slept together, most often petrified, in the same bed, the same tastes in food, the lemon curd with the soft folds of barely baked meringue over a queen of puddings, the same tastes in fashion, a penchant for the tweeds with the flecks of blue and purple, colors that summoned up hill and dale, the blue glass rosary beads from Lourdes that they prayed on together, each praying that the other would not die first, vowing to die together, inseparable, and yet sundered. Eleanora with a different lifestyle, men and Shakespeare and God knows what else, oh yes, a fine firmament in which there was no chair saved for mother.

Those letters she wrote on Sunday nights, after her husband had gone up to bed, mostly ignored, or perhaps burned. Eleanora's letters not at all in the same vein. Vivid descriptions of beautiful squares in Mediterranean cities, the warm blond of the buildings, palazzos, people gathering of an evening for their coffee and their aperitifs, orange groves, lemon groves, olive trees with their trunks deformed but their leaves young and whispery. Picturesque things, but never the pith, never why her daughter was in those blond squares or whom she was with, not the letters a mother would have wished for, not an opening or rather a reopening of hearts, such as had once been.

Bart

DILLY IS WITH BART in a little nook, where he has asked for her to be brought to talk in private. He has been led there by a nurse, his mittened hand reaching out to find hers, then groping for the chair on account of his sight almost gone.

At first he reminisces about her husband and their place, the lorry loads of sandstone that he and another brought from the ruins of an Englishman's house to build Rusheen, her husband and him on the best of terms when they met at horse fairs and horse shows. He has sent for her, as he says, for a bit of advice, she and her husband being educated people.

"What's wrong, Bart, what is it?" she asks as she watches him, his agitation, sucking the air between his teeth, muttering curse words.

"He banjaxed my spray, missus . . . the spray for my heart, thought I was finished and if you saw me you'd think it too, without my spray . . . the phone ripped out of the wall and in the yard what did the bucko do but pull the rug I had over the van to keep the engine warm, pull it off . . . no car, no phone . . . no spray . . . it's what drove me here and why wouldn't it. My own cousin. Highwayman with his highwaywoman. Coveting all I have. Manus was an all right sort of fella till he married her. Thomand no less. She began to come around a lot after she saw the sight going on me. It went by degrees. Cute. Cute. She'd pretend she'd left something, a brooch since Christmas night and that it had to be somewhere. Left no brooch, only an excuse to rummage, to root in drawers and wardrobe, to see where I'd be hiding my little bit of money. It has to be somewhere, she'd keep saying, describing the brooch, a marcasite leaf, a gift from a Yank. A stunt. No brooch at all. Picking out the glasses from the glass cabinet, that queer sound of tinkling glass that says a sailor is dying at sea. What would I want with Waterford crystal, she'd yell. Put them back, I says, and I hit out with the stick. Oh, I was just giving them a dust, she'd say. Then the husband come round one evening, saying it being so wet he'd put the animals in for me. Sat himself down. It's about time, says he, that you'd be thinking of making your will. Who says, so says I. If you die intestate the government gets their hands on it, it'll be no good to anyone. That won't happen, says I. He had a few more excuses up his sleeve such as that my memory might be going. I knew she was behind it. Madam Thomand. A bad breed, a no-breed, her father tramped the roads. 'Twas I gave her husband the site to build his house before he met her, before she came on the scene. When a man marries a woman she turns him into her own likeness, her own crooked likeness. My two brothers and me never married. I have a niece of my sister's out foreign in Vancouver, she's all I have in the way of blood. Manus an all right sort of fellow until he met her, the biddy. Gave him the site because I thought he'd be company, a voice passing by, bringing milk or wood for the fire and keeping my fences up. No such luck. All he wanted was to get his hands on my place. I'll make no feckin' will, I says. He began cursing and swearing, began to smash all before him. I go to the phone to pick it up and I declare to God didn't he pull the gadget out of its socket to prevent me. They knowed I have a niece and were afraid I'd give it to her. A few weeks after he comes back all pie. We'll do a boozer, he says, and brings me up in the van to the pub. With them sleeping pills that I was taking the drink got up to my brain box too fast and there was no bread to soak it up. We were in the parlor.

He'd plonked a bottle of whiskey down on the table and glasses. Declare to God, Thomand has a smart fountain pen and a bottle of ink and says she has a trusted witness in the person of Mrs. Deane, her first cousin that owns the bar. Next thing she produces one of them forms you get from the post office to make a will easy, without having to go to a solicitor. Drunk as I was I wouldn't sign. I jumped up and I says, I'll go into the bar and tell the trick you're pullin' on me. They were bucking. 'Twas after that the war really began. My fences pulled down. My little terrier poisoned. I got the guards onto them, but they couldn't prove it, couldn't prove a thing. The jubilee nurse telling me Thomand was odd on account of being childless. Not odd but bad. I tell you, missus, that's only the skim of it. Now I'm here and I'm nearly stone-blind and day and night I'm thinking what will happen to my little place. I dreamed twice of smoke coming out the front door. Only a few years left and a bitch begrudging me my three fields, my little boat, and the house I was reared in. Better not have chick nor child nor blood relative, because all they think is grab, grab—turn you over when you're gone to rifle your pockets."

Walking back, Dilly thinks she sees on the several faces that same predicament, that fret, thinking of their shops, their herds, their holdings, and what will become of them, puzzling what they must do and do smartly, or else . . .

Nolan

"FRIGGING CHEST OF DRAWERS no effing good, two more stuck and the snib in Castleknock telling Larry that all it needs is oiling and Mrs. Lavelle . . . nearly bolted . . . up at the hall door in the middle of the night, tomfooled a driver, asked him to give her a lift out, and he fell for it . . ."

It is Nolan with the daily installment of news and happenings. In the week Dilly has heard of Mrs. Lavelle and her bids to escape and of a man from Kerry dressed to go home suddenly asking to be let sit down and never getting up again. "Beyond the beyond" as Nolan puts it.

Dilly is not listening, not heeding, caught up in her own stew, her affairs topsy-turvy, her daughter not answering the telephone, and a presentiment that she will never get out of there now.

Nolan sees tears but thinks, because they have become friends, that she can dispel them with chatter: "Didn't tell you about the fella that proposed to me. A bachelor. Two-story house, five miles outside Loughrea. Used to do B and Bs. Jesus. Him doing B and Bs. 'What d'you give them for the breakfast,' I says. 'Tay and flakes and orange juice.' Says if I shack up with him he'll will me the place . . . I'll be a big shot five miles outside Loughrea . . . following the hounds, the Galway blazers. He'll will me the place, my eye. He has a will here and a will there and when they're gone, relatives fighting and shooting each other and that's the holy alls of it. I'll string him along, tell him I'm thinking it over just to get a rise off him. You won't believe it but this morning he asks me to put my hand in his pajama pocket. 'I will not,' I says. Trying to get me to tickle his fandango. Next thing there'll be a document on a bit of ruled paper saying, 'I of sound mind and so forth.' All bull. Poor bugger, poor buggers, married or unmarried they're all longing, they're all dying for a grope."

Seeing Dilly so listless, she leans in to cradle her, wipes a tear and then another, dries them with the corner of her teacloth, and says in a whisper, "Ah, missus, you're not the worst off . . . strokes is the worst . . . strokes is the end of the road altogether."

Cornelius

DILLY IS FINISHING the dish of jelly and custard when she looks up and then looks away, startled. Her husband, whom she is not expecting, is coming down along the ward, carrying oranges in a mesh bag and a tin of sweets. Billy the ex-blacksmith skulking behind him, one hand in the pocket, both men hesitating, like they're going to be ordered out of there.

For one awful series of seconds she thinks her husband has gone on the batter again, he and Billy being erstwhile drinkers at races and shows, but to her relief when Con stands over her she realizes he is completely sober, sober and that bit constrained. Their arrival has in some way discombobulated her. She has slid into the hospital routine, into limbo, as she calls it, waking very early, a pewterish light, the pigeons rustling in the trees, their throaty murmurs, then the slow advance of dawn, the little dickie bird poised for a gust of wind and Nolan arriving with the illicit cup of tea in a special china cup, a wet flannel to freshen her face, the second cup of tea tasting like senna, and deliberations with Nolan as to what to have for lunch and what to have for dinner, various doctors converging with an air of importance, and students trooping behind them, not uttering a word.

Now with her husband standing there she remembers home so acutely, her twelve or thirteen hens, their nests most likely sodden because she is not there to put the clean sops of hay in, ashes not emptied, another bill for oil, and Rusheen beginning to look neglected.

"Ye needn't have come," she says somewhat shyly. Billy was coming anyhow, she is told. Billy having to see the eye doctor in a different hospital about his cataracts. Billy is down for an operation three months hence, the waiting list being that long. Regardless of his poor eyesight Billy is a speed merchant and Con tells her with a certain pride that the journey door-to-door was under two hours, one that would take Buss closer to four.

"He always drives as if he's going to a funeral," Billy says with a snigger. There is still that unwashed look to him, his face blackish from being in the forge for over forty years, smelting horseshoes and lengths of iron in the roaring fire.

"Two hours is far too fast, it's dangerous," she says.

"Well, we're here," Con says and clumsily hands over the gifts.

They sit awkwardly, unaccustomed to hospital noises, the phones, the ringing bells, the wheeling of trolleys, vacillating between bouts of talk and bouts of silence. The dog misses her, has stationed herself in a hole under the hedge, eager for her return. They rack their brains for news, a bank robbery, Tilda, a young girl tied up, a new priest saying Mass, rumors that Father Gerrard is out of favor with his bishop due to drinking habits and frequenting a hotel in Ennis for ballad sessions.

Seeing her husband in his everyday clothes, a bit unkempt, his cuffs hanging loose, she asks if he is eating enough, as she might ask a child.

"He is not," Billy chimes in, and there follows a contest about the number of cigarettes Con smoked on their journey, Billy insisting that it was at least twenty and Con taking the packet from his pocket to show that there were still a few left, which meant he hadn't smoked the full twenty. They talk of the weather, the weather in the city and the weather down the country, her husband telling her then that Crotty has agreed to sleep in for the weeks she is away, her husband a grown man, afraid to sleep alone in his own house, he who for many a year struck terror into her and Eleanora.

"What do they say is wrong with you?" he asks her.

"What do they not say?" she answers with a sarcasm, then tells him that all her tests had to be retaken and re-sent to the laboratory. Billy with his own private and scornful agenda pipes up to say that doctors know nothing, that doctors chance their arms just as much as gamblers do.

They have been treated to tea and biscuits, the conversation stilted, when Dilly comes up with a brainwave. From the small leather wallet that she herself had thonged at night classes, she produces some ten-pound notes and says that it is a grand opportunity for him to go down to the town and buy himself a pair of shoes.

"I'm fine as I am," he says.

"Look . . . go down to O'Connell Street . . . Billy and you . . . you'll be glad of the little stroll after sitting in that car," and Billy thrills to the idea, recalls a hotel near Parnell Square where he drank with hurley players after an all-Ireland hurley final.

When they are gone she commences on the letter. She reminds Con how dear Rusheen is to them both and how fortunate at their not losing it, managing to cling on, doing their sums, as she says, in times of adversity, proud of that and prideful when motorists stop down at the gate to look up at it, the fine house of warm sandstone, trees of every denomination girdling it. She reminds him of the flurried and coercive occasion when she made her will, he acting as witness, but neither having the gumption to object. Would it not be fairer, she asks, then answers, to divide things equally between both children? If anything should happen to her she is appealing to him to honor this final wish. It is the first letter she has written to her husband in over fifty years, an admission that makes her choke back a tear. Fifty years. The golden jubilee that neither remembered. Fields let for grazing. No more the proud neighing thoroughbreds in the fields, the thoroughbreds on which his hopes centered and his fortune lost.

They return overcheerful and talkative.

"I only had a mineral," Con says, reading the anxiety in her eyes at the fact that Billy is staggering because he has had a few, waving his arm to praise the lineaments of a young nurse hurrying by.

Con is wearing the new shoes and asks her to guess how they differ from all the other pairs of shoes he has bought over the years. She cannot. They have a feature that is unique. What is it? Shock absorbers. What are they? I'm telling you, shock absorbers. He removes one shoe and points to a nodule of raised metal, guaranteed to absorb any shock, then re-dons it and does a circuit around her bed for her to admire them. She guesses the price almost to a shilling.

"Jaysus, they didn't give us the box of free polish," Billy declares. When Billy bought a pair of shoes in distant times there was always a box of polish thrown in and a spare pair of laces, but times, as Billy says, though skittishly, are tougher.

"We should hit the road, I suppose," Con says, not looking at her.

"Rightio," Billy says, overeager. Then, emboldened from drink, he raves on about shadows lengthening, mist on the rivers creeping in over bog land and headland, blinding headlights, woeful altogether, and their engine ready to conk it at any minute.

"Are you sure you're fit to drive?" she asks.

"Sure! Haven't we a chauffeur?" and she learns how they'd hired a youth from the factory to drive them. What with scolding them about the extravagance, thanking them for coming, and reminding Con to give the dog a bit of something when he gets home late, she forgets altogether to hand him the letter.

Holding it after he has left she thinks of the many crucial things left unsaid.

Buried Love

FOR THREE NIGHTS in a row, Dilly has dreamed of Gabriel, a look of yearning on his face, the clothes hanging off him, making no attempt to come to her and yet making his presence felt, standing on an empty road, like he was waiting. Three nights in a row.

"It must mean that he's trying to reach you," Sister says.

"It doesn't," Dilly answers and says that she believes he is dead. A letter she wrote the year previous was returned, having gone to various addresses across America. Sad, she and Sister concur, when things of that nature are left unfinished. She recalls their last encounter, or rather their last, missed encounter.

"I was back in Brooklyn with Cornelius, a bride, much more palatial lodgings than Ma Sullivan's, his lordship off in the bars every night, spending all before him, when one evening the landlady taps on my door and hands me a box with a ribbon round it. A glass dish, a red cranberry that resembled a jug he had won in Long Island long before, and a note wishing myself and Cornelius every happiness. I ran down the stairs in my bare feet and ran out into the street to ask anyone if anyone had seen the tall bearded man, but it was already dark and no one had sighted him. Back upstairs, I studied it, the color like the color that summer's day, but the P.S. on his letter so blunt, so final: 'I am not in the place I was anymore.' That was all. That was Gabriel. I'd wronged him and he paid me back. I'd been told that he was going with another girl when he wasn't, at the time he was sick, unconscious, after an accident in Wisconsin hauling timber, but these two girls, these two friends, deceived me into believing that I was jilted, which I wasn't."

"Wasn't that very bad," Sister says in a voice of commiseration.

"Worse than bad," Dilly replies and muses aloud on the crosses that beset love.

Sister nods, hesitates, then she sits and recounts, in a voice quite other to her everyday chattery voice, her downfall, the one time when she reneged on Christ the Redeemer.

"I, who had consecrated myself, I who had offered my life, my thoughts, my desires, my long black hair, my everything to Him. In the bodily garden the apple lurks. It was ward seventeen. Six of my urinals gone missing. I knew the culprit to be Sister Xavier. Sent to try me, always poking her nose in my business. I went straight across to have words with her. Words. A flaming row, first she denied it then said I'd have to make do with jam jars. My patients reduced to jam jars. Shame on you, Xavier. Oh, we tussled. Like two washerwomen jawing and then, then, this arm came around my waist and a male voice said, 'Don't worry, I'll see that you get six more' and I laid eyes on him for the first time, a new junior doctor, handsome, with that Cork lilt, an Aengus, the name of the wanderer. I was called over the coals after night prayers, Matron saying there had been a complaint about me, I had upset another sister. I was given penances, made to lift the heavy patients, turning them over in the bed, sponge them, and then turn them back again, having to scrub the stone stairs and the porches three times a week with Jeyes fluid. That's where I met him. Again and again. He had a little dog in his car, a cocker spaniel that he had to let out twice a day. Buttons was its name. Buttons, a whiz at hunting birds, knew all the places down in Cork, in the briars and the undergrowth where the pheasants hid and in the reeds where the coots and the moorhens were, flushed them out. Each day Buttons perched on the bonnet of his sports car, ears cocked, lifting one paw and then another, like a ballerina. Buttons, our accomplice. Aengus plying me with questions. At what moment in my life did I realize that I had a vocation? I told him how I came home from a dance one night, I was about seventeen, a bit wound up from the dancing, and I sat by the fire and read the paper and came on an article about the foundress of our order, Catherine McAuley, an heiress who might have led a butterfly existence but instead opened Coolock House to the poor and set herself a crusade to help the children in the lanes and alleyways of Dublin and at fifty entered a novitiate and became a nun.

"As time went on things got more dangerous, those telling looks, whispering in my ear, who cut my hair and how often did I change my habit, wanting to know every single thing about my habit, the material, the veiling, the length of the train, the dimity, the guimpe, the cincture, the inner sleeving, the outer sleeving, the pocket handkerchief, the night cap, and the night veil of cotton calico that we nuns wear for sleep. Had to know it all. Then on the spur of the moment he picks up my rosary to look at the black beads with the two crosses, the ebony and the ivory, then the ring on the marriage finger that signifies betrothal to the Lord. Soon after the gifts, harmless at first, bars of scented soap, a paperweight that housed a universe of flaked snow, and then the tantalizing one, a little blue bottle of perfume, my daring to unscrew the top, prizing out the pink rubber nozzle and basking in that profane smell. *Oh, Blood of Christ, save me. Body of Christ, inebriate me.* Doing everything to avoid him and yet and at unexpected moments walking straight into him and blushing; having to abstain from the sacraments because my confessor must not learn of my sin, Mother Superior summoning me to her private parlor for a stiff talk. Why had I not received the Holy Host for five weeks? Was it the sin of pride? Me unable to answer. Punishments. Not even allowed to listen with the other nuns to the ballad program on the radio of a Sunday evening, I who loved those ballads and doing my tasks always hummed them. Then the fall. Agreeing to meet him in the pharmacy where he would have to go nights to collect the sleeping drafts for the patients and where I would also have to go to collect my medicines, suppositories, or whatever. He would shut the door, softly. We would each ask how the other was but not answer. He put it in writing to me, tucked the letter up inside my inner sleeve, saying I could read it in seclusion. Read it a thousand times. The last line crucifying me: 'Why are you staying when you do not wish to stay?' In three months he was leaving for the States, he had secured a post in a hospital in Buffalo and was asking me to go with him as his wife. Instead of a silver ring, as he remarked, I would have the prouder gold wedding band. If traveling together was too awkward he suggested that I could follow in a week. 'Why are you staying when you do not wish to stay?' He gave me time to think it over and promised to deprive himself of my company. He would not seek me out, far from it, he had himself transferred to the new wing that had been opened down the street. Looking up Buffalo in the globe atlas in the office, spinning it round and round but unable to find it. Voices telling me, 'Consolata, this is the time of your trial.' It was clear to all my sisters in God that there was something wrong with me because the weight fell off me and I walked around like a ghost. The Holy Office that we are obliged to say twice daily, merely mouthed, the beautiful words of the Psalms wasted on me. Asking myself, what would I look like in street clothes, the habit gone, the veiling gone, the yards and yards of camouflage material stripped away, and my white legs that he had never seen. Shoes and stockings having to be bought in Buffalo. How many letters did I write to my archbishop to say that I wished to renounce my vows and leave the order. How many letters did I write and then tear up. I would rehearse the interview with Mother Superior. I would see her face, grained like wood as I broke it to her and worse was the breaking of it to my mother. Writing a letter, her reading it in the kitchen and most probably having a seizure. I went from one chore to the next, asking the good God whom I was betraying to see me through. At moments I would savor the joys ahead: Buffalo, Aengus, cooking a dinner and going out to the cinema, high heels and a handbag. Sisters from the various convents were brought to persuade me, harsh and compassionate by turn. The worst was a mother superior from our branch in Liverpool, a very tall commanding person of whom it was rumored that she suffered night and day with migraines and never slept. She did not mince her words. They would not release me, at least not for five years, and then if I wished I could go my infidel way. Did I not see, she kept insisting, that I was being tested, did I not see the honor the good God placed on me by allowing me to immerse myself in the way of the cross. She cited the path that led to Calvary, Satan leading Judas to betrayal, Peter's denial, Pilate washing his hands of the case, insisting that Satan had singled me out by sending me this temptation, Satan had contemplated the masterpiece of crucifying Christ all over again by my defecting. 'Did Christ shrink from sacrifice?' 'No, Mother.' 'Nor must you.' The curtain of worldly desire must be ripped in half and I must look into my own soul and overcome the pit of hell. 'I am in hell,' I blurted to her. She almost struck me with her raised withered hand. After that it was banishment. I was sent to a sister house in Ballinasloe, silence and meditation, excused from all manual work, alone with myself, no patients to occupy the welter of my thoughts. A card was forwarded at Easter. From him. Yellow buttercups and yellow chicklets, not the image of the Christ on the cross. He was waiting, he was fretting, while I meanwhile was being watched for the sea change that would transpire in my soul. One day a young nun, a postulant in her white habit, came and sat next to me on a garden seat, sat by my side, the two of us facing a cherry tree coming into flower and knowing that I was under the vow of silence she did not utter a word. She just sat there and began to cry softly and earnestly. To this day I do not know if she cried with me or for me, all I know is she had been sent in some miraculous guise, because not long after I wakened saying and re-saying, 'In the juvenescence of the year came Christ the Tiger.' My turning point.

"It seems like only yesterday," she said, rising, then placing her hand on the damp of the misted window brought it to the guimpe that covered her forehead, pressing on it, then back to the window again and to her forehead, too overwrought to say anything more.

The Visit

"OH BEAUTIFUL DAY, beautiful day altogether, such a change, my my, such a change after that bitter wind, that bitter March wind that would go through you and the temperature has shot up after being minus what and thank God, a nice crisp morning and little shoots on the trees, little furls and the bushes atwitter with the birds."

How they laugh, how they fuss, their fussing and laughter filling that end of the ward, overflowing, one bringing a chair for Eleanora, another a cup of coffee, marveling that at long last she has come, they fearing, as her mother feared, that she had gone somewhere as far-flung as Peru, but at least it was only Denmark and for a conference, as they'd been told, to do with her work.

Her mother is propped on several pillows, her hair neatly swept up with side combs, her face heavily powdered, the too-pink powder not patted in. She twirls the two blue ribbons of her bed jacket, unable to contain her pride and joy in the fact that her daughter has come. Nuns and a nurse have converged for the welcome and what a welcome it is, compliments at the beautiful bouquet of flowers, chocolates and macaroons and fudges in a gift basket, mouth-watering, and look at those dates so moist, so luscious, all the way from Gibraltar.

Then it is to Eleanora's smart outfit, ultra feminine, the color suggestive of the fuchsia in the hedges and one of the nuns, flushed with excitement, marvels at the resemblance between mother and daughter. It is Sister Consolata to whom she is ceremoniously introduced. Sister touches her lapel and says she'll stay a month, be a balm to her mother's brooding, and listen to her mother's fund of stories, maybe put them in a book.

"I knew you'd come, I knew you'd come," Dilly says, tears and joy striving for mastery in her. Sister Rosario, a postulant in white, her face pale and chiseled like ivory, stops on her way by to meet the visitor and admire the beautiful fringed shawl, the gift for Dilly that has been spread over the bed, the better to study the colors and the patterns, birds and branched tracery. They surpass one another in deciding on its exact color. Is it brown, is it cocoa, is it cinnamon, arguing, then conceding that it is all these colors, the warm colors of the baked earth where the sun beats unfailingly down. The shawl is draped over Dilly's shoulders and yielding now to tears she says, "It's too good for me, it's far too good for me" to which Sister Rosario with a petulance asks why should it be too good for her, she a mother like every Irish mother, sacrificing her own life for her young.

"My cup it brimmeth over," Dilly says, tasting one of the chocolates, saying that unlike Eleanora she has a sweet tooth, had it all her life and consequently a spare tire. Sister Consolata rebuts with a nonsense, nonsense, still a slip of a girl and such a crop of hair, a feature that she passed on to her daughter.

Sister Consolata then draws attention to Busby, the yellow dickie bird on his tall wooden perch. Had Eleanora noticed his lordship, the little mascot, out there in the garden, harking for wind, for gusts of wind to get his propellers rattling, to get moving, to get himself noticed. Yes, the propellers did the talking for him, did his singing, the little beak never uttering a note, but nature, as Sister said, always bettering, always surpassing the mechanical. Yet Busby, as she concedes, such a nice little guy, a feature for the patients to while the hours. An older sister, Aquinas, as she is told, had the gardener install Busby on some whim, but oh Aquinas, a contrary creature, always complaining, didn't like this one or that one, couldn't stand onions, complained if there was onions in the stew.

All the while Elcanora is wondering about the time. She has not come for long but her mother does not know that yet. She is not wearing a watch. Siegfried is waiting for her, salt fish and crayfish, a ladder stairs to the loft room, setting out for the airport probably around then from the lair that he has borrowed for her coming.

Sister Consolata senses this restlessness and whispers if maybe she needs the facilities and upon being told not, claps her hands, joyous, resolute, says that it is time for mother and daughter to be left alone to retrace the sands of time. As she swishes the curtain around on its metal runner Eleanora relives the terror of the sliding wooden hatch of the confessional, in childhood, being drawn back, and the beefy face of the priest looming through the dark grille.

She has said nothing about leaving and yet it is as if her mother senses it, her face beginning to look sadder, squashed, the pride and jubilation of earlier eking out. Eleanora does unnecessary things such as altering the tilt of the lamp above the bed, resetting the paper doily over the jug of barley water, moving the flowers once, then back to their original place, saying that only the greenery smells, only the eucalyptus leaf had any smell.

Ten more minutes, otherwise she will miss the flight. She will have to send a telegram asking the Norseman to make the same journey on the morrow.

Blessedly she finds a little novelty, something that may interest her mother. It is a sewing kit from her hotel bedroom in Denmark where she and Siegfried had met, where they had flirted, walking at night after dinner in the cobbled streets, cyclists weaving in and out between them, church bells, his hair sometimes touching her cheek where he had bent to almost kiss her, though not actually kissing her, and afterward back in their hotel, occupying the pair of ample green armchairs on the landing, smitten and unwilling to be parted so early. They laughed at all the pairs of shoes outside all the doors and once as a prank he changed a few pairs to engender a little confusion the next day.

She unfolds the scarlet pouch of the sewing kit. There are needles of different sizes, a minute gold safety pin, tiny pearl shirt buttons, and strands of thread folded tightly together, their colors lapping into one another like the colors of the rainbow. Dilly reckons it would be difficult to thread those needles, the eyes so small, especially with her cataracts.

Eight more minutes. A nurse with steel-gray hair, large in girth, her elbows angled out, comes to see the visitor, stands with a sharp questing look and slightly mockingly says, "So this is Terence's famous sister, is it," then goes.

Her mother tells how Nurse Flaherty rules the ward with an iron fist and how between them it was hostilities from day one. She still seethes, as she says, from the way she was bullied, was made to take sleeping pills by that strap of a nurse, forced to swallow them, her mind rambling, back in Brooklyn, bumping into people she had not met in years. It is from that to her dismay at Terence's visit, so hurried, so callow, Madam Cindy choosing not to come in, but to sit in the car outside because hospitals upset her.

"No nature in them, in either of them," Dilly says and then putting her hand out asks for it to be held and asks what Matron had told Eleanora when they met in private downstairs. Were they keeping something from her?

"They're not . . . it's just that they can't operate until all the fluid is gone . . . until you're fit enough . . . until you're strong."

"I'm not right, love . . . I'm not right," Dilly says.

"You will be right . . . you will be," Eleanora assures her, and then Dilly draws her nearer and whispers that she wants to give her Rusheen, she wants to go out home just for the day and go back to the same solicitor that she has already been to and make a new will giving her Rusheen.

"There's no hurry," Eleanora says.

"But you love it, don't you?"

"Yes, I love it."

"Then it's decided . . . go downstairs to the matron and tell her we're going out for the day . . ."

Eleanora looks rapidly and frantically about for a way to say it and to be excused for saying it and then in a hesitant voice says, "I have to go back to that conference . . . it wasn't over when I left" and recognizes by the needlelike flicker in her mother's eyes that she is not believed, the eyes cold and blue and repudiating, robbed of hope.

From under the pillow her mother takes a torn clipping, handing it to her assertively, all gentleness and docility gone. The time seems to crawl in that ghastly hiatus, her mother recognizing her glaring untruth.

"Read it, read it," her mother insists.

Eleanora reads, somewhat stilted: "Often called the silent killer, ovarian cancer claims six thousand lives a year, yet the symptoms are almost undetectable. The cancer develops in the cells of the ovaries, two almond-shaped organs found at either side of the uterus that produce eggs; the more eggs your ovaries produce during your lifetime the more the cells need to divide and so the more opportunity for things to go wrong."

"The silent killer," Dilly says.

"But the picture is of two women who are cured."

"As many die as don't die," Dilly says, flatly.

"I'll be back in forty-eight hours," Eleanora says.

"Do that . . . do that," she is told.

Then Dilly raises herself up and is out of bed, panting with a rapid breath as she embraces her daughter, holds her in a tight, clumsy, angry, desperate, loving, farewelling embrace.

Eleanora moves, then turns, and the last thing she sees is her mother's arm raised, her nightgown sleeve raised also, sawing the air, the bone of her elbow the loneliest blue and the pity she should have shown earlier has started up in her then.

Siegfried

A LOW WOODEN HOUSE, like a barn, the entrance door tarred black and the straw from the thatched roof straggling over the eaves and the minute windowpanes. To one side there was a stack of chopped wood, an ax stuck rigid in the huge round log that obviously had failed to sunder and next to it a water barrel with a wooden gourd hanging on a bit of wet brown string. Everything bare and spartan in a gray sulky light.

Far from anywhere, in the north of the country, a cottage that he had borrowed from his friend Jakob, set down in a flat featureless field, similar to the flat fields that they had passed on the way from the airport, fields and occasionally a configuration of tall stones in some sort of ritualistic commemoration, then one tiny yellow-washed chapel, itself like a pilgrim that had been left stranded. They saw no animals but the smells from pig farms along the way were stifling.

He was not the same as the Siegfried who had flirted with her only days before; there he was charm, affability, with his hair shocking gold, like a firmament in the dreary room, and because it seemed to have been carelessly hacked, women were offering to trim it for him, many women at his beck and call.

The door opened into a room with a ladder stairs that led to an upper loft room and the walls gave off a faint smell of lime. Above the black iron stove on a rack are his socks, his shirt and pairs of gray underpants, a wool blanket, yellow and ocher, stretched ceremoniously along the banister. The table has been laid, it would seem, for breakfast, mugs, a coffee flask, and small knitted bonnets placed beside the squat wooden eggcups.

Something has happened in the little time since they parted so wistfully.

She has left her mother and regrets it now, wants to leave at once, but is too nervous to tell him, he being so tetchy and critical. She guesses that he is married and that probably there were scenes at home before he left, guesses this because of his looking in several pockets for something, possibly a letter, and then making an initial on the whitewashed wall. It cannot simply be the eye shadow, she keeps saying, somewhat irked, to herself. The moment with the eye shadow had crushed her. As she walked toward him in the little airport lounge, he, wearing a flat cap with a fur border, alone and watchful, like a lone hunter, did not shake her hand or kiss her, merely ran his finger across her eyelids to erase the glaring terracotta that was an affront to him.

She recalled the previous week with a pang, the functional tables, the blue and white plastic chairs, jugs of water, and various speakers courteous and earnest, expounding on the future of the novel, the future of the cinema, drama versus documentary, the tedium of it made bearable by the fact that whenever she looked in his direction, he beamed at her, so young, so boyish, with his tangle of golden hair. When they filed out for lunch and took off their name tags and obligatory red cotton jackets, he would make sure to find a way to sit next to her and there she heard of the white nights, people sleeping outside, people getting crazy because of the endless daylight, then of the autumn in the forests, he and his friends eating the mushrooms and stripping naked to dance like dervishes.

When his turn came to take the platform, he chose to speak in English as a courtesy to the foreign guests, but she knew that it was for her. On a screen they saw haunting images of his landscape that he had been filming for many years — islands, fjords, lakes, forests, and people old and young, children on sleighs whizzing with abandon. Afterward he was questioned as to why he had not made a film for some years, because many had seen the one that had made him famous.

"They call me a genius at the time . . . everybody calling me a genius for one month," he said and laughed and assured them that he was no longer arrogant, no longer a genius, only a bum. The film he wished to make was too esoteric. It was the story of the poet Hölderlin, sick in his mind, imprisoned in a room in Tübingen for thirty-seven years, where he played piano night and day, carpenter Zimmer his surly guardian.

On their last evening, he and she played truant, did not attend the farewell reception in the small café inside the main door, but met instead in the sumptuous dining room on the third floor, a galaxy of welcoming lights, coronets of candles that swung low on hoops of wire, the reflections of stars racing across the ceiling, stars the size of big blooms, and elsewhere lagoons of lit candles, hosts of waiters and waitresses all in black, like fledgling birds, swooping to be of use.

It was during that dinner that he decided he would ask his friend Jakob to loan him the summerhouse and somehow she pictured it differently, rustic and hospitable. The young waiter explained the dishes to her in a singsong, recitative voice: "You have the pig with the apple inside, you have the red hare with the baby hare inside, you have the roebuck with the juniper berry inside, and the crayfish hot or cold with potato dill." How flirtatious it was, Siegfried touching the silk of her sleeve, her pulse, whetting her longings, the color rising in her neck and in her cheeks, as it did in all the youthful faces around, the white complexions a mere gauze, housing the blood beneath, the blood pink and fresh and very innocent.

But now in the cold kitchen with its orderliness, its pipes and pipe cleaners, various pairs of boots and clogs that obviously are Jakob's, every moment of the hospital tableau keeps appearing before her eyes, those last seconds, the bone and joint of her mother's elbow the famished blue, and she wants to tell him all this, to reach and be reached, to cry in his arms. She keeps walking to get warm, runs her hand over the dank wall, and stops before a blown-up poster of a pair of wolves, their gray-green coats perfectly flecked with snow, the dugs of the she-wolf drooping with milk, and she reads, "The alpha male follows his mate around faithfully before and during the heat period waiting for a chance to copulate. After mounting the female and inserting his penis the male dismounts while still attached, swivels one-hundred-and-eighty degrees and faces away from her. The pair either stand or lie locked together for a period of up to half an hour and this is when the actual bliss comes in, by the alpha female releasing her sex hormones." He sees her reading but does not pause, moving hurriedly, swift and purposeful, bringing in wood, emptying it with a thud into the basket, and then taking a bicycle pump from the windowsill, telling her that the water in the pipe has frozen and that it can make a lot of trouble for them if they have no water.

It was when she asked for a drink—anything, whiskey, brandy, aquavit—that he flinched and enquired if she was an alcoholic, then was irked by her not appreciating his little joke. Except that there was no whiskey or brandy or aquavit, there was milk that he had brought from the city, along with pickled herrings, pumpernickel bread, spaghetti in a packet, and a tin bearing an image of ripe meaty tomatoes.

"I ate my dinner cautiously and without schnapps," he says, quoting Strindberg, poor Strindberg with his deathly melodies. They are drinking schnapps and washing it down with beer in an isolated pub, ropes, chains, and anchors hanging from the ceiling, memorabilia of seafarers and an old battered jukebox with its bellied front. A dried white orchid scummed in dust. The owner, a sullen full-breasted woman, is behind the counter, her hair the same color as Siegfried's, but unwashed, her face with that same pallor and rising blood, eyeing them with suspicion. At the large wooden table there is a group of young men, loud and laughing, and by the fire an old man in a faded military jacket muttering to himself, the fire being nothing more than stubs of used candles thrown in over a thick log and some pinecones encrusted with lichen, the flames fitful and with a ghastly greenness.

It was in the cottage not long after they had sat down to dinner that it happened, that Strindberg came to the rescue. Why, he had asked her, did every woman he ever met have to bring her bloody mother into the bed, every bloody woman, including his own wife, Siri.

"You have a wife," she had said.

"Of course I have a wife . . . everyone has a wife," he answered wearily, then told her of his wife, Siri, aboard a ship in the south seas with her then husband, a radio engineer, who knew with a certainty that her mother had just died in Cologne and even guessed that her mother had taken her own life, all done with such propriety, such consideration, the bed not slept in, her mother choosing to die on a mat on the floor.

"But my mother is not dead . . . she's not even dying," she had said.

"How do you know?" he said, the words carrying such a ring of doom and the glass of milk leaving her hand, traveling across the room, not fast, not meteorlike, mapping its course, before it chose to crash against the windowpane, where it made a pattern of a jagged, bursting star.

"Strindberg! Strindberg!" he had said with soft and beautiful surprise.

And now they are in the pub and he drinks to Strindberg, in that cold room in Montparnasse, with his utensils and his smelting furnace, trying to wrest the secrets of matter, choosing science as he believed over love, yet consumed by love, a first wife, a second wife, a third wife, his hands black and bleeding from his experiments, remembering a child of his, white-clad with a toy

216

sloop, somewhere in a castle in Austria with its mother, mistletoe on the Christmas table, poor Strindberg, outcast and torturing lover.

"I have been a pig to you," he says and takes her hands, leaning across the table, almost to kiss her. It is the cue that one of the youths has been waiting for. Since they sat — Siegfried having his back to them — she has been aware of him, blond, podgy, lewd, soliciting her with grimace, with gesture, running one of the pinecones over his tongue, his friends spluttering with laughter.

Now he is at their table standing above her, his eyes small and drained, eyes full of nothing, and without uttering a word places a gift on her lap. It is a cigarette carton and it feels warm.

"I don't smoke," she says, says it several times, then to Siegfried, "Tell him I don't smoke" and the two men exchange heated words. The youth refuses to push off, instead and with a skittish aplomb opens the packet and allows a shower of warm ash to spill onto her skirt. Proud of this feat, he picks up Siegfried's cap that is on a table. It is a special cap, far grander than his, with its rich trim of fox fur, brown and reddish-brown, the neat V-shaped panels of the crown in differing, sleeker furs, ending in a topnotch of ocelot.

"UFO, UFO, UFO . . . flying saucer, flying saucer," he says, veering it to simulate the snout of an airplane and having made an impression with his friends, he dons it and walks around, enquiring how he looks. Siegfried crosses to retrieve it and suddenly they are all standing, all shouting, the burliest one with a bare arm coiling, uncoiling, asking that it be broken or do its breaking. The jukebox has been turned on and she is pulled up by the podgy boy into an ugly dance, jounced about, the sweet, banal words of the song, "I do I do I do I do I do," ropes and chains from the ceiling conking her head and the old man holding up a chair, the dirty legs forked out in defense. It would only have been moments, except that it seemed far longer before the woman behind the counter bestirred herself and came among them, wielding a crowbar, prodding them as she would prod cattle, calling them by their first names, sending them back to their table, ejecting the two unwelcome visitors, his mauled cap tossed onto the road for him to retrieve.

The road was black, the sky black with it, and not a single star, the wind whipped their faces as they hurried along, he faster than she because of her high heels, and not a word exchanged. As the first sound of a motorcycle, only a few hundred yards away, reached them, he grips her arm and leads her through an opening in the fence into a flat plowed field, where they stagger like drunkards until they find a hiding place behind the high earthen bank. They listen as the sounds of the engines draw nearer, then the screech of the brakes when the riders stop directly on the other side, as though they have smelled their prey, splotches of light out there and raised voices, he and she listening with every pore of their being, breathing almost as one, but not holding on to one another, separate and tensed as they listen to the wheels pawing the ground outside and the engines puttering in an indecision.

Then a name was said. It was the name Henrik. It was either one of the group or the One who waited for them, but whatever its significance the engines started up and as if in answer to some more daring warrant they rode off, yelling, to give notice of their next maraud.

In the thick confounding darkness, he kept pouring gourd after gourd of freezing water from the barrel over his head and down onto his face, cursing, shouting, goading them to come and find him and she pleading with him as he bellowed, but her entreaties going unheard.

・　・　・

She sat on the bed without undressing. The wind tore around the house, inside the room the tarred beams creaked and sagged, while outside a weathercock rasped and re-rasped on its metal socket. He had not come up. The wind had many voices and she sat there listening to it, discharging its furies, the slow mournful notes as it subsided then rose and swelled, the very howls purposing to wreck all before it. Had it, she wondered, chased across the North Sea in the wake of the little airplane, or was it from the far-off tundras, making its way to the hospital grounds to send the dickie bird on its mad maraud. Much later, as she leaned over the banister, she saw that he was asleep on the floor, the gaudy rug over him, his arms folded penitentwise.

She sat waiting for daylight, waiting to leave, when suddenly the window flew open, swung back and forth on its hinges, as if something was about to come in, and she waited in dread for what that something might be.

Storm

A LITTLE FIGURE, slight and fidgety, is at the end of the bed, whispering, "Did I waken you, missus?"

"No, I'm awake . . . the wind kept me awake," Dilly answers.

"Pat the porter asked me to bring this up . . . your daughter left it . . . there might be jewelry or valuables in it . . ."

"What's all the rumpus?"

"It's the wind and the hooligans out of the pubs . . . they smash all before them . . . we're lucky to be indoors," the girl says, plonks the bag into the woman's hands, and creeps away.

Dilly turns on the overhead light to see. It resembles a tapestry bag such as she herself once had, a salmon pink with little figurines and two bone handles the shape of a crescent moon. What happened to it? What happened to so many things? Unthinkingly she has opened it. Inside a journal with a mottled green cover and the insignia of a brown eagle on a plinth. Always in America there were eagles, gold eagles, silver eagles, brass eagles, on a coin, on a dollar bill, above the doorways of the big banks and insurance offices and in that inglenook where Mrs. McCormack's fashionable portrait hung.

She read at a glance the sentence so arresting: *The milk thou sucklest me with hath turned to marble.*

She lay still but wide awake, the words in Eleanora's favorite gentian-colored ink slanting away under the light and her heart like a wild beating bird in her chest.

Part VI

❧

THE JOURNAL

SHE, THE MOTHERLESS MOTHER, I, the motherless mother, the million zillion motherless mothers with their skinless mysteries.

When she coughed blood we stared down at it, together, down into the well of the kitchen sink, the cream-colored porcelain with millions of little black strokes, like charcoal strokes; stared at it, the small clots so bright, so impudent, striking fear and doom into us, the presage of her untimely death. Death for her meant death for us both. Thinking that if I picked primroses and put them in a jam jar to cheer her up that she would not die.

Much much later she gave me flowers, shop flowers that she had had sent at considerable expense from the city, shop flowers and a glass of oversweet German wine, to win me back to the fold.

Her eyes a range of blues that could search out the slightest miscreance and then seethe with anger.

The two feelings pieced together and forking like the wishbone. Break one and the other snaps, or vice versa. You came again last night or very early this morning and the terror was if anything greater, magnified by your frequent visitations. You determine to strangle me. Yes, it is you . . . it is no one else. I do believe that I stop breathing for an instant because even in my cowardly cre-tiny I prefer to die my own death, rather than have it inflicted upon me by you. After you have departed I am paralyzed, too afraid to open my eyes lest you have lingered in the doorway, too afraid to alter my wan clutch on the sheet, or the counterpane, or whatever. Legs like spindles. It takes an hour or more during which I think of crying out for help. I too have children but am ashamed to make that cry, that suppliance.

I waken from the dream, haul myself out of it, and think of you, also alone, a summer's night, alone in the bedroom with the periwinkle-colored linoleum, the garish holy pictures, and the choking smell of broken camphor balls. You are no longer young, old in fact, yes old, in a blue crocheted bed jacket, missing your former life, maybe missing the mother that gave birth to you, maybe missing your children, filled with the morbid thoughts of the growth, dreading the growth growing inside you. Insects crawl through the open window and naturally veer toward the slightly warm fleshy mass that is you in which you fear decay has already left its calling card. How I pity you. You sit up and try, mostly in vain, to seize and exterminate these insects, to clap them between the palms of your chapped hands, saying to yourself, "All that is left in the end is yourself and these mites that you are trying to kill." Words. Pitiable words. Pitiable plight. The growth on your mind. The growth, afeasting inside you. Your anti-lover, your anti-child, your anti-self. You took steps to eradicate it. You sought out this person and that. All hushed up. Buss, the hackney driver, to meet you at the hall door and help you into the front seat and chat to you about the foul weather and the scarcity of tourists as a consequence. You searched out a seventh son of a seventh son. He ran his hands over your body and then his hands stayed on the belly and he told you that he could see the green slush within, green bile at his touch turning to gold, and that you would go home cured, a spring in your step as of old. But you were not convinced. The next place was in a great furniture mart. Group healing. You recoiled from those around you, their eczemas, their coughing, their phlegm. They disgusted you. When all knelt and sobbed in a stupor of emotion you prayed to escape, back to your own bed, beneath your own quilt, the dog in its hidey hole under a bit of rusted hedge, letting out the odd yap, your last companion, or as you so quaintly put it, your one remaining pal.

You ask me in the name of God to go to you, to comfort you, and I would dearly like to, except that it entails going back, back to that frankness that can lead to murder, that frankness that we only allow in in the madness of dream.

Someone has only to say roses or violets and I feel these transports ... emanations so sweet, so fugitive, the flowers of long ago, seas of them, blue in bluebell time, yellow in buttercup time, carpets of color flung down there in the trampled fields and the honeysuckle with its flutes of nectar to suck from. White thorn and hawthorn, white and pink confections, the fallen blossom soaked with rain, mornings of such rapture, diadems of dew, evenings less so, raised voices then night to come, "Blanketstowntram," the vaulting staircase, rooms, more rooms, creaks, sobs, rungs, a judder, juddering, feuds out there in the fields, the dogs getting their own back on their masters and on each other, discordant, the keening quiet.

That bit of rock made my hair stand on end. Appeared mysteriously in one of my cupboards, found its way in there somehow and nestled on the fleece, settled in as an animal might. It had not been there the day previous. I thought it to be either good luck or bad luck, being prone to the auguries. It was grayish and nobbled, a lump of slate and a veined substance halfway between marble and soapstone. Held at a certain tilt it had a face, the face of a man, solemn, one-eyed like the god Lugh or the giant Balor, who was able by the gaze of one eye to strike his foes dead. I could tell it was from home, something pained and disputing about it. There in one of my cupboards. I threw it out, then had a change of heart and in the middle of the night went down to rummage in a dustbin to retrieve it. Things have as much a hold on us as people. Talismans maybe.

I'd met a young boy, a quite disturbed young boy with a series of bandages around his head in a waiting room, and he told me that he had gone to a hypnotist about his phobia, his disgust regarding his own nose and the noses of others, gave him the bejeebies they did. This hypnotist ordered him to write on a clean sheet of paper the saga concerning his phobia and give it back to his mother, rather to put it in one of her drawers, not a kitchen drawer but a drawer with her undies and lavender sachets and so forth and presto, his phobia went. He was in a waiting room, his head bandaged, a vindictive look in the eyes.

I was there for my own vacillations, wrongs, slights, frozen friendships, jiltings, the road not taken, and so forth. Friday's appointment. Fifty minutes of every Friday devoted to raking up the past. Herr Inquisitor on a chair behind me stock-still. Sometimes I couldn't talk at all, the influx was too much. Once I lay on that couch with its unassuming cottonette blanket, the doctor on a chair behind me, when something unfortunate happened. A sort of seizure, everything flooding in, truths, half-truths, limbs, litter, and of all things a shell-less egg that was mushy in the hand and that our workman Drue called a bugaun. He remained stock-still and seated. Then it was a descent down, down into this bloodied abode, blood and water, both, a door very low, swimming into view, a shut door, no entrance, no exit, no in, no out, the watery regions thrashed by hell's flame and the gift of speech ebbing, then gone.

Everything gone. It was death without being dead. Nearly nonexistent, yet clinging on by mere threads of blood. Talking, prattling, to keep seizure at bay. No use. It came, in waves, in waves and that infantile cry for a hand, any hand, his or another's. The begging bowl. God almighty, what mendicants we are.

I don't know how I got out of there, possibly I staggered. The street a bedlam, but a quiet in all the treetops, the laced uppermost branches nodding, nodding gracefully, and the pavement soft as osier.

It must have been winter. Strange how all the sessions ran into one another, whereas the fifty pounds a go piled up. One check I paid got lost. I had to pay again. Someone I will never know benefited from these ravings.

Intemperate forays into the social melee. Salons lit as by showers of sunlight. Pearls. Sapphires. Platitudes. Choirs of laughter. A red-faced gent with spotted dicky bow and booming delivery assuring me there were not as many trees in my emerald isle as of yore, he had seen the whole country from a helicopter, went to stay with Teddy, lovely new wife, the azaleas absolutely splendid, absolutely ravishing, but the old Irish oaks thinning out.

My "turn" shook the inquisitor, because the following week the receptionist whispered to me that he had sent her out to the waiting room on the q.t. to see what sort of state I was in. She wasn't supposed to tell me but she did. She liked me. She gave me a picture that she had painted, tore it from her artist's jotter. It was a sunny field with a gate, a swing gate that led to heaven. She died suddenly not long after. The swing gate that led to heaven.

The inquisitor had moved to his own flat, further to the north side, away from the salubrious street of doctors, consultants, healers, and quacks. One went up in a lift dreading its rumbles and the way it lurched. He'd meet me at the doorway, see me in, where I sat, constrained, in a room that had fairly indifferent furniture, three irises in a vase, no knowing if they smelled. In the wings, the living area, there was a constant clatter, someone making its presence felt that I guessed to be his wife and that she resented he and I in there together, wondering what was transpiring in their sitting room where he and she sat by night. I had caught a glimpse of her once getting out of the lift, caught her peeping from the end of the hall, a small neat woman, her hair tied back in a chignon, with a slightly nervous, perplexed expression. Lo and behold after a few further sessions I meet her. She is out on the street walking up and down past their gate, hair long, loose, painted like a streetwalker, gaudy-looking, walking there in order for me to see her, to confront her. Rivals. I found it funny but also sad. I wanted to say something to her, say that she belonged in a Chekhov story, a woman parading her foolishness, her jealousy, out there on the street, looking for her lost beauty, her lost paramours and so forth, but I did not say a word.

I can't remember when I left him or perhaps he died. It just goes to show how callous I am as well as how craven.

There was a chenille cloth that I kept seeing in all its sumptuousness. Rich reds with lagoons of turquoise. It was where I did my homework, the ink bottle tipped on its side as it got down near the dregs, ructions if it spilled over. Then strangely a catalogue was put through my door. A tablecloth of the same terracotta reds, random slashes of blue, and long deep russet fringing. The shop was in an emporium of shops all housed under one vast glass dome so that it entailed going up flight after flight of stairs, taking side stairs, twice going astray, and praying that it would not have been sold since it seemed so necessary to me.

Then at last finding the right showroom, quite a large space, bales of carpeting, cushions, hanging tapestries, and in the furthest recess a dozy young man who did not bestir himself, simply ignored my call. I had to shout to ask the price and he came forward, reluctantly. I pointed to it in the window. It looked fetching on a round table in an alcove of the window with place settings to give the semblance of a gathering. One small disappointment was the feel of the material. It was a taffeta; it did not have the sumptuousness of velvet or nap, flimsy to the touch. Again I enquired the price. Either one hundred pounds or one hundred and fifty pounds. Which? Somewhere between those figures. He could not say for certain and the lady who owned the shop was abroad. Might he look up the price in a ledger? There was no ledger. The lady herself kept the books. All he wanted was to get rid of me, to retreat back to his nook, to burrow down in the mounds of cushions and mope.

White Frost. Black Frost. Hoar Frost. Jack Frost. The family of Frosts, late for Mass, my mother and I. The first bell gone, the second bell pealing, the high grass plumed, starched, the cow-pats iced over, and the ice in the puddles like the frozen sugar in the green and orange candied peel that was kept for flavoring the Christmas cakes. Helter-skelter. My mother and I. Late for Mass again.

At the chapel gate neighbors pushing through, smiling or sullen, icicles on the black spears like drop earrings, danglers, and inside on the altar an array of white flowers, the petals shredded, like the white shredding in the coconut biscuits, flowers that must have come from a shop in Limerick because not even weeds throve in winter. The cross priest that gave the cross sermons spoke first of sins mounting ever upward, of penance, then the message of the gospel according to Matthew, Mark, Luke, and John, concluding with some innovative farming tips.

Holy Communion. Up to the rails, one and all, except the three men, the pagans at the back, renowned for their nocturnal prowls, and when the moment came, up there, bowing my head to abstain. *Oh Lord, we are not worthy to enter under your roof.*

Back in the pew dagger looks from my mother, who kissed and re-kissed the medal of her rosary beads and brought it to my lips in chastisement.

"Young lady," my mother said as we went up our own avenue. *Why had I refused the Eucharist? No why. There must be a why, there is always a why. Why. Why why.*

It was what happened some evenings. Three or four of us go-

229

ing to the bridge at dusk, well knowing that the man in the plus fours would be there. Intrigued by him, his plus fours, his cigars, his scorn, casual chatting that then led to the game, the game of him swinging us round and round in turn, ending in a kiss that tasted of cigars. Innocence and wrongdoing. Then his knowing look to Oonagh, the gamiest of us, and she following him over a heap of rubble where the corner of the bridge had been blown up, over the steppingstones by the edge of the river, to be alone with him in the lime kiln, in the dark, where couples who were not married went.

Would you believe it, Mother, but one of these specialists had the cheek to ask if there was a history of insanity in the family. I denied it. Stoutly. Yet could not forget our little turns, not to mention our big turns. I thought of the moths, the way they feasted on woolens and angoras and the furor the day we saw swarms of them. It was in the blue room with the walnut furniture and the cherished souvenirs, an alabaster china bowl cracked down the middle, and a bone vanity box, with, for ornamentation, the bald severed head of an infant. Yes, inside our clothes, into our hair, into our armpits, into every nook and corner of our being as we writhed and cried out helplessly to one another.

Every so often there would come on you this yen to find a particular brooch from the Brooklyn days. It was amber. It contained the shriveled threads of a gnat that had got trapped inside it.

You stood me on a chair to reach the top shelf of the wardrobe and pull out clothes that had been flung there, kept for no reason except for the keeping of them—squashed straw hats, cardigans, scarves in flitters—and there among them I came on the green snood that led to the fits. It literally crawled with moths, moth eggs and white larvae. It sent shivers through us. Deciding you must take action, you went and fetched the goose wing and a bit of cardboard to sweep them up, whereupon matters became far worse. The goose grease that had saturated that handle must have imparted its juices to them, because they acquired new life, new momentum, and began to circulate.

"Jesus, they'll eat us alive," you kept saying and threw off your jumper, believing that they already nested in it.

Of what were we so afraid? We did not know, all we knew was that life and quasi-life had been transpiring for years in that wardrobe.

Marching down the stairs, you held the strip of cardboard at arm's length and I hummed to create a distraction. It was not onto the old rhubarb bed that you flung them, that would have been too near to the house. We went down the field, past the clothesline, to the old fort where bad spirits and bad secrets lurked and you cast everything, wing, cardboard, and crawling snood, into a swamp, itself foul with matter.

Yet in that same swamp the blue irises streaked with yellow would eventually flourish.

"Don't let on," you said as we walked back. So many binding secrets.

One evening we set out for your mother's house in the mountains. I knew it must be a crisis. We took the back road, said to be shorter, a stony road, hard on the feet. I would beg for us to sit down but you discouraged it, knowing that sitting was fatal, because of the willpower required to get up again.

Your mother, a distant creature, draped in black, a black head rag, a consortium of black petticoats, and a black cloth purse that she sometimes took a threepenny bit from and gave to me, with a warning not to squander it.

There was fluster when we arrived, my grandmother, slightly huffed, saying why hadn't we sent warning and you reasoning that a letter would have taken two days. My aunt tried to placate her mother, said what did it matter if the kitchen was untidy, if there were no dainties for us, were we not a family who didn't stand on ceremony. You hinted about there being a sword hanging over Rusheen. My grandmother asked if my father had broken out again, meaning was he drinking. You pretended not to hear her. There we were, in that dark flagged kitchen, an open fire, pots of water to boil or reboil, an Aladdin lamp stationed in the middle of the table, its coned mantle sooted, not yet shedding, but not plump, letting out a little purr. Three grown women, with evident strain between them. My aunt spoke of a new crop of potato that they had planted and said we must carry a few back because there was nothing to beat them for flavor.

The walk back lay ahead of us, the darker night, dogs, cats, badgers, pine martens, foxes, not to mention the sinners that might waylay us.

When you asked outright, there was disbelief. Five hundred pounds. Five hundred pounds! Where in God's name would they get five hundred pounds? What did you think they were — millionaires? My grandmother was furious. You mentioned a Damocles sword hanging over Rusheen. My grandmother said, *As ye sow so also shall ye reap.* You held out your worn hands, attesting to the hard work they had done. Matters came to a head when you broached the matter of your dowry, the amount that had been promised that February morning, when you set out to marry, your husband-to-be already in the city, almost two hundred miles away, having gone hence with bachelors for pre-wedding celebrations. My grandmother picked up the tongs and vented some of her anger on the various sods in the fire. *A dowry, my lassie.* The way my grandmother said *my lassie* was most stinging. You had a cheek in coming to ask for such a sum, showed a terrible absence of nature, not to mention ingratitude. You said feebly that you had never asked before and made a mistake of reminding your mother that when you had it, you gave in plenty. My aunt concurred but my grandmother, too irate, had already launched into the telling of the time my father had descended upon them in the middle of the night, roaring drunk, throwing stones up to the window, shouting to my grandfather to get up and come down and hand over the five hundred pounds that had been guaranteed prior to the wedding, years before. She detailed my grandfather in his nightshirt, trembling, begging for time, also afraid and incapable of tackling my father, being as he was by then an old man, infirm, and my father belting the table with his stick, repeating his demands and putting the fear of God into them. My grandfather went to the three hiding places where their nest egg was stowed, one out of doors in the stable, for fear of the law, parting with their entire savings, so dear to them, dear as their blood. You had not known of it and the shame that overcame you was heartbreaking. You stood, then you staggered, your voice breaking, and you said, "As God is my judge, I never knew of it."

In the subsequent dismay, tears, wailing, and hand-wringing, my grandmother swearing that she would sooner have cut her tongue out than have told it. Being of a good nature, albeit contrary, she limped off and fetched her black cloth pouch, then thrust it into your hand, said, "Take it, take it."

We slept, you and I, on chairs by the fire and at daylight set out with the money and the new potatoes, their stalks still on them as my aunt swore that the leaves also had flavor and to add them to the pot for the makings of a broth.

Lacedaemon's lovely halls were not so temptingly depicted as Rusheen in the months as my mother kept inveigling us for the annual visit. It was the summer I had not wanted to go.

Quentin was the cause.

Months of teetering joy when he would come from the Highlands to my house in London, the anticipation of his arrival so intense that often I would have to go out for a walk and leave my front door on the latch in order for him to allow himself in. He carried very few belongings, a smart leather bag in which there were a few spare shirts and a best pair of shoes with clumps of paper tissue that his wife had put in. His wife packed for him. His journeys were ostensibly about work. Yes, he would be there in my house, by the fire, as if he lived there, so at home in it, the spill of his hair, a violet evening light, the lamps not yet lit, and Quentin both shy and amorous. During those months, there had been several scenes at home, tears, threats, the ransacking of pockets, possibly reconciliations, though he was gallant enough to spare me those. He did mention a fancy-dress ball that he and his wife had gone to, fearing perhaps that I might have read about it in a magazine. It was a grand event in a castle. His wife went as Norma and he chose to be Sinbad the Sailor because that was the only costume that remained for hire. Yes, scenes at home, visits from cousins, parents, parents-in-law, all pleading with him to see sense. Weeks of agonizing silence and then a postcard — "Suddenly I meet your face" — our romance resumed and he would be back with his crushed leather bag, his hair spilling over his face, reconciliation, the bounty of kisses.

But in the end the imperatives of home and hearth won out.

Yet I clung.

He had mentioned wanting to bring me to Holland, to a museum, to stand before a favorite painting of his. It was of a swan with wings splayed out, protecting her nest of seven eggs against a marauding swimming dog. So strongly did I believe in our destiny that I made the journey alone to Holland and felt with all my being that he would be there in that museum staring at that swan and her unhatched young, sensing I had come in and turning he would weep with joy. I had no difficulty in finding the painting, it found me, stopped me in my tracks, the girth and fury of the swan's wings, the hungry dog, but no Quentin.

At the start of the summer holiday, my children and I broke the journey in Dublin and there I did a shaming thing; I had the manager of the hotel where we were staying phone Quentin's house and ask to speak to him. It was a hotel where he and I had spent a clandestine night in a four-poster bed and where a

234

man, ghost or intruder I know not, appeared in our room wearing a stockingette nightcap and matching drawers, like a sprite in a fairy tale, and my lover who had mounted me saying quite insouciantly, "I think you're in the wrong room, old boy," and the man giving a leering and loathsome laugh.

I knew that by asking the proprietor of the hotel to ring him that Quentin would twig the call had come indirectly from me. His wife answered the phone, called out the proprietor's name, which she also knew, because of having visited the hotel to check the register after she found out that we stayed there. It seems she replied with peals of laughter and said, "Sorry, darling, but my husband is over his little fling."

Then it was home. I would go from room to room, sit on beds fiddling with the chenille roses on the bedspreads, dipping my hands into the china holy water fonts that had long since dried up and then out of doors, anywhere, to escape the questioning of my mother's cobalt-blue eyes. Out there under some tree or some clump of trees I would re-imagine it, Quentin unnerved by the telephone call, possibly some tart exchange between them, and his wife's bitter laughter.

My mother, observing my moods and the barely withheld tears, decided to go into action. It was suppertime. I was staring down at a plump pork chop, glistening in its bed of gravy, and at a potato that she had gone to the trouble of peeling for me in order to encourage me to eat. She called my son away from the table and into the room that smelled of apples, because of her storing them there each autumn. He returned somewhat quashed. He was silent and a little cold with me. Under the table I squeezed his knee to assure him of something, of anything, but he ignored it. Prior to bed he told me what had occurred. My mother had sat him down, then sat opposite him and asked him was he aware of how upset his mother was and how it had infected the whole holiday. He said nothing. Then there came from her the damning question: "Is she at fault?" Was I at fault.

When he told me I said that we would have to leave there and then and he remonstrated, spoke of how awkward it would be and how hurtful, and in the end we arrived at a sort of compromise, which is to say we walked to the village where I knocked on the hall door of a public house and was admitted by a widow whom I slightly knew. She led us into a parlor where we would not be seen by the local clientele in the bar. In a heightened and incensed state I could barely speak to her, could barely register her offer of wine and of cake, hearing only the same sentence — *Is she at fault?* — hearing it and biting my nails down to the quick.

Back at home, I lay awake conspiring how I would gouge out my mother's blue eyes, leaving nothing but cavities. Then I remembered that we had stowed a doll, a large pasty china doll, in the well above the wardrobe and dragging a chair I climbed to get it, to do damage to it, feeling the bulge that was its stomach, the chipped excrescences that were its nipples, the metal wires that moved its hands, assaulting it, in short visiting upon it the punishments that I wished to visit on her.

My children had gone to a boarding school in the country. The house was ghostly, with nothing but their belongings, clothes they had grown out of, and a broken guitar. Every second Sunday I would visit them and they could see by my eyes that I was losing my marbles. I was. Asking for no particular reason why Shakespeare left his second-best bed to his wife, Anne Hathaway. Errant nonsense flying out of my mouth, such as the poor drunken Marquesa asking her little maid Pepita to fetch her a bowl of snow for her temples. A woman friend came with me. I would bring them hampers, cooked chickens, jellied hams, sherry, and port, all in a big basket covered with tempting red paper, and thrust it into their arms for their midnight binge, the woman trotting out the excuse that we had to go because we had an urgent appointment in London. But they knew. "Is Mumsies going away forever?" my elder son asked and made a to-do about the farewell, waving a handkerchief in order to hide his true grief.

That was when I took in the defrocked monk to be a companion. He'd been in a commune but got kicked out, claiming that others were jealous of him because he made himself so useful, not only in the kitchen but also doing repairs and maintenance throughout the building. I met him in a park. He looked famished in his khaki-colored robe and tattered sandals.

I can still hear him out in the hall the day he had to leave, the groaning and gnashing, waiting for the taxi that I had ordered, crying, then retching, then an avalanche of prayer, in the hope that I would come out and say, "You can stay," the reprieve that a condemned man or woman hopes for, up to the very last moments. Things had gone swimmingly at the beginning. He was spic and span, wore a clean white tunic every day and a loose khaki robe, the flapping of his worn sandals so reassuring on the stairs. He would count his blessings, say if he had not met me he would have been a mendicant, left to wander the world with his begging bowl. I'd offered him a room in return for which he would cook, do the shopping, and yet have enough time to get on with his sketches, his sketches all identical, harmless hazy foregrounds with flecks of gold doing their sturdiest to shimmer through. Still, my house was filled with a semblance of cheer, him pottering about, going off with his rush basket every morning, traveling far and wide for bargains, scouring bazaars for the special herbs and spices for the special dishes that he cooked. Tempting smells wafting out from the kitchen, the evening ritual, the laid table, candlelight, and conversation in which he talked of his departed wife and the subsequent sorrow that led him to join an order of lay monks.

It must have been something as simple as a pair of green jade earrings, danglers. I had sent a wrong signal. On the landing where we usually bade goodnight formally before retiring, he clasped me, a strenuous clasp, and declared his feelings. Next morning he shook, his complexion, which was the fawn brown of a walnut shell, had become a stark white overnight and his sighs were momentous. When he put the cups and necessities down for breakfast, he made such a rumpus. Later he knelt, wanted me to know he was sorry, but that he had not held anyone since his beloved wife passed away fifteen years previous, or had not believed it possible to fall in love again, but in love he was. It was pitiable. It was awful. It was ridiculous. He began to do a million unnecessary things for me, such as leave flowers or scraps of paper with endearing mottoes, lit incense sticks all over the place, and were I to be returning of an evening and it happened to be raining, he rushed out with a massive golf umbrella that he had procured somewhere.

At night he would spend hours bathing, either to purge himself of his desires or to capture my attention. I hated the gurgling of the water in my ancient doddery pipes, hated the thought of him lolling there, willing me to show some compassion. And on each morrow he would use every little excuse as he put down a plate or a vessel to almost touch me, though of course never actually touching me. It got to be that I could not stomach the meals that he prepared. That hurt him. I had to feign sickness and then indeed did fall sick, nauseous. I would take a few oatcakes to my bedroom and mull over the dreaded procedure of asking him to leave.

Talking of my bedroom, I would find him at all hours outside the door, in the lotus position, praying for a return to our harmonious ways.

The morning I asked him to go, he took it like a man, bowed, said how lovely it had been to have known shelter for those hospitable months, and I was grateful to him for accepting the money, the Maundy money that I gave him.

It was only when the actual moment of departure came that he broke down. As I waited for him to leave, cooped up in the kitchen, the chair to the door lest he burst in, I prayed that the taxi I had ordered would be in time. The doorbell was rung and re-rung and I knew that obviously he was incapable of answering it. I almost had to walk over him as he lay face-down on the hall floor. The hour had come, the hour that for him ritually constituted the moment of death. He had found love and a haven or thought he had found love and a haven and the removing of it did him in.

The taxi driver and myself got him standing, had to help him into the back seat with his few belongings, his cloth bag, his praying mat, and a calendar with the picture of a laughing girl with a red bindi on her forehead. His farewell gaze from the back window best forgotten.

It was a Lady So-and-So that informed me of his death. She had found my name, my telephone number, and a photograph of me in his belongings marked "Secrets." He had been her and Sir Anthony's cook for just over three weeks and had acquitted himself very well. She said that she knew I would feel wretched at hearing of the sad news. It seems it was a Sunday and being let off duty from them he had gone out of the city to have a little picnic by himself, somewhere in the country. He had got off at some isolated railway station, delphiniums, hollyhocks, and so forth, it being the month of June. He betook himself up a steep hill to have his picnic and commune with nature. Either, as she and Sir Anthony both surmised, he fell asleep, then rolled down the hill and lost his balance, or else he was walking down and missed his foothold, but the upshot was that he was rolled all the way onto the tracks and was made mince of by the wheels of an oncoming speeding train. The last line of her letter shook me, knowing what I knew, knowing my criminality. "Poor thing," she wrote, "he would not eat, he was weighed down by some great sorrow, had he eaten he might have been stronger and withstood the fall."

The doctor farther north beat all. A large house, a large sitting room, dining room, kitchen, magazines, a bowl of fruit by way of simulating hospitality. His wife was in the country. I had heard him say so on the telephone, heard that she was in Lincolnshire, and thought, uselessly, of Lady Deadlock, dreading the footfalls on the ghost walk.

Yet despite the receiving rooms with view of garden outside, his patients were put to wait in a cupboard where you wouldn't put a dog. A kitchen chair had been wedged in there, an abode so dark, so dismal that it could only help to further the heebie-jeebies.

The day I brought my suicide dream he got quite conversant. The dream was thus. I had gone to Holland to avail myself of their suicide hospitality. It was a sort of garage, the light from the fluorescent tubes ghastly bright. We were told to sit for a given time. The waiting was perhaps to allow the sufferers to make peace with themselves or maybe write a last letter to kith and kin. Not once did we acknowledge one another. Then a few minutes prior to the appointed time there was a warning bell, like a bell at the interval in the theater, and we all stood up and formed an orderly line to go in and meet our end. At the very last minute I panicked. I realized that my children would see it as an everlasting betrayal and so I went to an attendant and asked to be excused, to be allowed to turn back, except that it was too late.

When I told him he mulled, looked at the notes he had already made on my condition, and came up with the crassest explanation imaginable. A few weeks previous I had wakened one morning to find that in my garden there were several pairs of men's shoes thrown about—some polished, some not, some without shoelaces, and all black. Moreover an apple that had been growing on a young apple tree was also missing. It had not fallen to the ground and there was no butt, no pips, just a tiny wound on the trunk where it had been snapped off. Naturally I was apprehensive, twenty or twenty-five pairs of shoes thrown into my garden and an apple mysteriously consumed. Someone had been in that garden while I slept. I was certain. He ignored that. According to him the dream mirrored my anxiety at coming to him, a new doctor, and that perhaps I had wanted to taste one of the apples in the bowl on his kitchen table. Pure balderdash. I was at my wits' end trying to explain to him the most horrific part of the dream, the moment when I changed my mind but would not be allowed back. Herded into a cul-de-sac where a team of women stood, some holding white kidney-shaped enamel spittoons and others with cutthroat razors. I even tried to describe the scream, how endless it was, and in the aftermath, getting up, quaking, going down to boil milk, because there was something about boiled milk that seemed normal.

I only sat in that cramped cupboard for one more appointment and he was offended at my decision to quit.

A swish dining room, orange trees and lemon trees in big terracotta urns. A sepulchral maitre d' who assigned me to an obscure table. As fate would have it a gentleman, also unaccompanied, was at a companion table, two solitaries, in the wide curve of the bay window.

Ere long, he began to send the Portia "fair speechless messages." Then the maitre d', to my surprise, came over and with a courtesy that had not hitherto been evident, asked, "Would madam wish for a glass of red wine?" Madam drank white wine. The gentleman bowed by way of consent. Rhone, Rhine, or Loire? Either. Something with a nose in it perhaps? Yes, something with a nose in it. A bottle arrived in a pewter ice bucket, beaded with dew, and he made much of offering me the cork to smell. A glass of red wine and a glass of white wine raised in mutual salutation. *Salute. Sante. Skol.* Cheers. *Slainte.* The west's awake, the west's asleep, and down the hatch.

Presently and with an alacrity, monsieur's plate, cutlery, and glassware are plonked down at my table, he himself bowing obsequiously, charmed at the ease and glide of it all. He was a coffee maestro, went into raptures about coffee beans, their nuttiness, their taste, their aroma, their aftertaste, their after-aromas, the different soils they throve in. He was from Turin. Was the Turin shroud, which was said to be placed over the face of the crucified Christ and bore his image, authentic or a hoax. Who knows, Bellissima! It was not a topic to his liking. The wines, coffees, and cuisines of the regions in which he traveled were his forte. Studied human nature and female beauty from the vantage of many a dining room.

He ate heartily, jambon with artichoke, duck à l'orange, and then announced exuberantly his craving for zuppe Inglese. The waiter was uncomprehending, then scornful, holding up the carte where there was soufflé, crepe au poivre, or tarte citron. No no. The coffee maestro must have his zuppe Inglese. A contretemps. "A little joke, monsieur, a traveler's joke."

Afterward a digestiva and a night stroll. A very select street, high shuttered windows, the shutters swinging open, the dwellers walking their small dogs, the last word in respectability. Back in the lobby a courteous goodnight as he betook himself to a bar in the cellar, no doubt to order a liqueur, having done the gallant with Bellissima.

The unfinished bottle of wine had been sent up to my bedroom. It lay there, wobbling in the ice bucket, and my sky-blue nightgown was draped decorously across the largest, fattest white bolster I have ever seen. There were two doors to the bedroom, an outer door padded with red leather and studded with red buttons, then a second door that led to the inner sanctum and guaranteed silence.

Tap-tap-tap. There was even a little miniature knocker on the outer door. He had changed into a blazer, stood with a certain braggart air, his eyes keen but slightly contemptuous as though to say, "I always know when a woman wants to get laid." Without any demur he leaned in and switched out the bedroom light, confining us to a dark and speechless confessional, the unfamiliar mouth, the unfamiliar cock, the unfamiliar cunt, the lunging thrusts, swift and loveless and sinuous, in which nothing was allowed in, not even you, Mother.

The woman doctor I consulted was less of a wall than the two ponderous gentlemen. Bertha was her name. Her eyes were soft and dark as sloes and the fact that she was Eastern held out even greater promise. I thought that she, or maybe another, could reach in and pull out all the tribulation and the mountainous bile. These thoughts often became fanciful and I pictured different methods, many surgical, then recalled my mother putting wire down the throttles of young chickens to cure them of their pip. She would cure me of my pip, I thought.

I would arrive early and walk up and down her wide, windswept street. I say windswept because there was always building work and hence rubbish and grit flying about, along with loose bolts from the scaffolding that were a hazard. They were white stucco houses, several stories high, with basements, one of which was her consulting room, number forty-eight.

I would keep my eyes on her door — it was a black door with a knocker that jammed — and wait for the patient preceding me to be helped out. She was a younger woman in a wheelchair and a chauffeur came to collect her just minutes before she was due out, then carry her up the steps. There was something so poignant about this young woman being carried up those steps, making sure always to smile, and then as he went back to get the wheelchair she looked out the car window, gazing and forlorn.

After me there was a man, tall, owl-like, with owlish eyes and metallic gray hair, shoulder-length, which I reckoned was a wig.

One day the Owl man was there ahead of me and, to my consternation, as soon as the chauffeur arrived and descended the rickety stairs, he followed and stationed himself in the doorway. He spoke to Bertha after the chauffeur and the young woman had gone and in those moments I became frantic at the prospect of losing my precious appointment. She was nodding, listening, as he was obviously giving her a cock-and-bull story about having to catch a train or an airplane and she was falling for it. She saw me, saw my importuning, and presently he was coming back up the steps, muttering and with a galled expression.

Months later I did something extreme. I rang Bertha up one evening, invited her over, implying that it was important.

She came, muffled up. What a thrill it was, what a clandestine thrill it was to see her remove her garments and throw them off one by one, her scarf, her hat, her coat, and her black kid gloves with their zillions of little wrinkles. She crossed from the land of wide streets to the narrow street where I live, rows of Victorian cottages that adjoin or face each other but remain secretive, in one a window box with a few geraniums that survive the frosts, another with a dusty paisley curtain up against the window and wisteria on the double-fronted house, twice blooming, the trunk in winter pared back to the bone, bony and with a sallow thinness.

She was glowing. The fur collar around her throat brought to my mind a painting Rubens did of his second wife, who though clad in white ermine seemed stark naked. Bertha had taken trouble with her makeup, kohl under the eyes and the amethyst choker deepened the dark pools of her eyes.

We ate and drank and lolled, sat on big cushions by the fire, she so plump and languorous and confiding, telling tales of a childhood in Alexandria, a rocking horse with jade stones for eyes, orchards of pomegranates that when ripe she and her sister would trample on, visiting uncles, all of whom had a thing for her and she knew even then just how much rein to give them, then the dancing in the evening in the drawing room, parents and children and guests and cousins, dancing to an orchestra that had been summoned from the city. The fact that I had not danced was of no consequence to her. She said I would find such a freedom in it and even, perhaps, such pleasure. There we were dancing, my doctor Bertha and me. Her womanly arms soft but firm as junket, the musk smell of her perfume new, dancing as though in the fields of youth, the steps as wild and as fluid as she decreed them, in and out of the various downstairs rooms, rooms that had been crying out for a bit of life and thence into the garden, regardless of the season, where, in the aftermath of a shower of rain, the air was damp and refreshing.

Soon as she got her breath back she broached it, but very tentatively. I had said on the phone that her coming to see me was important. How could I tell her that it was, but now that it was not. How could I tell her that for the twenty-eight years since I first read it as a young wife, I had clung to the fable of the Steppenwolf, believing that his redemption would also become mine. I had thought and thought of Harry Haller as he chanced on the black sheen of wet asphalt in an unfamiliar quarter of the old town, chanced upon fallen lettering that when pieced together read "Magic Theater for Madmen Only." Going inside he encountered Hermine, the mysterious hermaphrodite who taught him the tango and many of life's sweet poisons. But sitting there with her, I knew that Harry Haller's magic theater was not our magic theater, no more than Proust's hawthorns in all their pink and tender effulgence could be our hawthorns, my mother's and mine, our hawthorns and our selves belonging off there in that sacral and saturate place and just as dearly as I had longed for her to come, I now longed for her to be gone, so that I could allow in the wolf of loneliness, at last.

Human begetting raw raw raw. A scorching day, the smell of the elderflower sickly, sickening. I was inside of you. Being banished. Wave after wave of it, hour after hour. Your blood, your bloodshed, and my last stab at living. Between us, that blood feud, blood knot, blood memory. How can I know? I don't know. I do know. It's what we know before the words that is known. At the end of your tether, alone, alone as only the dying are. Except that it did not turn out as you had planned. So little does. I picture you walking back, the heaving desolation, blood running down your thighs, down your legs, jellied blobs of it, and the drops here and there spangling the dry grass. Your Gethsemane. *Oh Father, oh Mother, forgive us, for we know not what we do.*

Part VII

Dilly

DILLY IS SITTING UP, her bed made, partly dressed for a journey, her face pale and drawn, dark shadows under her eyes, and a hunted look.

All she needs is her coat, hat, and shoes to be brought from the cloakroom. It is only a matter of a day; she will have returned before nightfall. These are her words that she repeats again and again, fearing she will be thwarted. The young nurse puzzles, thinks it ought to be okayed with someone higher up, whereupon Dilly asks to see Sister Consolata, only to learn that Sister had to fill in on a two-day retreat for a nun that got mumps.

"I'm my own boss anyhow," she says then quite commandingly and asks for her garments and the walking stick that Sister Consolata had put aside for her husband.

"Is it a funeral?" the little nurse asks kindly.

"Listen here . . . do you know anyone who could drive me?"

"I know one man . . . Bronco . . . he'll get you there and back but he's a terror on the road . . . umpteen crashes . . ."

"Like a good girl would you ring him for me . . . just do it on your own bat," Dilly says, then foolishly and contrary to her resolution she tells how she is going home to see her solicitor, to change her will, because as things stand, it could only lead to trouble. She delves in her purse for the coins for the pay phone, the little nurse refusing them, saying she can use the office phone as there's no one on duty yet.

"Are you sure you're strong enough to go, missus?"

"It's a flying visit."

She drinks the tea without tasting it, eats the toast without tasting, without chewing, her mind like that hold-all in the pantry where things were flung, sharp knives, scissors, razorblades, implements.

"Making our escape, are we?" Nurse Flaherty says, materializing, in a raincoat and plastic bonnet, obviously having been informed of this defection.

"I'll be up and down in a matter of hours," Dilly says, determined not to be ruffled.

"I won't allow it."

"You can't stop it."

"My good woman, if anything happened to you on that journey we'd be responsible, it's us who'd take the rap . . . so get back into that bed and I want no argument."

For an instant they face each other, sworn enemies, but Dilly is determined to be unflinching.

Seeing the little nurse return with her clothes and the walking stick, she asks as calmly as she can, "Did you get Bronco?"

"I got his wife . . . he's out on a run . . . we're to ring back."

"Who gave you leave to ring Bronco?" Nurse Flaherty asks her.

"No one," the little nurse replies, cowering, waiting to be thumped.

"Take off that hat and coat, Mrs. Macready, and you'll be brought your breakfast," the nurse says and hearing that she has already had a breakfast, she is told that she can't bolt it anyhow until the consultant comes on and that won't be for at least an hour.

As she goes, vehemently shaking the rain from the plastic bonnet, Dilly reads menace in the cut of her back.

Dilly sits in the outside porch by the front door, gathered into herself, not looking at those who come and go, her hands fingering her rosary beads, just willing Buss to hurry, imagining that by now he must be more than halfway, it being well over an hour since she rang and implored his sister to ask him to come post-haste. The porter, with a croak in his voice, keeps coming in and out of his booth to tell her she is in a draft, urging her into the inner hall because the March wind is bitter.

"I'm fine here . . . I'm fine here," she says and pulls her collar that bit higher so as to be inconspicuous.

Her husband will think she had been discharged, will welcome it, back to their routines, the blended soup, tomato or mulligatawny, the fire laid each morning but not lighted until six, their routines, their hard-won harmony. He may even bridle at the thought of being brought off to a solicitor, but she will remind him of being dragged for that crooked outing, afternoon tea in a deluxe hotel, a big reception hall with a black papier-mâché dog, its orange-rimmed eyes, and a card that read "Collection for the Blind," the drawing room so opulent, loveseats, armchairs, china shepherdesses along the mantelpiece, painted water lilies on the glass firescreen, a roaring fire, a picture window that looked onto a millstream, the big mill wheel stationary, tea for four, the white and the brown sugar cubes mixed into the one bowl, scones with jams and clotted cream and then the bombshell, Terence asking them did they love him as a son and if so would they show it, prove it by willing Rusheen and all its lands to Cindy and him. What with the strangeness, the grandeur, and the bluntness, they put up no fight at all, just acquiesced in it, he presently announcing that he had made an appointment with J. M. Brady & Co., the well-known solicitors.

When she sees her son come up the steps, flushed and agitated, she knows there has been foul play. She knows by the rage in him, the way he swoops through the swing door, not allowing an elderly woman to pass, his overcoat unbuttoned, and she smarts at the sarcasm in his voice, "Well, ma'am, I hear that you were thinking of creeping out on us."

"I want to see the homestead . . . to walk round it . . . it's a small thing to ask at my time of life."

"Nothing crookeder," he says, refixing his rimless glasses to see her all the clearer.

"Nothing crookeder," she answers.

"So why does it have to be so sly, so underhand?" he asks.

"I'm sick, Terence . . . make no scene here . . ." and as she says it she sees the expression on his face, savage and infantile, her own son, her once-upon-a-time white-haired boy, ready to strike her dead.

"Don't strike me, Terence . . . not here," she says and as if by prompt, Nurse Flaherty appears waving a thermometer and a plaid car rug, a soul of solicitude, saying how the little daft nurse had forgotten to take her temperature, something that is a must before any patient is allowed out.

Silenced, cowed, she is made to sit on a chair, the glass pipette in her mouth, unable to speak, hearing them expound on the unwiseness, nay the madness of her decision as her eyes cast around for the sight of Buss. Her temperature is slightly up as Sister Flaherty says, but her pulse is racing, in fact, like a dynamo and they each take her arm and she is conducted into the inner hall with the heave of the defeated. She does not struggle, she has lost her battle, listening in disgust to their false concerns about bad roads, rotten roads, trees down everywhere, a freezing vehicle, and the likelihood of her catching a cold that would undoubtedly go down to her chest.

They have reached the bottom of the staircase when she turns and sees Buss come through the door, doffing his cap as if he is entering chapel, and springing backward, she runs toward him with a surge, saying his name, her hat falling off and with it the two tortoiseshell side combs, her hair wild, disheveled, when she staggers, then stumbles, Buss's big slow hands and arms opening but failing to save her from crashing onto the hard, vast archipelago of colored tiles.

252

Bells, nurses running, two men in white coats, like two butchers to her stunned eyes, being lifted onto a wheelchair, and Nolan, as from nowhere, shouting, "What's happening to the missus?"

It is Nolan's hand Dilly reaches for, not theirs. It is Nolan to whom she whispers to keep them away, and it is Nolan who hears her last baleful utterances, again and again: "It's beyond the beyond the beyond now."

Moss

THERE WERE TWO MEN, an old man and a young man. A few stars still in the sky but pale and milky as stars are in the early hours before they slip away.

Ned, the young man, garrulous as if he were drunk, which he wasn't.

Climbing the mountain road, a godforsaken stretch, the odd carcass of a dead animal, ruts and runnels, and in the fields of richly bronzed bracken a few scutty Christmas trees that never flourished.

They park the van by the television mast, a steel god looking down on the valley below, the cable around it juddering in the wind, the threads and messages within, passing unheard, and then a tramp over toughened heather terrain until they arrive at the boundary wall and climb it. Already feeling like felons.

Flossie knows the owner and has gone there on the quiet umpteen times to shoot woodcock and even once shot a wild turkey, which Jimmy said had come all the way from the Appalachians. Flossie was an apprentice then and Jimmy was boss. Going together, because the loveliest and most luxuriant mosses throve in that wood, so many varieties, the oak moss, the brook moss, the stair-step moss, and the green-gold moss that has no equal for color, not in any curtain, not in any carpet, not in any mountain range.

The owner, a bachelor, the last of his tribe, living alone, confining himself to kitchen, scullery, and pantry quarters, holy pictures on every wall, walls covered with Sacred Hearts and a medley of saints, a mammy's boy who never married and who keeps a shotgun in case of trespassers, but loves his trees, loves his woodland, and honors a covenant set down by his great-uncle, which was that no tree should ever be wantonly cut down.

Ned stands, then walks, then stands again, flabbergasted. He has seen woods, he has even worked in woods, young woods, putting down spruces and the like, but he has never set foot in a place like this, the peacefulness of it, spooky, the way the trees seem to have stood there undisturbed for generations, have a greater claim on the place than either man or woman.

For the best part of a year he has been pestering Flossie, asking when can he go with him to gather the moss to line a grave, to learn the trade and be the one to pass it on. Flossie only does it for close friends or relatives or kids crashing on their way home from discos. But each time he has been turned down, Flossie in his gruff way saying, "You see I'm not Jimmy" and nothing more. Flossie learned the art from Jimmy, who learned it from a Cornish man, and the Cornish man having got it from a Breton, and the Breton from God knows where, maybe the Appalachian Way.

With Jimmy gone, Flossie preferred going alone, gathering the moss for those creatures that have meant something to him and now for the woman he scarcely knew but had a bond with, a bond never acknowledged by him and never ever by her.

A ghostlike mist hangs over and above the trees and above that, pockets of it run and frisk about, like the Pooka man playing hide and seek.

A hush and the two men advancing into the very heart of the forest, where even Ned has had the sense to pipe down. Flossie knows the trees with the best hangings, can already picture in his mind peeling back the beautiful copious strands, the green, the wetter green, and the orangey yellow, some meshy, some compact, some, even in winter, with little pinky purply flowers bedded in them. He already thinks what a beautiful sight it will make on the four walls of the woman's grave. He has brought six black plastic bags, two for Ned and four for himself, and instructs the young boy not to rush it, the one thing he must not do is to rush it or the mosses will crumble, fall apart, and be useless. Slowly and with infinite care he begins to peel from the roots of the trees, the beech, the oak, and the elm, as Ned watches and follows, unfurling strand after strand, yet now and then Flossie has to shout, "Jesus, don't rush it, you're destroying it" and painstakingly they gather their crop and lay the strips along the boulders to dry off.

"'Tis a pity to be taking it," Ned says, struck by the rich colors, now that the sun is half up.

"Ah, 'twill grow again . . . 'twill grow even better . . . that's nature for you," Flossie tells him.

Ned doesn't know death, doesn't want to know death, yet he is proud to be gathering a carpet that will be cut and trimmed and hung on lines of wire, then pegged to the grave to make it splendid. He knows their house with the rhododendrons and piles of trees around it, two avenues, the back avenue completely overgrown, a haunt for the courting couples. Once he saw the woman with a man's hat on her, painting the bottom set of gates a silverish color.

"Was she a cousin of yours?" he asks.

"Mind your own feckin' business," he is told.

"Sorry, sorry," Ned says, cowers, and after an awkward silence asks what color dead bones are and is told that they're a dirty brown and all broken up, except for the skulls, the skulls stay intact, often three or four skulls in the same grave like they're one family, still fighting it out.

"Did you know her?" Ned asks.

"Sort of" is the answer.

Only a kid when he saw her cross the water park and head for the river. He could tell just by the way she walked back and forth what was on her mind, pacing, not saying a word to him, eyeing him, wanting him gone out of there, to scoot it because of what she had come to do. Only a kid but he knew and he knew that she knew he knew, him standing there with the two big goose eggs that barely fitted into the palm of his hand, goose eggs that he had just stolen and she pacing and the river so wild and free and sporting, hungry for anything to be thrown into it, a stick, a rake, a person. She was white as a sheet and fuming at the gall he had by not moving off, her shoes in one hand and her stockings in the other and the waterfall a hundred yards away, spouting a yellow-green foam. He can still see it and hear it and all else, for it was something he had never forgotten nor ever would forget, the picture had never faded, the pallor of the woman, her eyes desperate, darting, wanting him gone because of what she had come to do and without the words begging him to show her a kindness by going away. But he didn't go because he thought he shouldn't go. Only a kid but he knew that he must stand his ground. The roar of the water so gushing, the power of it, the thick curdling surface ready to suck anything into itself and go its willful way. He stood his ground, he could still recall it, he with the two big white goose eggs in his hand, the one about to drop, and she with the saddest look he had ever seen and without the words imploring him to let her do what she had come to do. But he wouldn't and he didn't and after a long time or after what seemed a long time she walked away, away from the river and back up toward her own place, Rusheen. Not spoken of ever again. How could it. Seeing her at Mass and things over the years. He owed her the moss.

"You see I'm not Jimmy," he said aloud, and the boy looks at him with a baleful look that is full of wonder.

The pelts of moss are drying out in the bit of sun, the sun's warmth seeping into them, making the colors to quicken.

Cortege

THE WET GREEN WORLD into which the rain has poured and now sunshine lighting upon everything, fields of grass a pulsing green and rivers overflowing, swishing the shores, black-green at the bends, branches forking this way and that and where the odd leaf had clung on, brown and hunched like brown hunched birds, yet the crows swooping and joyous, the rained-on roads drying out, ranges of mountains in the distance a molded blue, at one with the horizon.

Bringing her home to the woodlands she knew.

The hearse is in front and the two mourning cars behind, having made their way cumbrously through the suburbs that sprawled out of Dublin and beyond, picking up a bit of speed on the motorway, then losing their bearings in the first big town because the eejit of a driver, a Dublin jackeen, took the wrong fork, took the Cork road rather than the Limerick one, and her father's mood changing from one of lament to a scalding irritability. Her father, his friend Vinnie, and Eleanora are in the front car, Terence and Cindy behind, playing their car radio so loud that music could be heard when they came to a standstill in the market town enquiring if a hearse had been sighted, passing through.

"My mother is dead, my mother is dead," she kept saying it in her numbed state, because it had not sunk in. It is outside of her, it is a figment, both because it is so sudden and because she cannot pinpoint the exact moment, it being such and such a time in one land and a different time on the clock of the other. It had happened in lost time.

The three previous days are jumbled, the hospital bed that she fled from, the famished blue vein of her mother's elbow, the thick vinegary consistency of the rollmops herring, the motorcycle brigade, the tiny airport with its paltry souvenirs and Siegfried's rueful goodbye, then the air journey through fog, trough after trough of fog, strapped into their seats and full of foreboding. Then arriving through her own front door to a ringing telephone, picking it up, she heard the voice and recognized it as being that of the sister with the steel-gray hair, telling her that her mother has died and the remains were being brought down home on the morrow. Coronary thrombosis — in other words, heart failure.

Her father in the front seat is lighting one cigarette from the other and repeating the same mournful sentence, his eyes welling with desolation and wrongedness, "I didn't think she'd go so fast . . . I thought she'd pull through" and Vinnie doing his best to console him.

Vinnie is a big man, an ebullient man, keeps touching Con's shoulder, points to houses, farms, and gateways that they pass, telling how such and such an owner came home from the States with a load of money and opened a takeaway joint and made another load of money, tastiest chicken in the land, but the health not too good, so money isn't everything. "So money isn't everything," he says and suddenly Con turns on him, not wishing to hear baloney about takeaway chicken, saying Christ Almighty, his wife is dead and will no one throw him a crumb of pity and then turning to his daughter asks where are her tears, where are the natural feelings for a mother.

"Ah, you poor man, you're gutted . . . you're absolutely gutted," Vinnie says to Con, knowing how to humor him, having humored him all his life, in drink and out of drink, and nudging Eleanora, but for her father's benefit tells it as he has told it numerous times: "I'd buy a horse for some big shot but your daddy would come with me to look it over . . . a genius with the horses . . . an absolute genius . . . he'd see the potential in one and he was never out . . . by God, he was never out, knacker, hunter, thoroughbred, he could tell what stuff was in them . . . he and me, by Christ, we made the jackpot for other men but not ourselves, but not ourselves . . . am I right, boss, am I right?"

"Oh, right as rain," Con answers with a dreariness as Vinnie points to other farms owned now by foreigners, or Dublin people, solicitors and accountants, chaps with thesises, buying farms for their weekend shoots, aping the gentry of long ago.

It is Vinnie who suggests that they halt for a snack and Buss having beeped to the driver of the hearse waits, sees him reverse, then follows as they loop off the road and through a long winding avenue, dense with woodland on either side, big trees, leafless the upmost branches in lacy sway, the littler trees like foot soldiers with blousy buskins of ivy.

A girl meets them at the wide entrance door, her fingers twiddling delicately to wave them off. She is a young girl in a bright embroidered tunic, her high black boots draped with black fringing, the expression on her face apologetic — "We are very sorry . . . we cannot serve you . . . it is midwinter time" — and to emphasize it she points to the scattering of curled bronze leaves that have blown in under the heavy door and are strewn all over the great hall into which the travelers are looking with longing. It is empty except for a carving chair and a skeleton of bog oak, coal-black in color, on a center table, its limbs forking in all directions and to one side a huge copper gong lamentably mute.

Vinnie pleads with the girl, leads her around the side of the house where the hearse has been discreetly parked under a canopy of beeches, alludes to their grief, and wonders if she could see her way to make them a pot of tea.

They troop into the large dining room, the several tables laid with white cloths, mostly free of dishes except some cruets in which the damp salt has hardened. They sit in different places, the undertaker being a stranger to them, choosing to sit apart, and Buss being the last to have seen Dilly, simply repeating what a great lady she was. Terence and Cindy sit side by side holding hands, her father asking for a brandy and after much wrangling between him and his son, a tumbler of warm water and a tot of brandy are fetched.

From behind the folded shutters a butterfly, disturbed either by voices or the heat from her father's cigarette, appears, opening and shutting its wings in a quick shuddery motion, the tortoiseshell brown unfolding to show a tinge of vivid orange, its suckers moving wildly as though indecision dogs it, but then nature or perhaps folly prevails and presently it does a giddy pirouette around the room and roams into the cold hallway.

The young girl has returned with two branches of laurel that she has just plucked and that she lays down before them in a gesture of welcome and perhaps commiseration.

"The kettle, it boils slow," she tells them.

"And what might a beautiful girl like you be doing in the wilds of Ireland?" Vinnie asks her.

"It is poor wage in Latvia so I cannot live," she answers.

"I bet you live now . . . I'd say the fellas are queuing up in the woods at night."

"I am queen alone in my castle," she says proudly and suddenly draws their attention to a herd of deer that have come to look, to enquire, the dusk of their shapes at one with the dusk of the shrubbery, curious and furtive, the shrubs not stirring and the animals not seeming to stir, just watching and then without warning and in a beautiful elongation, disappearing, apparition-wise.

"The gamekeeper he say they are getting too many . . . we shoot some," the girl says.

"Which ones do you shoot?" Vinnie asks.

"The old ladies," she says and giggles, then realizes the faux pas, puts her hand to her mouth, and does a little curtsy.

Cindy in a show of false sympathy asks Con if he would not be better sitting elsewhere as the sun is in his eyes and again he flares: "What blasted sun in my eyes? What would you know? An ignoramus," at which Terence takes her arm and leads her solicitously away.

The girl has returned with the tray, different mugs chipped and putty-colored, apologizing for not being able to unlock the cabinet with its nice china. She has brought a cake of soda bread that is defrosting, the small beads of frost like hailstones on the yellowish crust. She does not sit with them, simply moves among them, remarks on the chilliness of the room, but brightens at the fact that they will open Easter week, except that she will no longer be queen alone in her castle.

As she wanders through the hall Eleanora hears her brother and his wife celebrate the fact that Rusheen is theirs, marveling at the good fortune that got him to the hospital in the nick of time, and the good friend Flaherty that had the acumen to tip him off. It was theirs on paper but it would always be her mother's, and in time her mother's ghost would demolish it, for the wrong done. She thinks of the three days ahead, mourners, endless pots of tea, endless plates of sandwiches, the low Mass, the high Mass, boats to the island grave, the first boat with the flowers, as is the tradition, the other boats following, and in her mind she goes upstairs to collect a few mementos, a gauze fan and from the blue room a bone box with the severed Bakelite head of an infant as ornamentation, in which there were old necklaces. In that instant it happens. It came first in her gut and thence to her thoughts and she knew before knowing. A tapestry bag belonging to her mother, with its birds and its griffins, seems similar to the one she had left in the porter's keeping at the hospital. Then a terrifying tableau as she sees it being handed to her mother, the bent fingers rummaging and the words jumping out, as might an animal. She runs from the hall, through the porch, pulling back the heavy oak door, around to where the hearse stands so stately under a canopy of beeches, a few stray husks fallen onto the glass roof, her mother in her cerements inside the new, too-yellow coffin, all quiet, so quiet save for a stirring branch, and she kneels, praying that it be not so, prayers rapid, incoherent, and jumbled.

For the farewell, the Latvian girl escorts them, two metal ice buckets wedged into her arms that she bangs, the music loud, brazen, and tuneless, something reckless about it, breaking the veiled and somber hush.

Pat the Porter

THE PORTER WITH the croaky voice is on duty inside his glass cubicle and seeing Eleanora he runs, having waited, as he says, for the last four days to tell her, his hands raised helplessly and in futile anger: "Shure, he made her cry ... her own son ... it was him that caused her to fall." Then he mashes her hands in sympathy. He saw it all, heard it all, with his own eyes, with his own ears, the poor woman sitting in the porch, by herself, minding her own business, waiting to be collected, her mind clear as a bell, going home for a private reason, except that there was an informer. Her son arriving, livid, ordering her down to bed, brooking no excuses, and a demon of a nurse in cahoots with him.

"Shure, that's what did it," he says and drags her into the inner hall to reenact the misfortune, them linking her, tugging, then he stops suddenly on the tiled spot where she turned round and saw the driver from home and bolted, but too hastily and in her flounder fell; pandemonium, bells ringing, nurses flying it, and the poor helpless woman collapsing, then lifted onto the wheelchair.

He tells her that wicked though that was, it was not the worst moment, the worst was when they tripped her up, caught her out in a lie, and she denying it stoutly, then her son throwing down the gauntlet, asking her was it not so that she had confided to a young nurse about changing her will and caught red-handed the creature blushed having to own up to it, pleading to be forgiven, begging him to let her go home anyhow, will or no will, if only to see the place, if only to walk around it, because Father Time was winding down her clock. But they wouldn't. And they didn't.

"Shure, that's what did it," he said, proud that he was there to be a witness but vexed that he failed to prevent it, staring with pale, watering eyes.

"The bag I left with you . . . could we get it?" Eleanora says gesturing to the glass booth and he not registering the question. She takes him by surprise as she goes there, into his little bivouac, where none are allowed.

"A bag with bone handles . . . it must be here," she says, rooting in corners, in which there are stacks of newspapers, boxes, his raincoat, and a man's black hardhat.

"Ah, I sent that back up . . . I'm never here of a Tuesday," he says, proud of the fact of having remembered but shocked by the sudden eruption in her voice.

"Find it . . . find it," she is close to screaming, when to placate her, as he thinks, he produces the death notice that her brother had in the paper, and the sickening opening words: *To our darling Mammy who will be sorely missed.*

"Where did you put it?" she asks, her face now only a few inches from his, his fluster, his tremor.

Then it dawns on him and he smiles, a baleful childlike smile. He has remembered.

"I sent it up . . . little Aoife brought it to your mother . . . you see I'm never here of a Tuesday," he says, at which she exclaims at the bungle, his denseness, his stupefaction, telling her the same useless thing over and over again, about never being there of a Tuesday.

She is no longer listening.

She has fled from that hall to the inner hall, down the corridor, heading for the ward on the third floor, where she last saw her mother and where she pictures the bag at the foot of the wrought-iron empty bed, with a ghastly white coverlet over it.

He is behind, trying to catch up with her, the impediment in his voice worsening, pleading to be heard, explaining how there are thieves everywhere, women's jewelry swiped off them, hooligans coming in off the street to rob.

"At least hear me out," he begs, but she can't. The frenzy to find the bag is all-enveloping.

He stands a gaunt, abject figure, apologizing for his foolish mistake as the steel doors of the lift meet and shut him out.

The Little Parlor

SISTER CONSOLATA was expecting me, the electric fire turned on, a tea tray with a mohair tea cozy with a picture of a quaint cottage, sandwiches and assorted biscuits, and on the circular table, written immaculately on a ruled sheet of paper, was the inventory of my mother's belongings.

I longed to ask her to go at once and get the bag but decency forbade it. Word had reached her that I had been hasty with Pat the porter and she regretted that and assured me that there was no kinder or more trustworthy person.

The room felt icy, even though the fire was on. It was one of those tall electric fires fronted with a simulation of logs, broken chunks of coal, lit from within by a red bulb that gave a semblance of heat, but not real heat.

Rain rushed down without warning. It came plopping through the trees and plashing onto the grass, sheeting the flowerbeds and then smack up against the glass pane as if there were hailstones in it, frozen beads of water running down the long double windows that rattled. How they rattled.

Her voice though very low was full of rapture and as she spoke her tiny hands kept darting in and out of her wide, black, capacious sleeves. She described being called out of the chapel of the retreat house to be given the urgent news, then being excused by one of the fathers and tearing from the south side of the city in rush-hour traffic, the young nun, her chauffeur, jumping traffic lights, nearly mowing people down, only to come through the front door five minutes too late. My mother was already in the operating theater. She and Nolan, as she said, outside, both with hankies, pacing and praying and poor Nolan distraught because she had been the last to be with my mother, had helped her along to bed after her tumble in the hall, had gone to make her a hot drink and come back to find her missing, found her nearly unconscious in the toilet, poor Nolan shouting, shouting, the cardiac team with the crash trolley arriving in seconds, one giving her mouth-to-mouth resuscitation and the other with compressions to her chest and Nolan calling, "Say hello to Elvis, missus." She said how one of the doctors had told her afterward how my mother's mind came and went, one minute lucid, the next minute flustered, saying the dinner wasn't ready and asking if for marmalade you double the amount of sugar. They waited in order to put in the pacemaker, sometimes her pulse was there and other times it had almost gone, and they feared that she was dying on them. Father Conmee was sent for. He anointed her and gave her the last sacraments and it seems she got very highly strung and asked for the courage to go bravely and for forgiveness for any wrongs she might have done. Then she whispered to him to come a bit nearer and take off her wedding ring, which he did, but he couldn't hear her last wish as the breath had gone. After that it was very fast, very fast.

"A little clot to the brain most likely," she said.

"Is that what she died of?" I asked ashamedly.

"She died from her heart, child," she said, her single caustic note.

It seemed an eternity before she went off to get the belongings. I kept thinking—as before an examination—that if I registered every feature of that room that I would be absolved and that my mother would not have read the journal. I noted the damp senna-colored stains on the blue border of the wallpaper, pictures of saints so very pensive, a more cheerful picture of the foundress of the order, and interred in a green glass bottle, ears of corn and grass stalks that had long since withered.

In a cardboard box there was my mother's angora beret and fawn coat, her shoes, odds and ends, her wedding ring in a small manila envelope, and her white rosary beads inside a prayer book along with a prayer composed by a Trappist monk that the Sister had copied out for her. On impulse she read it, said it was bound to be efficacious:

Anna was something of a local phenomenon in Jerusalem. Everyone knew the story, how as a young widow she had come to the temple one day to pray and had been there praying and fasting ever since—for all of sixty years. She was a tradition, they used to say. Simeon was only some old man down by the gate but no one took note of him. Anna, the temple figure, and Simeon of no renown yet Providence chose both as the Savior's childhood prophets. The somebodies and the nobodies equally the instruments of God.

Snatches of prayer, ejaculations, as she moved to the window, her hands on the dark sheen of glass and her wide sleeves winging out as if she were shielding us against the infernal hosts.

The bag looked exactly as I had left it, the two handles clasped together and the diary snug in its place, the mottled brown binding like that of an old dictionary or a prayer book. I leafed through it rapidly. There were no marks, no tear stains, but I could feel that my mother had read it, her spirit seemed to permeate it, and in that instant I found her glasses, steel-rimmed and mended in several places with cellophane tape that had yellowed, the little lenses so comical, like child's goggles peeping up at me. There was a cry that must have been mine because it was not the sister's, stunned and silent as she was, gazing upward as if questioning those legions of angels she had so confidently implored.

It was terrible. A moment of pure terror at being found out, forever damned.

She came across and took the glasses out of my hand and put them in their metal case, which she snapped shut, then tucked everything into the cardboard box to be rid of them. She did not attempt to soften matters, she simply said we would not know, not now, not ever. Except that we did know. The very chill in the room seemed to confirm it, as did the pockets of dark in the four corners of the high ceiling, and from everywhere there seemed to descend little accusing hisses, legions of them.

The mystery remained as to why my mother, having read it, having felt, as she must, such a violation, still determined to give me Rusheen. Was that love or was it despair? I put it to her.

"That's her secret and she has taken it to the grave with her," she said and in a gesture of clemency, she took the wedding ring out of the manila envelope and slid it onto my finger, as though to bind past and present, land and story, to effect as it were a truce between living and dead.

"Let's sit," she said after some time and I crossed and sat, the two chairs side by side, beneath the window, the freezing cold creeping in through the cracks of the wooden frame and the rain now soft and subdued, almost a comfort.

She spoke in a whisper. My mother had told her many things, had opened her heart, things that could scarcely be uttered, the milestones, our life together, my mother's and mine, the night my father held us hostage for several hours with a loaded revolver in that crazed and reeking room, that other time when he almost burned the house down, we flinging furniture and pictures and linen out into the garden, and then his sojourn with the monks, contrite, eating milk puddings and swearing never to touch another drink. She had heard it all. My mother not wanting ever to let me go, but having to let me go, having to bear it, having to bear everything, her one indulgence the letters she wrote on the Sunday nights, asking to be heard, asking to be understood, crossing the sea to be with me.

"She knew you loved her ... she knew how much you loved her," she said, her voice full of faith, the stark white of her dimity and her guimpe so ghostly in the thickening shadows and it was then I cried, cried for the fact of not having cried and for the immensity of tears yet to be shed.

We sat for a long time, the room filled with a soft weeping, hers and mine, the single drops of rain blinking, then gliding down the windowpane in serried succession. Somewhere not too distant a bell was rung, light and silver-tongued, then after an interval it was rung again, perhaps a supper bell except that there were no tramping feet, there was only us, in a freezing cold room, the encroaching shadows, and the moment when I would have to get up and take my leave of her.

At the hall door she said we would have to be crafty and she pointed to a little madwoman, elderly but with a childlike canter, jumping up and down, the small hands in vain trying to wrestle with the stout wooden knob to escape. Sister scolded her, ordered her back to bed at once, Mrs. Lavelle, then told me how Mrs. Lavelle was forever trying to get home.

"Call in, when you're back," she said and took both my hands in hers, held them with an intenseness, and it was as if we had lived a lifetime up there in that cold parlor, which in a sense we had.

The cars whizzed by and with a vengeful glee puddles of water were swooshed onto the pavement.

Part VIII

Letters

MY MOTHER'S LETTERS, heady and headlong, forgiving and unforgiving, lay in a box, or rather in a series of velveteen boxes, in which there had been bottles of toilet water or talcum powder and hence gave off a faint lavenderish or lily of the valley smell that sometimes prevailed and sometimes did not.

Dear Eleanora,

Another photo of you in the paper, your hairstyle more sophisticated but maybe not as natural. Still you are your own mistress now. The youngster we got to help doesn't know a thing about farming but how could he, worked in a garden below in Monasterboice and then went to England, came back a drifter, asks me the most stupid questions, rushed a cow, and she slipped on a timber gate that had fallen and could have broken her neck. Your father was away I didn't tell him or won't. As one gets old there is less to look forward to the only pleasure is to be with one's own and that is not always how life deals the cards. If you want any garments sewn bring them when you come, as we can get them done here more easily. A nurse here saw you on a stage in Dublin and said you looked lovely but she'd never know it was you only hearing your name, said you were very capable at handling the questions. The pace is too fast for you. As for the second heater you say you want to get us, winter is almost done and there will be twenty-five percent off them so far wiser to

275

wait than dishing out the full sum. Always after Christmas everyone is broke and Santa Claus gone back to Elkland or wherever he's supposed to hail from. Sheila, the chiropodist that knows my feet, was off sick and the new one, a strap, had to cut my big toenail down the side to keep it from in-growing, cut it and jagged at it, a real demon but then we're not all born to be alike. The things you do for me and God grant that you will be repaid one day.

Dear Eleanora,

The mare ran last week came third only thirty pounds for us as against three hundred for first. The galling part is she can win if she likes but she's temperamental, there were twenty in the race and twelve were near-winners, she can be last and out of the blue pass them out if she feels like it. Horses are the ruination of everyone, your father has a craze for them but then we all do crazy things. You work too hard it'll get to your nerves in time. I haven't got the same energy but didn't I do my bit for ye all and maybe God will give me a few more years though I'd be no loss to anybody. Sad to say, years and months seem all one now, the same pattern, eat, feed the animals, sit at the fire at night and brood. The coat you sent me I wear all the time, I hate to put on anything else, I had an old Persian lamb collar from a black coat of years back stitched onto it and people rave about it. The horse did not run well yesterday, when one sees that they are losing and losing it's time to say Enough but I don't utter a word as it would lead to civil war. The weather the past week bitter cold with frost. I went all day with my old coat on and a headscarf on me but it's not so bad if we don't get the snow. I don't think I could do a slimming fast even a bit of dry bread would suffice. I barely eat cake now. The one I'm sending you, make a hole on the top with a knitting needle and pour a glass of whiskey into it to keep it moist. Last week I drew I don't know how many buckets of water and sprayed the whole avenue to kill the weeds. It's sad if things get neglected but I should have sense enough not to bother but when you spend your whole life in a place you like to see it as spic as it can be. Since I came back from you from London I haven't been out, only to Mass and Tom Holland's funeral. That restaurant with the fortunes in the cookies was just out of this world and the spice in the Moroccan lamb so individual. The new shoes you got me will have a rest for a while. You didn't tell me if they exchanged the sideboard for you or if they were canny enough to find some mark on it. You had great pluck asking them at all, being as you had it a week. I like little bits of news: is the black lace frock you wore that evening we went out an antique? I do hope you get to come soon. I sent you yesterday eighteen large lace doilies eighteen small ones and four center ones, I am praying you will make use of them if not you can give them to someone. Cold sores all around my nose and mouth for a week and the last bit I had to eat was in a hotel the day your father had to see a trainer about the mare. The moods since diabolical. I suppose he longs for drink sometimes and isn't he great to have given it up, to have conquered his weakness.

Dear Eleanora,

Thanks a million for your all to me and may the New Year bring you what is best for you but remember love is all bull, the only true love is that between mother and child. All them paintings Italians do with mothers holding their infants and angels above them like the beautiful one in the chapel in Limerick can't be for nothing. I needn't tell you as you know from your own experience men think five pounds should do for a year. We were hit hard with the foot and mouth disease, no fairs, no marts for three months so that we couldn't sell an animal. If I were young again I'd find a job, I haven't your brains of course but I always thought I'd do well in hotel business, meeting people and showing them around. I confess that I shed tears with the cold it was that bitter. I had to ring the electricity people to come and install a storage heater but the man got sick and had to go to hospital and his wife was dead two mornings after so we all have our troubles, heat or no heat. My darling, I might have sounded odd when you rang but sometimes I get distracted, I forget now if there was someone in the room I only wish I could see you oftener. I used to like style when I was young, the world my oyster. Horses will be here I suppose long after me.

Dear Eleanora,

    This is to tell you I had a bad turn. I got very stunned for a week and nothing mattered to me but don't worry you won't bury me this time come what may. I wish I could see the Statue of Liberty once more and my old favorite haunts of Brooklyn which I loved and where I loved. The skirt you sent me is too narrow I am trying to get it let out. I dream so often of you, thinking you are not happy and it makes me sad each night as I lay in bed, but I know you love your children, little princes, may they never renege on you. Put your trust in God, He is the good shepherd the one man who will not let you down. Our beautiful sheepdog, Rover, got killed and I think it's not long before Dixie his partner joins him. Nature in animals is a remarkable thing, far superior to humans. Did you ever put up the chandelier I sent you? If any part got broken I can get it fixed. I am mailing a blouse I had crocheted for you, the work is very tedious, you may have to put a little pleat under each arm if it's baggy. The only snag is I could not get another done as she who did it says she'd never do another, too trying on the eyes. Don't you know I am constantly thinking of you, many don't know the first thing about loving a child. Here I was, wondering if you went away for your work. My prayer was answered as your letter came. My little needs are well taken care of with the money you send and now the extraordinary pleasant surprise that ye'll be coming in the sum-

mer so herewith questions to be answered: for ye'er meal on
Sunday when ye arrive is it to be hot or cold fare. I do not
want ye to have even a cup of tea at Shannon Airport, complete waste of money. Since you said you might build in the
kitchen garden I go up there more often than I did and try
to picture you in a new house and the old stone wall of the
garden to protect you, back to your roots where your heart
is. I pray that I live to see it up. There is so much red tape in
passing on a bit of land but it shall be done. The surgeon who
does the veins wouldn't do mine, told me to get a pair of elastic stockings and wear them permanently, my age no doubt.
Four people buried here this week a Mrs. Whiley in her thir-
ties and three that died of some flu that's going around, Hong
Kong or Kong Hong, or whatever it's called.

Dear Eleanora,
    Your brother called with his darling wife stayed one night.
I got up at three in the morning and found them in the hall
arguing, God knows why. The plants you put in the front garden are doing all right. We had the man from the council, the
Gate Lodge has to be demolished and they won't give a penny
but it must go. Mrs. Noonan was buried last week, a massive
funeral down as far as the Rock. We've started the fires, only
for the television it would be so lonely. Your Christmas cake
is on its way, a bakers will ice it, for if I iced it it would get
broken. When you wash my cushion covers do it yourself as
you don't want the colors of the embroidery to run, don't ever
fold them up wet that's what happened the last time. Do you
still wear the grosgrain black dress and the turquoise brooch
from Tibet? I went to Dublin with your father just to be sure
he'd come home okay, sold three horses but the stud farm got
most of it. I'm happy they're disposed of, trainers and jockeys
telling him he'd win races, all bull, the sense you pay for is the
best sense. I walked Dublin to try and get you a white counterpane of long ago but I failed so do not blame me. I didn't

buy a thing only four side combs. I wouldn't live in the city for love or money, it's a rat race. Thank God for the fresh air and the quiet, fears come on at night that never do in daytime. In years to come cities will be overcrowded and life so very mixed up that a peaceful spot will be impossible, so make your plans for the kitchen garden, it will be yours and no one else's, it's a home for the future. I got a good cough bottle with some of the money and thanks for the beautiful velvet jacket but to tell the truth I am bursting in it, even the armpits are too small. I will take off the buckle and put it on another garment. Four boys here coming home from a dance drove into a stationary lorry, the road a battlefield with dead and dying.

Dear Eleanora,

The electric blanket you gave me conked out and they said in the factory it wanted a new control. In case I should pass away we will get the mapping done for the kitchen garden when you are here. Somehow I have been thinking of you every moment. I went to a drama in the town hall but see one drama and you see the lot. A fella on his way to a ballad session called in, said he wanted to send you poems of his a bit simple I had to tell him for a finish to go he's not all square. I don't think he had eaten for a week. Never again will I rear a chicken. Another colt has been bought, it's a disease. With your money I got one and a half tons of anthracite. People here say they'll take an action against you for putting them in books and the dead people would take an action against you if they were alive. Your father gets tired from tearing after horses, he has to sleep on a board bed for his back. You seem to be traveling a lot but maybe it agrees with you. Land and houses here are sky-high. My old friend Mrs. Veller is blind and has to be led across the street. They moved from Foxrock out to Wicklow, her daughter went to Australia and is lonely there, the nearest neighbor one hundred miles away.

I wish you'd come oftener, it would be a change for you. You said you have thought of moving to America, well I had a man here visiting who spent forty-five years in it and his account is frightening, your life in danger even in daytime. He couldn't get over how nice Rusheen is. I never want to think of it all weeds and briars and overgrown, never. I keep a few guests now for B and B, I am not materially minded but they fill in a few lonely hours. I would not like you to live in the USA but if you go for a visit I will ask you to locate somebody for me. I was given an address but the letter returned after six months having been interfered with, steamed. Television in and out of the repair hospital. Your enclosures are a godsend, to have a pound is pure freedom but I don't let on you send it. I am enclosing you a little ivory letter opener as something tells me you don't open my letters regularly. I staggered and fell on the back kitchen step, took me an age to get to the phone to call a doctor in emergency and that's not like me. He said I was carrying surplus water and surplus weight, a pure eejit, it turned out it was cataracts in both eyes. The girl in Todd's showed me a cashmere cardigan at the old price of twenty pounds but needless to say I wouldn't spend that on my whole body. I went to an eye doctor because of fainting and told him that I'd lost the sight in my left eye for five or six minutes and he said it was a stroke and lucky the sight came back at all. A big ashtray I bought you got crushed on the way home. My eyes are better now but not my feet. If I had good feet I'd walk down the avenue to the gate to see folks passing. I dream of you most nights and the other night I thought you had turned into a beautiful black cat that spoke. I got the breakfast room painted a buff yellow.

Dear Eleanora,

The birds are singing gloriously all day but I can't say that it's spring. You'd go to your knees in muck and wet in the lawn and your father having to fodder cattle in the night when the youngster comes from his factory work, it's impossible to get help anywhere. The domestic economy instructress swore to me that she could get the stain off my first piece of embroidery, done fifty-five years ago, but instead burned it with whatever acid she applied to it. I've had to do a little invisible mending before I give it to you. Your brother rang, I could tell from his voice he was full of alcohol, they think of nobody only themselves, they covet this place but they have another guess coming. The little shrub you planted is flowering, an orange bell flower, I talk to it because I know it's part of you. Please put some savings aside for your rainy day.

Dear Eleanora,

We got two new pups, mischief-makers. I had left clothes on the line all night, the ground in the morning pure white like it had snowed. They had got to work on the sheets and the pillowslips, chewed them to bits. I could have killed them. The chimneys are full of crows' nests even though they were cleaned last spring, they clawed the pots off. We are four weeks sitting up close to an oil heater and the paraffin gives off a foul smell. Yes, your brother thinks Rusheen is his, all settled, she's the one driving him on though he was born selfish. If he got it you or your children would not be let inside the bottom gate. He was so vexed last Christmas night that he drove away from here and killed one of the pups and we cried and cried. He didn't even stop, only drove on and didn't tell us until we found out about it for ourselves. He loves neither man or beast. Some have nature and some have not. The comrade mourned her pal, couldn't get her into the kitchen to warm up and when she hears a dog barking in the distance she listens to see where the sound is coming from. Your father weeps and so do I. The paling around the house is all rusty and the posts will take forty pounds' worth of paint. That house you thought you might buy, Gore House, is a disaster. We brought a man that knows all about timbers, he said it's only fit to demolish, roof also rotten. A German man bought it many years ago but never came back, saw it from the air, so forget about it. I'd like you to persevere and build in the kitchen garden, an old stone wall all around you. No price for cattle, people killing their own beef now as most have got deep freezers. Do you recall the leak above your bed in the blue room when you were here, well I woke and saw a light shining and I couldn't believe it and went across and found the light on though the switch was off and when I went to turn it off I felt a current. Got so alarmed that I rang Graham and the creature came at midnight and found the carpet and boards of the floor all wet, all rotten and said lucky I didn't stand on that spot or I'd be in Kingdom Come. Your brother has never said would I or his father like a drive in one of their two cars, he isn't worth worrying about.

Dear Eleanora,

I have the head of that statue you gave me worn from tapping it; you won it for catechism, a black saint, blessed Martin de Porres. It will be laid on my breast and buried with me. At seventy-eight it's time to think. If I ask you something don't be cross, can we be buried in the same plot? I know you love this country in spite of the ugly things people have said about you and we could be near a nice grassy corner under trees, could you promise me that, if you can't then we won't worry. I have a nice Dutch man staying, the only thing is he has to have his breakfast at six-thirty. Your brother and herself called and said they wanted things here settled once and for all, shameless at getting what they consider theirs, said his beautiful wife did not intend to be a caretaker for you and yours. We sang dumb. Earlier he'd offered to bring me to Limerick to a specialist, the next day going out your father said, "We'll see you tomorrow" and he said, "You'll see me no more." He said you had pots of money from scribbling and I said you'd have pots of money if you didn't part with it so easily. They live for road and big hotels and race meetings and she going around buying clothes and furniture nonstop. They don't see their parents' plight and what their parents did for them. There was a time when I could go up to the yard to boil pots of meal ten times a day and still do the cooking and baking and have the house spic and span and pick the elder-berries to make the wine unbeknownst, to have for visitors. I hope you didn't tuck those cushions away in some press, that you weren't ashamed of them, I wouldn't want you to deny your mother like Peter who denied Christ as the cock crowed thrice. We make a good fire and sit by it, me thinking and your father thinking and scratching his head, the wind going all around the house fierce. My father used to tell of the night of the big wind in 1839 a poor man and his poor wife with their roof shot off he tying his wife to a tree to go back in and collect their utensils and when he came out again neither trace nor tidings of her swept away. But maybe death is not that terrible, no more fight, no more fighting but I do want to see Coney Island before I die. I heard it's not as big an at-traction as it used to be but for me it has associations.

Dear Eleanora,

Michael Patrick died and we have learned on the grape-vine that twenty-three first cousins are remembered in his will, your father being one, but as you would expect, rel-atives in close touch will have got in there quick. What we want to find out is if your father is mentioned in the residues which would be worthwhile as the farm is very valuable. He'd moved in with neighbors since he got feeble and most likely they'll get the major portion. Also we don't know if there is a second will there could be and we mightn't get a look-in. He'd lost three stone and was waiting to see his solicitor when he dropped dead. My wants are few as I grow older but there are things we could do by way of improving the place, phosphate and lime for the fields, good gates and fences as

animals are breaking in and breaking out at all hours. We had
Michael Patrick prayed for on Sunday at the first Mass. I hear
on good authority that your brother is hitting the bottle and
so is she, we are trying to put them out of our minds completely, all they think of is racing, drinking, and hotels. Poor
Ellie had a three in one operation, slow to heal. Henry Brady's
funeral miles long. Miss Conheady the cookery instructress
is very sad. She lost her only sister Moira who died on her
eighth baby. It was the saddest thing I ever saw to see her laid
out in the morgue and at her feet was this little dead baby.
Men and women in tears. Price of postage, telephone rental,
and electricity all gone up. Your father went to Lisdoonvarna
for the waters and your Aunt Bride and I went for the drive,
people singing and dancing down at the wells all day and all
night, some hoping to find husbands. Our puppies are getting big and oh so mischievous. They got up on the table for
a fletch of bacon, got their teeth into one of my Dr. Scholl's
elastic stockings, two good nightgowns, and a pajamas. They
jump feet high. The tea-maker you sent us is a gift, especially
in the mornings. Tom Lahiffe died milking a cow, sister of
his broke her neck running to him to pick him up. Your last
week's enclosure was too much but I am getting the dining
room papered. It's sixteen years up and was done badly and
I put emulsion over it two years ago, a botched job, so I am
hoping it will pass your admiration test. I often wish I had
a bank account like you. We never seem to be able to keep a
pound, I reckon we are fools. I think of you hourly. Got another flu and then relapse and didn't know or care if I died.
Bride had it too, all crocks, but I'm up and even made jelly,
a tedious task as sometimes it doesn't thicken. I wouldn't
have made it at all only the apples were knocked down in the
wind and rain and I thought what a sin and the world starving. Cattle down to twenty pounds per head, six of ours gone
with tuberculosis and the Department bought them for half
nothing, newborn calves have been sold at a pound whereas

a chicken costs one pound fifty. Didn't someone ring up to wish us happy anniversary and that's how I remembered the fifty long years, no big party. I'm not able to cater for anybody and bad colds and cold sores and itch is woeful. If I could feel like myself I'd thank God but I don't feel and never will. Had a crowd of men making silage for three days and had to feed them, nearly killed me. We have a heat wave now and it's sweltering. Silage making is more practical than saving hay. When you watch an animal die you think how sad it must be to see a human die. My best days I have seen out.

Dear Eleanora,

I'm sure you will be pleased by our news. The mare won in Limerick, her second time to run. I enclose the cutting. Your father was thrilled, as Sabre Point was a sure winner and people had bet thousands on her and also there were two other great horses and nobody gave our Shannon Rose even a chance but she surprised many and disappointed many more. The trainer's son Bobby was about to get on her for the race when a demon, a trainer that she was with earlier at huge cost, went up to him and said that's the greatest pig of a mare was ever ridden and she's liable to run against a wall and throw you off, well had it been a strange jockey was riding her he wouldn't have gone out into the race, but Bobby knowing her so well after two months knew her to be the gentlest creature alive. The Galway Hobo never wanted her to win and absolutely starved her when he had her. After the race a couple of prime boys wanted to buy her when they thought your father couldn't pay for her any longer and that he'd sell her cheap. He is absolutely ecstatic. It's not what she won, the two hundred pounds, but it will put up her value and he'll try her over hurdles now and if she takes to them he'll race her again. We were invited out to the trainer's house for a cup of tea, a mansion. I hadn't been outside the door, only to Mass and the henhouse. Sometimes I'd love for a spin on a Sunday evening but no such luck. People preach about Christianity and all the rest but how many act like Christians? When I'm dying I hope you will be with me, I always hope for that. The green chaise upstairs I'm getting new legs on it and plush cover, maybe red, maybe purple. The carpet sweeper you got me is a boon, better than the electric, they pick up more. Everything twice the price since decimalization came in. You'll find this strange but I was in Limerick recently and was introduced to a lady as your mother and she said I saw your daughter at Phoenix Park races two weeks ago with two very good-looking men. I said you are mistaken it wasn't my daughter as she was not home and she said the friends with whom she was with said it was you and as a matter of fact she said you wore a velvet coat very long and very unusual and that was what attracted them to you so I said you must have a double. The only peculiar bit was concerning the coat, velvet with gold braiding, the image of yours. Were you or were you not at Phoenix Park races last month? Strange that and I not to know it. Please do not fuss too much to keep your figure; your health must go before all else. God help anyone dealing with tradesmen, they come and go as suits them. There was a letter in the paper saying your writing is tripe, written by a man in Carrick-mines. I did see a lovely picture of you taken at an oyster festival; so near and yet so far. I like your hair down. It will be exciting to go to Finland but I'm always frightened for you in airplanes. Your father can't go anywhere as there are a couple of cows to calve and sometimes young cows don't calve right. We had one a week ago and the calf was dead and we have to find another calf to suckle her but they don't always take on to them; so many drawbacks in farming. I have to herd in cows and calves with him, it's beyond me. I can't run but it has to be done. I enclose medals of Saint Benedict blessed by the mission fathers at the rails and they carry a special blessing so keep one in the house and put the other on your clothing as you travel so much.

Dear Eleanora,

Your father has been gone now for fourteen days. He was asleep after the operation when we got to the hospital so we went out for a cup of tea and went back and stayed twenty minutes. He looked worn. The surgeon said it was a very big operation, two thirds of his stomach taken away. The ulcer was very far up and hard to get to, but that it was well it was taken out as malignancy had set in. Your father says he'd die before he'd go through it all again, you'd feel sorry for him to see him all tubed up, the nurses are very rough and the matron who knows him would be kind except she's on leave. Many pints of blood had to be put into him. I suppose I wasn't really sympathetic for a long time, I felt it was nerves and contrariness but now I see I was wrong. I am so relieved to see him well. Do drop him a line when you can. Another sick cow was taken away to Limerick on the lorry for the knackers yard. Farming is an utter nightmare. You are lucky to have brains and to use them, not like the foolish virgins in the parable. I go for a checkup next month, I should have gone long ago. It would be worse to be out on the roadside like our forebears were. A Cecilia Long who nursed in the USA for thirty-five years took retirement and came home to nurse her sister Lilly a cripple. Last Sunday a niece visited them but by the time she'd got home in the evening word awaited her that Aunt Cecilia fell going up the stairs and broke her neck. Pitiful. I felt so sad after Ellie's death I couldn't bring myself to go to the funeral. I went to see her sick and when I went into the room I took fright with the roaring of her, I'll never forget it. I'm tired from nothing and then tired from something. I did ring Bea Minogue one morning for the locum's number and before I knew it she was here on the doorstep and drove me over to him. He gave me an injection which pained me for one and a half hours but I suppose it helped because I slept and I raved all day. Bea said he came again to make sure the fever was abating. Bea is the soul of kindness.

I fear you are mixed-up about things which is why you did not come this year. The teacher said he will look for the book you want, he will try a trunk. The breach has come with your brother: they want too much and assumed there was no one else in the family.

Dear Eleanora,

Now for the bombshell, we might have to sell Rusheen. Things are getting on top of us. Your brother is making demands. We know it's her, she's cracked but he is not man enough to stand up to her. We have said goodbye to them for the last time. We might build a bungalow. He demanded ten thousand pounds immediately and let everyone else go to hell. We hear now they have gone to Spain to recuperate. We're not the only ones who had to sell their homesteads, nobody ever counted with him only her and I believe his life is hell, a brother of hers let it out at a funeral. The animal that won the race is now one and a half years in training at seven guineas a week plus jockey's fees, plus stablemen, plus fifty pounds to the jockey every so often, a dead loss but if I say anything there's ructions so I sing dumb. Some critic commented that you as a writer are trying to present a false and malevolent picture of your country, said your works will not live on. Another critic to outsmart him wrote that your work is hocus pocus so you see how controversial you are but sometimes we get the sting of it. I regret to tell you that more trouble is brewing regarding your most recent book. Some have written to publishers to say they are going to take an action against you. Of course they are money mad but they are also out for your blood. I say that I do not want to hear about it but they are evidently upset and very sore with you. They did not expect you to go back years and years to make them objects of ridicule and humiliation. Your father and I do not discuss it as I feel it hurts him too. Yet I know I can go to you if I am in need. I have heard indirectly that you were seen crying in public. I hope it does not bode some fresh disaster. With the last money you sent me, I'm going to buy myself a rocking chair and rock away for the remainder of my life. Gore House that you enquired after went for thirty-five thousand and you could drive a car through the woodworm in it, fungus all over the place and everything rotten. The report is you bought it and as late as last night three people congratulated your father on the purchase. When shall I see you again? You hinted about living in New York, but I pray you don't. A bank strike and shipping strike so tourists have canceled as they can't bring their cars. Your father cried a lot before his operation as he was afraid it would perforate at any time. I am telling you it would be better to be married to a man in a cottage earning a weekly wage as there is no money in farming. Last night I had a dream of being back at home in Middleline and looking from the field in front of the door in through the window and seeing a beautiful metal crucifix and white beads hanging on the wall and saying to myself the room is changed, it means change and what does it signify? When you have a minute, would you ever draw a sketch of your black jacket with the grosgrain reveres, I am getting one made like it as I have black skirts but no good jacket.

Dear Eleanora,

Great news that you are coming for a weekend. I had to read your card twice in case I imagined it. I hope to have chickens in good killing order and have a new recipe with apples and chestnuts, for the stuffing. We'll go up the mountains to see the scenery like long ago. I must give you the tapestry picture of the Statue of Liberty as you will have it when I no longer exist, something you could never buy in a shop. This racing bug is a form of lunacy and he keeps getting into debt in the hope of getting out of debt, utter folly, he works for horses alone. I did more perhaps for your brother than for you long ago when I had a couple of pounds and went to

Limerick on a lorry, deprived myself of even a cup of tea to come home with a tennis racket or a new flannel trousers for him that never even said thank you. I have a little request but really it's not that important, if you can't get it don't worry, a copper bracelet for rheumatism to be worn on the arm and never taken off. A nurse told me about it, says it's miraculous. Even my toes are rigid and sore. I set out to pick a few black-berries and ended up with half a bucket, I made fifty pounds of jelly and only wish I could hand it over the hedge to you. So please bring baskets galore when ye come. The boys love it on scones. You must be lonely without them. Let us pray they don't grow up heartless and ungrateful and that they never take against you. The most unkindest cut of all, like you once read to me from some book.

Dear Eleanora,

The coat you posted is beautiful but it has one defective skin in the back which the manufacturers stretched to make it fit and I brought it to the furriers in Limerick to ask if they could put press studs in the vents down the back to make it sit but no go as it wasn't bought there. They even showed me where and how the skin had been faultily cut as if I wanted to know. I got you a supper cloth as I remember you saying you liked them. Our dogs fought Saxton's dog and ours got the worst of it, one had to be carried in, not even able to stand. The new fridge you ordered has been delivered, it's pure mar-velous as milk always went sour and meat kept only a day. I have a German lodger for six months but of course he has not two words of English. Great to-do here over your latest book, ninety-five percent shocked, they have borrowed from one another to see how revolting it is and ask why can you not write parables that would make pleasant reading. There are lovely teaspoons that I got for coupons out of cornflake packets and they are yours if you fancy them. Another death in the factory, an only son. So that girl you got to help you

did something dishonorable I am not surprised. The fire barrel of the stove conked out on me and I will have to go to Te-
resa O'Gorman's to have your Christmas cake baked. There
are many parts of my life I would not want to relive but I
must say I had good times of it in Brooklyn. New York I only
set foot in once and on a very unhappy mission, searching for
a friend who wasn't even there at the time. How I long for us
to have a big chat one day as there are things I'd like to tell
you. You have not forgotten us or our creature comforts but
there is something that bugs me. It hurts the way you make
yourself so aloof, always running away from us, running running to where. Are we lepers or what . . .

Or . . .

What

Or . . .

What

Epilogue

We were sitting by the kitchen stove, my mother and myself. It must have been September, too early to light a fire in the front room, but nevertheless a bit of a chill to the evening, even the dog, the old rheumatic dog, had gone into his cubbyhole and we had not the slightest difficulty putting in the hens, they wandered in of their own accord. After she'd bolted the door we stood to look at a most ravishing sunset, a shocking pink that spanned a huge panoply of sky, rivers and rivulets crimsoning all before it, ruddying the fort of somber trees, seeping into cloud that was erstwhile and sullen and straggly.

"There's no place like home," she said, and I nodded because she wanted me to think likewise.

Once in the kitchen she opened the two oven doors to let the heat out and we sat for one of our chats. Quite unselfconsciously she ran her hands along her neck, all along the sides and then to the back to feel the stiffnesses, and though she had not asked me I felt without the words that she wished me to massage her and I did, searching out the knots and the crick, then along the nape, under her swallow, holding the bowl of her head in my hands, entreating her to let go, to let go of all her troubles and she replying, "If only we could, if only we could."

Somewhat emboldened, she opened the top button of her good Sunday blouse so that I might lay my hands above the mesh of blue veins that were raised like braid over her sunken chest. She began to bask in it, her expression melting, a happiness at being touched as she had never been touched in all her life, and it was as though she was the child and I had become the mother.

Twilight falls upon her in that kitchen, in that partial darkness, the soft and beautiful light of a moment's nearness; the soul's openness, the soul's magnanimity, falling timorously through the universe and timorously falling upon us.

ACKNOWLEDGMENTS

So many people helped me in my researches that I sincerely hope I have forgotten none: the Clare Heritage in Tuamgraney, the Irish Folklore Commission in Dublin, the National Library of Ireland, Ulster American Folk Park in Omagh, the Brooklyn Public Library, the New York Public Library, the New-York Historical Society, and the American Irish Historical Society in New York.

Of the many people who not only answered my questions but also encouraged me to look elsewhere, I would like to include Eilis Ni Duibhne, Criostoir Mac Carthaigh, Chris McIver, Kevin Whelan, Niamh O'Sullivan, Bernadette Whelan, Colum McCann, Chris Kelly, Emily Stone, Mike Onorato, Ron Schweiger, Judith Walsh, Joy Holland, and Dave Smith of the New York Public Library, all of whom were tireless in their continued efforts on my behalf.

In my native County Clare, I am indebted to my nephew Michael Blake, John Howard, Paddy Ryan, a faith healer, and Gerrard Madden, who allowed me to quote from his magazine *Slieve Aughty*.

Sister Maura, who befriended my mother, gave so much of her generous time. Her profound insights into the journey of death were an enlightenment to me.

I wish to thank Nadia Proudian, who typed the manuscript again and again with such meticulousness.